NEW YORK REVIEW BOOKS
CLASSICS

SCHOOL FOR LO

OLIVIA MANNING (1908–1980) was born in Portsmouth, England, and spent much of her childhood in Northern Ireland. Her father, Oliver, was a penniless British sailor who rose to become a naval commander, and her mother, Olivia, had a prosperous Anglo-Irish background. Manning trained as a painter at the Portsmouth School of Art, then moved to London and turned to writing. She published her first novel under her own name in 1938 (she had published several potboilers in a local paper under the name Jacob Morrow while a teenager). The next year she married R. D. "Reggie" Smith, and the couple moved to Romania, where Smith was employed by the British Council. In World War II, the couple fled before the Nazi advance, first to Greece and then to Jerusalem, where they lived until the end of the war. Manning wrote several novels during the 1950s, but her first real success as a novelist was *The Great Fortune* (1960), the first of six books concerning Guy and Harriet Pringle, whose wartime experiences and troubled marriage echoed that of the diffident Manning and her gregarious husband. In the 1980s these novels were collected in two volumes, *The Balkan Trilogy* (forthcoming from NYRB Classics) and *The Levant Trilogy*, known collectively as *The Fortunes of War*. In addition to her novels, Manning wrote essays and criticism, history, a screenplay, and a book about Burmese and Siamese cats. She was made Commander of the Order of the British Empire in 1976, and died four years later.

JANE SMILEY is the author of *Ten Days in the Hills*, *Thirteen Ways of Looking at the Novel*, *A Thousand Acres*, and many other books. She lives in California.

SCHOOL FOR LOVE

OLIVIA MANNING

Introduction by
JANE SMILEY

NEW YORK REVIEW BOOKS

New York

THIS IS A NEW YORK REVIEW BOOK
PUBLISHED BY THE NEW YORK REVIEW OF BOOKS
435 Hudson Street, New York, NY 10014
www.nyrb.com

Library of Congress Cataloging-in-Publication Data
Manning, Olivia.
  School for love / by Olivia Manning ; introduction by Jane Smiley.
      p. cm. — (New York Review Books classics)
  ISBN 978-1-59017-303-9 (alk. paper)
  1. Orphans—Fiction. 2. Jerusalem—History—20th century—Fiction. 3.
Jewish–Arab relations—History—1917–1948—Fiction. 4. Jerusalem—Ethnic
relations—Fiction. I. Smiley, Jane. II. Title.
  PR6063.A384S36 2009
  823.914—dc22

                                        2008041415

ISBN 978-1-59017-303-9

Printed in the United States of America on acid-free paper.
10 9 8 7 6 5 4 3 2 1

INTRODUCTION

When Olivia Manning's novel *The Doves of Venus* was published in the United States in 1956—her first American publication in nearly twenty years—*New York Times* reviewer William Du Bois greeted it with a disdain that was cultural as well as artistic. "Our British cousins have been turning out a spate of peevish books this fall," he wrote, only to add in the next paragraph, "It is an almost classic example of how an imported novel should not be written if the novelist's hope is to capture American readers in sufficient numbers to pay for the American printer." Best-selling American novels in 1956 included *Peyton Place* and *Marjorie Morningstar*—Manning was not destined to be an American sensation. Her tone was too mordant and her observations too precise for the American market, and, perhaps, her characters and plots were too English in one way—not optimistic enough for the new American century—and not English enough in another way—no country estates or cozy parlors or tidy murder mysteries.

In England, Manning was known as the author of nine books of fiction and nonfiction, but there too she had not found the success she had hoped for. She was an integral member of the London literary scene—in part through her husband, Reggie Smith, who worked for the BBC. Her friends were writers, such as Stevie Smith and Anthony Powell. But in her late forties, she compared herself to more celebrated (and younger) friends and acquaintances, such as Iris Murdoch and Beryl Bainbridge. Her hard work seemed not to have paid off. Surely the reception of her work in the United States came as yet another blow to her ambitions.

School for Love, now finally appearing in America some sixty years after it did in England, is the best of Manning's early novels, and the one that looks forward to the great achievement with which she crowned her career, the Balkan and Levant trilogies, which together compose the vast roman-fleuve about World War II that she called *The Fortunes of War*. *School for Love* is set just after the war, in Jerusalem (Manning and her husband, who worked for the British Council, had lived there from 1942 through 1946). Read today, it seems a work of uncanny prescience. The grave concerns of our own age—religious fanaticism, passionate competing territorial claims—are here in embryo, set into the precisely rendered, everyday texture of an era that has vanished. The alien British feel that Du Bois complained of in 1956 was not, in fact, cultural—it is a characteristic of Manning's unique vision and style, her cool way of dissecting her world and her experience, in which even the most pitiable or terrifying circumstances are worthy of interested and detailed scrutiny.

The novel opens with a freak snowstorm, at once establishing the theme of surprise and displacement. Felix Latimer, newly orphaned, is in a taxi, having just arrived from Baghdad. His father has been killed in the war, and his mother has recently died of typhoid. He is in his mid-teens, but to us he seems younger, more naïve, and more vulnerable. His situation is described almost with a shrug, as if the author is consciously setting aside Felix's claims on our sympathies—after all, everyone in Jerusalem at the end of the Second World War is displaced, or about to be. Felix himself seems stunned. What he had valued about his mother—her beauty and her impractical artistic nature—are the very things that have left him unprotected and far from everyone who might help him. The taxi is taking him to a guesthouse in Jerusalem belonging to a distant relative named Miss Bohun. It quickly becomes clear that although Miss Bohun prides herself on her charitable actions, what she is really interested in is the money to be paid out by the British Council for Felix's upkeep while he awaits his return to England.

Felix, an affectionate boy, is prepared to be thankful and loyal to Miss Bohun, even though he does not quite comprehend why she always serves the same poor meals, why she never buys provisions on the black market, why she has assumed control of the guesthouse and reduced its former leaseholders to servants.

Miss Bohun is a brilliant and fascinating character, and in the English reviews of the novel she was compared to such great English literary monsters as Mrs. Havisham in *Great Expectations*. She is described as small and dried-up-looking, but her presence fills her guesthouse, and Felix is always aware of her predilections, her opinions, and her state of mind. There is a mystery about her—in addition to tutoring locals in English and running the pension, she heads a group called the Ever-Readys. The event the Ever-Readys are preparing for is the Second Coming of Christ—a fact that must strike the twenty-first-century reader as prophetic at first glance, but then, of course, as an "of course." Manning indicates that all sorts of religious sects are busy in Jerusalem, waiting for something or cultivating an eccentric theology.

Miss Bohun is a marvel, even a paradigm, of hypocrisy, always congratulating herself on her selflessness, always pinching pennies, always angling for more power and more pounds. After Felix has been living in the guesthouse for some months, Miss Bohun inquires of one of the other guests, the elderly and impoverished Mr. Jewel, whether he is packed up and ready to leave the following morning. It turns out that he has nowhere to go—the Bethlehem refugee center is closing down. Mr. Jewel says, "You'll have to put me on the street." Miss Bohun's riposte is, "You're taking advantage." She then waxes philosophical: "Surely you don't think I could go on keeping you indefinitely for...for a mere pittance. But that's always the way when one tries to do good."

Mr. Jewel must go to make room for Mrs. Ellis, a pregnant

young widow Miss Bohun hopes will be her bosom companion. Mrs. Ellis is another refugee of the war; Felix is immediately drawn to her youth, her beauty, and her mysterious reserve. Once their acquaintance is established, Mrs. Ellis allows Felix to accompany her around the nightspots of the city, and he gets to experience the strange atmosphere of Jerusalem in transition from one state of war to another. Mrs. Ellis soon proves a worthy opponent for Miss Bohun.

In Manning's *School for Love*, there is little love exchanged between the characters, and none at all shown for Felix, but Felix is unequipped to judge his new companions. Even as he grows fonder of Mrs. Ellis, she seems less and less interested in him. She, too, it is implied, has been stunned and hardened by her wartime experiences. Instead, Felix comes to love Miss Bohun's Siamese cat, Faro (modeled upon Manning's own Siamese cat). Faro is appealingly characterized—it is clear that Manning is a sharp observer of cats as well as people—but Faro is in every way a cat, arbitrary and independent, neither attentive nor affectionate.

Manning was both secretive and prickly. Born in 1908, in Portsmouth, the daughter of a commander in the Royal Navy, she gave out that she was born in 1914 (the same year as her husband, Reggie Smith, and a year after her brother, Oliver, who was killed in the war). Her education was nothing to brag of in London literary circles—she went to various schools in Portsmouth and Northern Ireland, studying literature and art (she showed considerable talent as a painter), but she left school at sixteen to work as a typist and a furniture refinisher. Once she had escaped to London, in the late 1920s, she worked hard to establish herself as a writer. Reggie, too, was a son of the working classes—his father was a factory worker and his mother a charwoman. Before entering the employ of the British Council, he had worked as an actor, a Christmastime mail sorter, and a part-time archaeologist. The British Council sent him to Romania in 1938. He and Olivia met while he was on leave in the summer of 1939—two years after Olivia had published her first novel (*The Wind Changes*). It was love at first sight, at least on Reggie's side, and after a quick marriage, the couple returned to his post in Bucharest, Romania. They were then away from England for six years, traveling and fleeing and observing the war in the eastern Mediterranean. It was in Jerusalem that Olivia gave birth to their only child, a son, who was stillborn.

Olivia and Reggie had a wide social connection with many famous English writers of the mid-century—Lawrence Durrell, Walter Allen, Louis MacNeice, Francis King, Stevie Smith, among others—but Reggie was the energetic, sociable, charismatic half of the couple. Olivia was more suspicious and retiring, and sometimes aroused antipathy in her husband's friends and in her own. Like Miss Bohun, she was a well-known penny-pincher, who argued over small sums in contracts; her biography, by her friends Neville and June Braybrooke, contains a telling anecdote: Olivia liked to frequent antique shops and bargain for pieces she thought were valuable, then resell them at other shops for a better price. The Braybrookes write:

> Sometimes, if she was selling something, a gallery owner would ask, "Do you know, madam, if this is an original?"
>
> Her inevitable reply was, "The family always thought it was."

School for Love is an idiosyncratic and neatly controlled story with sharp, uncomfortable characters, set in a large and volatile world. Manning portrays the paradox of Felix's life in Jerusalem—what is temporary feels permanent, what is permanent is on the verge of cataclysmic change. Manning's English characters act as though they feel themselves as at home as they would in Manchester or Shaftesbury. In this, they are almost, but not quite, unsympathetic, since Manning so carefully depicts their underlying unease—unease borne of the war, of repeated displacements, of treacherous circumstances and uncertainty about the future. In a novel of wartime, Manning dares to dismiss heroism and senti-mentality in favor of the mundane, but it is the mundane that is most revealing of individual character. *School for Love* still has the somewhat alien, British feel to it that Du Bois complained of in 1956. Because of that very thing, that odd insularity in the midst of overwhelming events and alien landscapes, it strikes the modern reader as unusually informative, not only about the era in which it takes place but about how our own era came to be what it is.

—JANE SMILEY

SCHOOL FOR LOVE

To Robert Liddell

1

When they reached the top of the hill from which the road snaked down in the Seven Sisters' bends, the driver nodded to the opposite hill and said: 'El-telq.' Felix knew that did not mean Jerusalem, although Jerusalem was over there.

He asked: 'El-telq?'

The driver smiled, shrugged, could not explain. Felix felt he ought to respond in some way. To show interest, he wound down the window and put his head out; the air, striking him with a glassy freshness, made him think of England. He had not been home since before the war when he was a small boy. That was the time his father had gone abroad alone and he and his mother had lived in Bath; the best time of all. Now, in spite of everything, the cold gave him a slight exhilaration. The exhilaration was painful, like blood returning to a cramped limb, for it seemed to him he had had no feelings at all since his mother's death. At once, of course, he was jolted by the realization there was nothing to feel exhilarated about. He would never see his mother again. Not only that – he had now to face the real Miss Bohun. Ever since the letter arrived inviting him to Jerusalem, an imaginary Miss Bohun, exactly like his mother, had been standing in a doorway with her arms open for Felix. She was still there when the plane touched down at Lydda and while the taxi was taking him from the mild, flat seaboard up into mountains where rocks overhung the road as though an avalanche had been arrested in mid-descent. Now he knew there was not a chance she would be like his mother. For one thing, she was years older; she was older even than his father, who had always seemed elderly and remote. Although she was not related to him – Miss Bohun had been an adopted child of his father's parents – Felix was afraid she might resemble his father. Another thing, Miss Bohun was a person whom his mother had not wanted to visit. Whenever his father had suggested a trip to Jerusalem, his mother had said: 'Oh no, dear one, not there. We'd have to see Ethel Bohun. I couldn't bear it.'

Felix shivered, not only with cold, but with a return of an old grief and sense of being lost in the world. He felt a slight nausea of apprehension. The driver, as though sensing this, drew his attention to distant, sharp-edged peaks, each tipped with a village and looking like a stronghold carved from living rock.

'All Arabs,' he said, 'and down there . . .' Felix gazed down into the valley where the settlements were green with cultivated fruit trees, 'down there all Jews.'

Felix, ignorant of the problems of Palestine, nodded and thought this was probably some arrangement agreed on by both parties. On either side of the road the rocks were like great flints, the earth pinkish and bare as desert, and over all a silver glimmer fell from a dark sky. In the distance, on the uneven top of the hill that was their destination, a few towers began to rise: 'El-Kuds,' said the driver, and Felix knew that meant Jerusalem, for some of the Iraqis called it that. The driver murmured again: 'El-telq,' then, remembering that Felix did not know what he meant, he distracted him by saying quickly: 'Here road very bad. These Seven Sisters very bad,' he was taking the bends at top speed so Felix was thrown from side to side as they zigzagged downhill: 'Turkish engineers think this very clever, yes, but I say no good. Bad for cars, bad for horses. Here in Turkish times horses smell their home and bolt, so very bad accidents,' he lifted a hand dramatically from the wheel and nearly had them off the tarmac on to the rocks.

'Very bad!' he shook his head sternly, then put two fingers into the pocket of the car-door and took out a caramel and offered it to Felix, 'Very good!' he said.

It was not until they had passed the first grey-stone houses of Jerusalem that Felix saw the cause of the brittle cold in the air and, even then, a moment passed before he realized what it was. 'Snow!' he said suddenly. The Arab nodded, pleased, and said for the third time: 'El-telq.'

It seemed to Felix he had seen snow before but he could not remember when. He had heard of it, had seen pictures of it, but now the sight of it touched him like a primordial memory; he could scarcely see the city for looking at the snow. They were driving down a long main street. Everything was built of stone, silver-grey, snow-capped, huddled under the blue snow light, looking like nothing so much as a wintry English village street. The driver ignored all this; it was not until they came to the centre of the new town and saw before them the Old City, walled like a fortress, the snow marking the crenellations and towers, that he announced again: 'El-Kuds,' then, swinging left, dropped down the hill to Herod's Gate. Without slowing, he stepped on the brake and the car stopped abruptly outside a gate set in a wall.

'Misboon house,' announced the driver.

Felix felt no surprise. In Baghdad he had seen, behind walls as unpromising as this, tiled courtyards full of jasmine and roses, fountains and little fretted platforms for musicians, and, opening on all sides, summer rooms painted like golden brocade. He hoped for as much within.

When he had settled with the driver and the car had backed with a rush to the main road and disappeared, Felix found himself alone for the first time – yes, for the first time in his life. In Baghdad, after his mother's death, there had always been the Shiptons; they had become bored by him and sent him off as quickly as they could when the chance came, yet they were there, people he knew and who had known his mother. Here he knew no one. He felt an acute loneliness that would have filled his eyes with tears had he not thrown it off, angry with himself because now he was a boy, not a child.

He knocked on the gate. While waiting, he bent and touched the snow. It was greyish, glassy and wet, but to him it was a wonder and, being a natural thing, a consolation. No one came to the gate. He knocked again, then, at last, lifted the latch. Inside was a small courtyard, undecorated except by snow. Doors opened off on either side and at the end was the facade of the house. A woman stood beside one of the doors staring towards the gate. She looked small and dark against the white ground, a bundle of dark, shabby clothes, with a dark face, her head bound round with a black woollen scarf and her feet in Wellington boots. She called out in a resentful, nasal whine: 'You are wanting somesing?'

'Miss Bohun, please?'

'Ah, so? In there,' she pointed to the front door of the house, then went on watching as Felix dragged his luggage over the step and latched the gate behind him. Someone spoke to her in German from a side room; she answered in German. Felix, shut into the small courtyard in the strange, uncertain light, felt as though he had entered an enemy country.

His suitcases were heavy. He carried one of them at a run across to the porch, then returned for the other. As he did so, the woman went inside and slammed the door. Almost at the same moment a window opened in the upper part of the house and another woman put out her head. A strong voice echoed in the noiselessness of the snow:

'Who is that? Frau Leszno, where are you?'

Felix called up: 'It's Felix . . . Felix Latimer.'

'Felix? Oh, dear!' The window rattled to and he waited in the silence.

'My dear boy, come in, come in,' said Miss Bohun as she opened the door. 'This snow has disorganized everything. Frau Leszno is so bad-tempered today. We must make allowances, of course; any variation in routine gives extra work to the servants. Wipe your feet. Now, if you can manage one of these bags, I'll take the other, and I'll show you up to your room.'

Miss Bohun was a tiny woman but she lifted the suitcase as though it were a feather. She hurried ahead while Felix struggled after with the other case. 'You've arrived between meals; an awkward time,' her voice sailed back to him. 'But you can get all nicely unpacked before tea.'

The front door had opened straight into a living-room. Here the floor tiles were marked with wet foot-prints. There was no fire and no light except a phosphorescent glimmer from a back window which was set, like a painting of iridescent whiteness, in the black wall.

'Oh,' said Felix, 'a garden! And the snow! Isn't it super?'

'You wouldn't think so if you had to do the housework.' Miss Bohun moved ahead with irritable quickness so Felix could not keep up with her. She paused on the stairs. Her face – featureless, like a long egg, in the gloom: her hair the same colour as her skin – was turned towards him but Felix was sure she was not looking at him.

'I'm so busy,' she said.

'Oh, sorry!' said Felix, trying to hurry. The stairs led up directly from the sitting-room to the landing. At the top Miss Bohun turned right and showed Felix to one of the two bedrooms overlooking the garden.

'Here you are,' she said, 'this is such a nice room. It gets all the sunlight. And my room's just opposite,' then she darted over to the window and closed it sharply. 'Don't want snow in here. When you're studying, you can have an oil-stove, but now you'll be busy unpacking so you won't need one. If you *should* happen to want me, I'm preparing the room at the front – but try not to disturb me, there's a good boy.'

Felix opened his mouth, but the door closed before he could speak. She was gone. Had she, or had she not, said she was preparing a room? If so, that meant someone else was coming to the house. The thought heartened him – he had been unnerved by the German woman, by Miss Bohun herself, by a muddle of memories of horror stories about houses as dark and cold as this – but he was uncertain if he had heard her right. With all the servants there were in this part of the world, surely she would not be preparing a room herself? He opened the door and, with his heart thumping, tip-toed out to the landing. Yes, there was a sound of brushing coming from the front. As he listened, Miss Bohun's voice rose strong and tuneless:

> 'I know not, oh, I know not
> What social joys are there . . .'

He hurried back to his room. Unused to real cold, he was chilled to the bone. Mr Shipton had said he would need an overcoat here, but there had not been time to buy one. As, with numbed, clumsy fingers, he struggled to unlock his cases, he longed for his mother to come into the room and give the world its normal look.

Reality was thrusting at him now through a sort of blanket of memory of her. As the 'plane that morning had passed over the dawn-lit Iraqi sands, he had slid into sleep; rather, he had slid back into the sleep from which he had scarcely wakened when Mr Shipton got him out of bed and drove him through the night silence to the airport. His setting out had been no more than a dream from which he had passed easily into that other dream still

11

clinging like an atmosphere about him. In it he had seemed to be sailing with his mother on the Golden Horn. Shortly before his father was killed, they had rented a summer house on the Bosphorus. He had had a little boat of his own. In the dream he and his mother were together in the boat, skimming the surface as smoothly as a swan. It seemed to be early morning. A mist lay on the sea, very white but thinning here and there so the water beneath could be seen looking like green milk. The mist hid the waterside buildings, but the cupolas and minarets of the mosques rose from it and hung as though baseless on the pearl sheen of the sky. The air was warm and delicate. A perfume of flowers came from the gardens so he knew it must be spring. When he smiled at his mother she smiled back with so much love and sweetness, he was filled with well-being. Transported by this delicious security, he moved to touch her, but his hand passed through nothingness. Then he saw she was fading out of sight. In an instant she would disappear. As he leant forward he wakened himself with his own cry. He had sat upright, surprised to find himself where he was, setting out into strangeness . . . Then, remembering, he had glanced round, shamefaced, but there had been only two other people in the plane, officers, both asleep.

Now, re-dreaming his dream in memory, a noise startled him awake again. Someone was moving in the room below. It was nearly dark. He switched on the light and looked about him and suddenly realized all over again that his mother was lost to him. She was dead. Whatever happened, he could never see her, never speak to her, never hear her voice. It was no good feeling sorry for himself. She would never come into this room. He would have to manage without her.

As he hung up his clothes, he thought he would not mind so much if it were even the Shiptons moving about downstairs. Anyone known to him, rather than the people of this house. Indeed, the Shiptons had been very kind. They had taken him to their home when his mother fell ill. She had been ill, with typhoid, a long time; everyone had said she would get better but, instead, she had died. He had to stay on in the Shiptons' flat. They did not say anything about his going, but after the funeral he had felt a change in their attitude. Before that he had been a temporary guest and every time they went to the American Hospital his mother had told Mrs Shipton how grateful she was; after her death there had been no one to appreciate their kindness except Felix and he obviously could not stay for ever. Mr Shipton wrote to Mrs Latimer's brother in England and tried to get Felix a passage home, but it was at the worst possible time. The ships were full of troops being withdrawn from the Middle East, and the few civilian passages were reserved for important people. Felix was put on a waiting-list; the weeks passed and he heard nothing. The Shiptons were still quite kind, but more and more casual. Felix was moved out of his room into the box-room because another guest came; then he was moved out of the box-room because Mr Shipton had 'flu and was afraid of infecting his wife, but when Mr Shipton got better he stayed on in the box-room. Felix had no room, nowhere of his own at all. A camp-bed was put up for him each night in the hall. Sometimes the servant forgot, and it was always awkward when the Shiptons gave a party. Even in his frantic need to get away, knowing he was staying too long, knowing he was not wanted, Felix did not think of Miss Bohun. Mr Shipton must have found out about her and written without telling Felix. When her letter came offering to 'take the poor boy for his expenses alone', Felix could have wept with relief that there was, after all, a solution. The letter came on the 27th December; it came when Felix was near despair, for the Shiptons had been invited to spend Christmas with friends in Mosul and had had to leave him in the flat alone. When they returned and found Miss Bohun's letter, they became quite nice again as though to make up for the long weeks of indifference, but within two days they had got him a seat on the 'plane to Lydda and packed him off.

Well, now, at any rate, he had a room of his own. He need not be in anyone's way. Except for its bareness and cold, the room was pleasant enough with its peaked Arab ceiling imitating a tent and its long, spear-shaped window let into a wall so thick that the sill made a window-seat. There was a small iron bedstead, a wardrobe, a table and chair, nothing else – but he could put up some of his mother's embroideries as she had done whenever they moved to a new hotel or pension. 'So dull, darling,' she would say, 'but wait till I put up some of my pretties and then these will really be our rooms.'

He wondered what he should do now he had unpacked. There had been no time for breakfast and no food on the plane. He was almost past feeling hungry. He peered from the window. The light outside was a pure, dark blue, as though he were seeing it through blue glass. Some sleet was falling and as he watched it, it began to turn to rain. From the room below came a chink of crockery. Oh, tea-time! It made Felix feel better and the house seem less strange. When he heard Miss Bohun going downstairs, he decided to go down, too.

Out on the landing, he heard something clatter in the sitting-room. Miss Bohun called peevishly from the stairs: 'Oh, dear, Frau Leszno, what have you broken now?'

The German voice, twanging like a flat string, more peevish than Miss Bohun's, replied: 'Just such a little plate. It is nosing. In Jastrow we had a hundred such.'

'Well, there aren't a hundred such here.'

'No,' agreed Frau Leszno with sombre contempt.

Miss Bohun went on down, clicking her tongue and saying sadly: 'Really, Frau Leszno, you might help me to save!'

'So? For what should I help you to save? You have here mine dinner-table and mine six chairs, and mine horsehair sofa, and for me – what? Even my room is taken for sis spoilt boy while my Nikky sleeps in the kitchen.'

'That will do.' The change in Miss Bohun's voice was impressive. Frau Leszno said nothing more, but the door slammed as she went. Felix turned the corner diffidently. Miss Bohun was sitting at the tea-table, her eyes hidden behind her hand. She sighed deeply as she heard Felix's step and began to busy herself with the tea-cups. A single yellowish bulb of light hung over her head. He had felt sorry for her as she sat there, a little, worried old lady with her hand to her brow; he thought how silly he had been to distrust her, but now he could see her face, he was disturbed again. Her face was so narrow there seemed scarcely room between the cheeks for the long, bone-thin nose and the compressed mouth. It looked to Felix like the face of some sort of large insect. Her hair, fairish and greyish, was bound in thin plaits round her head. Her eyelids, thick and pale, hid her eyes. She did not look up or smile as Felix sat down.

She said: 'I'm afraid Frau Leszno is being rather difficult – not

14

for the first time, I may say; but she'll get over it. It's the war coming to an end. The Lesznos had some money and a house in Eastern Germany – actually they're Polish Jews but they fled to Germany during some pogrom or other – and now she thinks the Allies are going to send her back to spend the rest of her days in luxury. Dear me, if all . . .' Miss Bohun broke off abruptly as Frau Leszno pushed the front door open and came in, her black coat tight and damp-looking on her stout little body, her boots trailing water, her round, red, commonplace face set in a brooding look of grievance. She wore black mittens, but her fingers stuck out cracked and red like a row of beef sausages. She pushed a plate of bread on to the table.

Felix moved uncomfortably under her stare. When the door slammed again, he said: 'Is she cross with me?'

'Take no notice of her.' Miss Bohun suddenly gave a decided movement of her shoulders that seemed to throw off Frau Leszno and everything to do with her. She lifted the bread-plate: 'Have a slice. I'm afraid there's nothing to put on to it but margarine. No doubt you fed very well in Baghdad. You'll find a difference here; none of the best people live much above starvation level here today. They have the satisfaction of knowing they are doing the right thing. I buy what I can afford and we always have something nourishing, even if it's plain, but I *won't* buy on the black market. That brings us to the question of your keep.' For the first time her eyelids rose and she fixed Felix with small, critical, reddish-brown eyes, then her glance fell again. She continued: 'I do not wish to make a profit on you, Felix, but I'm a working-woman and, of course, running this house takes valuable time. I can't be expected to do it for nothing: but there! after tea we'll try and worry it out. Do you feel cold? You can put the fire on for a bit.'

Felix, who felt very cold, bent and snapped on the switch of a small electric fire.

Miss Bohun said: 'I know no one can take the place of your mother, Felix, but I'm a sort of relative – the only relative of any sort that you have out here – and I want to do what I can for you. It's my duty, anyway.'

Felix said: 'Thank you,' and tried out of gratitude to feel responsive, but the space between them seemed to echo with emptiness. Miss Bohun was so unlike his mother, and, for some reason, he felt sure that when she had raised her eyes and looked at him she had somehow expressed disappointment in him. Perhaps she had imagined he would be older, or younger, or better-looking, or a more unusual sort of boy. Anyway, she retired now into her own thoughts, eyes hidden, and he gave his attention to the meal of grey, gritty bread and tasteless tea. Then he heard a slight movement beside him. He looked down and cried out involuntarily in delight. As the bars of the fire had grown red, a Siamese cat had come out from somewhere and was moving towards the warmth. It looked a sad little cat, as lost as himself, and his heart seemed to swell with relief at the sight of something – something he could love.

Miss Bohun looked up, startled by his cry, then, seeing the cat, she sniffed and said: 'Oh, Faro. She was given to me. An army officer and his wife going back to England. The thoughtless way people take on animals here! They know they've got to leave them behind. I didn't want a fancy cat. I just wanted an ordinary backyard animal to catch rats.'

'Doesn't he catch rats?' asked Felix.

' "She",' Miss Bohun corrected him, 'it's a "she". That's another nuisance. Yes, she catches them – I'll say that for her – but she won't eat them. I have to go to the Old City and buy camel meat for her.'

'She's very quiet.'

'She's learnt to be quiet. When she first came she was a spoilt thing. The Peppers had spoilt her. They had no children, you know. She wanted to sit on my knee and get into my bed at night. "Oh, no, young woman," I said, "you're here to catch rats. Out into the garden you go, the wood-shed's full of them." Then she tried to make up to the Lesznos. Well, they'd no time for her, either, so she stopped asking to be made a fuss of, but she still screams when she's hungry. They're selfish creatures.'

'I could get her camel meat if it would help,' said Felix.

Miss Bohun reflected a moment, as though about to accept this offer, then she shook her head: 'They'd cheat you. I know how to deal with them. I've been in this country twenty years.'

When tea was finished Felix knelt down beside Faro and stroked her. She scarcely looked at him. He whispered: 'Dear little cat, dear little cat,' and as though stirred by the affection in his voice, she looked up, her eyes intelligent, and blue as flowers. She let Felix lift her and take her on to his knee while Miss Bohun went into the question of his keep.

'Now,' said Miss Bohun, 'my idea is that we should share everything equally. I've made a list of household expenses.' She sat down at her writing-desk and found among the muddle in her drawer a piece of paper on which she had written things like: Rent, Light, Heating, Telephone, Wages, Kerosene, Food, Upkeep of Garden, Wear and Tear of Furniture &c. She did not hand him the paper but, peering at it over her arm, he noticed she had put Telephone and Kerosene down twice. He did not like to mention this. He noticed that the rent was only £5 a month and the wages of Frau Leszno, her son Nikky and the gardener together only £9 – but somehow, with one thing and another, the total in large figures at the bottom was £35. Miss Bohun ticked through the items quickly, read the total aloud, wrote it again and halved it: 'There! Now, shall we call your share £21 – that's £21 a month, of course. Actually, that's the controlled price here, and it makes a nice round figure and helps me to cover expenses.'

Felix nodded, a little stunned. He had not dreamt that life with Miss Bohun would cost so much. His mother's pension had died with her: obviously the Shiptons were right when they told him the lump sum left for his education and keep would not last long.

Miss Bohun smiled briefly and put the paper away. Then, hearing Faro's purring rising like a dynamo, she said quickly and brightly: 'Dear me, listen to that cat. I've never heard her purr like that before.'

'She only wants to be loved,' said Felix.

Miss Bohun frowned slightly, something odd in her expression: then, raising her eyelids again, she glanced at the boy and the cat and said: 'Oh, well, if you've got the time to waste. I'm afraid I've a pupil coming, so, if you wouldn't mind going up to your room, Felix . . .'

'Can I take Faro?'

'Yes. Yes, I suppose so.'

He wanted to add: 'And can I have an oil-stove?' but Miss Bohun seemed so occupied by the papers on her desk that he hesitated too long to be able to speak. He went upstairs, holding Faro to his throat for warmth. At the top he noticed another flight, no more than a ladder between walls, that led up to what must be an attic; a curtain hung at the top in place of a door and through the holes in the fabric sparkled stars of light. So there was already someone else in the house! Well, perhaps things were not as bad as he had feared. Anyway, he had Faro. He went to his room and began to put up his mother's favourite things. She had been a great collector of bazaar objects and had often said to people: 'I ought to have been an interior decorator. It's a gift, you know; I'd make a fortune if I were in Mayfair.' He had brought the little hammer and packet of nails which she always carried in her luggage, and now he hung over his bed a large Turkish embroidery, a repeating pattern of birds in gold thread on rose-pink silk. Over the desk he put a Persian painting of a gazelle-eyed girl holding a rose and, opposite it, a late Phanariot ikon almost entirely covered with brass. He went round hammering happily, imitating in his mind his mother's pleasure in these things, until, suddenly, his door burst open and Miss Bohun stood there looking very sour. Even so, she kept her eyelids down. This made her look strange, as though she were blind, when she raised her face to speak:

'What is this noise? Where did you get that hammer?'

'It's mine,' Felix breathed nervously.

'You should have asked me before doing this sort of thing. I don't want the walls spoilt.' That was all she said before she lifted her eyelids and saw Faro curled on the thin Arab carpet that formed a bed-cover. She crossed the room and slapped her off indignantly, saying: 'I won't have cats on beds,' and went out, closing the door on Felix's apology.

When the dinner-bell rang and Felix went downstairs again, he saw with a lift of his spirits that three places were laid at the table.

'Does someone else live here?' he asked.

Miss Bohun glanced at the third place as though unable to account for it herself, then she said: 'Oh yes, old Mr Jewel. He's up in the attic.' Her tone implied that there was something rather unpleasant about Mr Jewel. She clicked her tongue and murmured: 'Really, he's late again for dinner. I suppose one must excuse him, he knows no better.' She picked up the dinner-bell that stood at her right hand, gave it a sharp ring, then went on murmuring: '. . . and when he uses the bathroom! People have to grow old, of course, I'm not denying it, but . . . oh dear, I don't know!' As she ladled out the soup, she sighed, making Felix feel uneasy as though with guilt.

Slow and very careful footsteps began descending from the top of the house, but Miss Bohun appeared to hear nothing. She sighed again and said: 'I'm tired. You must not be surprised, Felix, if you sometimes find me thoughtful or tired. You see, I'm a pastor. I have my own little church, my own little flock, and I have to give so much to them. So much. Also, as you will have noticed, I have my troubles here as well – all the result of giving a home to those unwanted elsewhere. I have only tried to be kind, only tried to be good.'

Felix felt embarrassed, but he was also much moved. Miss Bohun had been kind to him, too; she had given him a home when he was unwanted elsewhere. She glanced up to find him gazing at her, his cheeks pink, his eyes round with gratitude, and a slight smile and warmth of colour touched her own face. 'One day, perhaps,' she said, 'I'll tell you about my religion,' then she broke off as Mr Jewel at last reached the lower stairs.

He was a little, old man, with a square, snub face that even now, grey and worn with old age as it was, looked more like the face of a school-boy than of a man. He grinned at Felix and gave a sort of salute by lifting a knotted hand to the grey stubble over his ears. Miss Bohun did not look at him or introduce him. Felix, smiling back at him, said: 'How do you do?' as though there had been no omission. Mr Jewel nodded in reply. He lowered himself slowly into his chair but, once in it, he set about his soup without a pause, making a lot of noise as it went down. Miss Bohun's mouth turned down. As soon as the soup was finished, Mr Jewel waited for the next course, holding to the sides of his chair and giving quick glances at the door through which Frau Leszno would enter. Felix watched him happily, feeling that Mr Jewel's presence had taken a weight from the air. It was evident, however, that Miss Bohun did not feel like that. Once or twice she sighed deeply and she had nothing to say. Frau Leszno came in with a plate of greenish mash.

'I hope you like beans done in this way,' Miss Bohun said to Felix, 'they're so good for you. When I was at school we used to be shown how beans burnt with a blue flame, just the same as meat. That means they're full of carbohydrates.'

Mr Jewel did not speak throughout the meal. After a long silence had followed Miss Bohun's remark about the beans, Felix managed to ask: 'Could I have a plug put in for a reading-lamp, Miss Bohun?'

She frowned down at her beans: 'You don't need two lights in that room.'

'I'd rather have a reading-lamp. I brought my mother's. It's a Venetian glass bottle, ruby glass with gold on it, and she made the shade herself. I'd like to have it. I'll pay for the plug, of course.'

'Oh dear!' said Miss Bohun as though beset on all sides. 'Well, if you mean to pay for it, I suppose I can't refuse; but only one light burning at a time, mind you.'

Felix promised.

When he had finished the last course, of bread pudding, Mr Jewel at once started the ascent to the attic. Miss Bohun said in very bright tones to Felix: 'Well, I must be off to my "Ever-Readies". Wet or fine, the "Ever-Readies" shine. Perhaps you'd like a hot bath after your journey? Just ask Frau Leszno to light the boiler. I'm afraid there's no electric light in the bathroom. You'll have to take this little lamp.' She put on a raincoat, bound her head in a ginger-coloured scarf, and went with a light step from the house.

The thought of the hot bath cheered Felix. When Frau Leszno came in to clear the table he asked her politely if she would be kind enough to light the boiler. She gave him a bleak stare from her pale, globular eyes, then seemed abruptly to shut off her expression. Hiding all she thought and felt beneath the humble whine of her voice, she said: 'I shall see.'

Felix wandered round the living-room that contained Frau Leszno's table and six chairs of cheap, varnished wood; her horse-hair sofa – he sat down on this and found it very hard; Miss Bohun's desk; a dresser to take the household china; and, placed on either side of the electric fire, two chairs with wooden arms. Hanging up on the coat-hooks beside the front door was a sheepskin coat that filled half the room with a heavy odour of mortality.

He found nothing to hold his attention except, on the desk, six shabby little books with titles like *Handbook of Rumanian, Russian in Twenty-five Easy Lessons* and *Hungarian Without Tears*. He wondered if Miss Bohun could possibly be learning all these languages. Later he discovered she collected these old grammars in order to use the phrases for her own dictation to pupils; now, impressed and curious, he took them to the table and studied them for want of anything better to do.

Half an hour later, when he supposed the water must be hot, he lit the lamp, got his dressing-gown, towel and soap, and crossed the wet yard to the bathroom that was opposite the kitchen. The rain had stopped but a damp, icy wind was blowing. The bathroom was a large, draughty, white-washed room in which a small bath and a boiler stood lost in one corner. The air was so cold he knew before he touched the boiler it had not been lit. He stood for some moments not knowing what to do, then he returned to the yard.

There was a light in the kitchen; his disappointment gave him courage to go over and open the door. Inside there was a dark, dirty-looking room smelling of stale grease and lit only by an oil-lamp, but it was warm. A young man sat on a back-tilted kitchen chair, his feet on the table. As the door opened, he looked up from his book.

'Is Frau Leszno about?' asked Felix.

'She has gone to bed.'

'She promised to light the boiler for the bath.' As he said this, Felix realized she had not promised; she had merely said: 'I shall see.'

The young man said: 'Did she?' with cold disbelief, and added casually: 'Speak to her yourself. She's in her room.'

The warmth of the kitchen held Felix in spite of the young man's dark, discouraging stare. He asked: 'Are you Nikky Leszno?'

'Yes.'

'Do you think perhaps you could light it? Or could you show me how?'

'I don't know how.' Nikky returned to his book and Felix had no choice but to go.

Out in the yard again, he saw that what he had thought was the second window of the kitchen was a separate small room. He knocked on the door.

'Bitte?' came from Frau Leszno.

'Oh, Frau Leszno, you did not light the boiler.'

There was a pause, then Frau Leszno agreed complacently: 'No, I did not light it.'

'Would you light it now?'

'No,' said Frau Leszno. She sounded pleased with her own decision, but could not resist adding in her usual whine: 'Why should I myself trouble with such a thing? No, I do not light it.'

Felix went back to the bathroom and examined the boiler. Under the tank there was a small stove to take fuel – probably wood. If he could find the wood-shed, he might be able to light it himself. He went outside and looked round. The sky was black but by the glimmer that came from the surrounding windows, he could see there was a passage running into darkness at one side of the house. That might lead to a shed. He followed it, touching with his finger-tips the wet, stone house-side, and came out to the garden at the back. There was nothing to be seen but a great black space. The rain had washed the snow away; the wind poured in from the blackness, steady and cold as a wind from the sea. He stood on the path, peering into the dark but unable to distinguish anything. He knew he would not be able to find where the wood was kept... Somehow this seemed at that moment worse than anything else that had happened to him since his mother's death. He had thought himself lonely at the Shiptons', but now it was as though he had never known real loneliness before.

As he stood he remembered a story he had read once about a peasant who, after his wife's funeral, had gone alone at midnight into the fields and called to her: 'Come back to me,' but when her voice from the remote distance answered: 'I come,' he had fled in panic back to his hut and barricaded the door. Felix knew if he could now call to his mother and hear her voice in reply, he would not flee from her. No, he would run, run into the black sea and fling himself into her arms. He opened his mouth and whispered shyly: 'Come back to me.' The wind swept his whisper into silence. Suddenly he shouted: 'Come back, come back, come back,' but there was no reply. There was no movement, no sound but the roaring wind.

He returned down the passage feeling that his mother, by dying and leaving him like this, had abandoned him utterly.

Back in the house, he could not find Faro. He went to his room and left the door ajar in the hope she might find him.

Lying cold in bed, he tried to return to his dream of his mother in the boat, but that now seemed as remote as she was. He stared into nothingness, thinking he would never sleep, never feel warm again. At last Faro jumped on to his bed and he felt her paws, soft and heavy, move with a cautious certainty up to his face; her whiskers touched his cheek as she sniffed to be sure of him, then, like an arrow-tip of ice, her nose pointed between the sheets. He raised the covers for her. Slipping like silk into his arms, she curled warm against his body and lay with her chin on his shoulder, purring contentment. He wrapped his arms round her. Comforted, kissing her between the ears, he whispered: 'I love you.' He pressed his face into her fur and said: 'Faro, darling little Faro . . .' but in a moment, when he meant only to say 'Faro', he found he was saying: 'Mother' and all the tears he had kept back that day streamed down his face until he slept, exhausted.

2

As the days passed, life did not change much in Miss Bohun's house. Felix was at a loss about it. Except for Faro, there was nothing here with which he could feel any contact. His longing for his mother was fixed like an ache in the centre of his chest and there was nothing to disperse it. From it the routine of his new life spread about him, winter bleak.

The garden was green and cold; the house colder. Most days the sky was stormy. Miss Bohun said the rains had been unusually heavy that year; indeed it had been an unusual winter altogether, for snow fell only about once in a decade and the Arabs were saying the Jews must have brought it from Europe. When she noticed Felix shivering, she told him the winter here was so short, no one bothered to combat it; it had to be suffered and let pass.

Felix would awake in the morning with Faro still in his arms and both of them would move reluctantly out of bed into the icy room. Each day seemed to lie ahead grey and purposeless. He would begin it by going downstairs in his dressing-gown and crossing the yard to the bathroom. As Miss Bohun saw nothing extraordinary about this, he supposed there was nothing extraordinary, but he caught the worst cold he had ever had. He began to remember his mother as warmth, comfort, happiness – things he must learn to live without.

Before he arrived, Miss Bohun had arranged for him to have lessons with a Mr Posthorn of the Education Office. Mr Posthorn was a busy man; he not only had his government job but tutored some Arab boys of wealthy family who hoped, when the war ended, to go to an English university. He had agreed to 'fit Felix into his spare time', which meant that some mornings Felix went to Mr Posthorn's office and was told to study this or that, while occasionally Mr Posthorn could spare an hour to drop in to

Miss Bohun's and give Felix some instruction. Most of Felix's day was spent in study in his bedroom. He knew he would not get far in this way and he knew also that Mr Posthorn would have been willing to give him more attention had he, like Miss Bohun, not been disappointed in him. Miss Bohun said or did nothing that gave Felix any clue as to how he had failed her, but Mr Posthorn, after testing his knowledge, spoke without hesitation: 'What on earth have you been doing with yourself since you left school in England?'

Felix explained that in Baghdad he had taken lessons with an old English lady, an ex-governess to a royal family, who had taught him English composition, French, drawing, geography and history. Unfortunately she had known less Greek, Latin and mathematics than he knew himself. His mother had treated lessons there as a joke and said: 'Never mind, darling, when the war's over we'll make up for lost time.' The Shiptons, like Mr Posthorn, had been shocked to discover how little Felix knew and had told him that as he would have to earn his living one day, he had better start studying at once for his Matriculation. Mr Posthorn said:

'Your parents ought to have been ashamed of themselves, keeping you away from school during the most important years of your life. I can't understand it. Your father was an educated man, wasn't he?'

Felix explained: 'It wasn't my father's fault. Mother wouldn't let me go back to England when the war started. Father was cross, but Mother said: "If he goes I may not see him again," and she wouldn't have, either.'

Mr Posthorn said: 'You'll never make up for it,' but Felix, although he knew it to be a serious matter, could not really care. It was as though the important part of his life were already over; only blankness lay ahead. Like the Jerusalem winter, it was only to be suffered and got over. Yet, before his mother's death, he had begun to feel excited about his life that was, he supposed, just beginning. The war was ending. Soon they would be able to go where they liked – there was the whole world to see. He had begun to have bursts of wild exhilaration. He felt then that something was growing within him that gave an excitement and brilliance and wonder to everything. But when his mother died, the

wonder had gone like a light snapped off. He could see no reason
for doing anything now. It would be like dressing up, or acting a
play, or writing a book, on a desert island. Sometimes, when his
own life flickered again in him and he knew the future was still
there, he wondered in desperation if he could try and please Miss
Bohun. Could he become something – a famous general, say, or
an admiral? – to impress her? There was no warmth in the idea.
And what would she care?

At meal-times he would feel drawn to stare at her face, which
was colourless as plaster, the eyes nearly always hidden behind
the thick, plaster-coloured lids. Even when she lifted her face to
speak or call Frau Leszno, she would not open her eyes. Her
mouth was never more than a minus sign drawn under the thin,
drooping tip of her nose. Often the sign drooped too, as though
something near her was distasteful to her, but more often she held
it firm and straight against her teeth. When caught staring, Felix
would look away at once, nervous, repelled, yet drawn to look
again as soon as it seemed safe. One day he realized she reminded
him of a praying mantis. A mantis had come into his room once
in Baghdad and hung motionless all night on the curtain – a narrow insect, like a green stick, silent, shut up in itself. This like-
ness made her even more strange to him, almost monstrous, and
she was the stranger for having a religion of her own. She told
him nothing about this; she seemed to have forgotten her promise
to tell him one day, she seemed for long stretches to forget him
altogether.

When she was not rushing off to the 'Ever-Readies' or giving
an English lesson, she was, he could see, obsessed by the dis-
agreement with Frau Leszno which was always carried on just
out of his hearing. He was rather glad of this quarrel because it
somehow made the two women seem more human – but it was a
negative consolation. He wished he had something, anything, to
which he could look forward. For a week or two he dwelt on the
new person who must be coming into the front room, but no one
came and the hope began to fade. He wished very much that Mr
Jewel came downstairs oftener, but the old man kept to his room
and descended only for supper, which he ate rapidly without a
word. Obviously things were not well between Miss Bohun and
Mr Jewel, but there was no open quarrel; she merely ignored

him, and when she was near there was about him something guilty, flustered, almost apprehensive. Felix was full of curiosity as to what Mr Jewel did about his other meals. One day he asked Miss Bohun. She kept silent, reflecting a moment, holding in her narrow spade-shaped chin so that two other chins appeared beneath it; then she lifted her face and said vaguely: 'He makes tea in his room, I believe. He's funny that way.'

'Oh! . . . and what does he do all alone upstairs?'

'I have not asked him.'

The extreme coldness of this reply silenced Felix. But it was not only Miss Bohun that kept him at arm's length – the atmosphere of the whole house seemed to him hostile. He was at home only with Faro or in the garden or at the cinema. He wondered sometimes if things would be any different for him anywhere. The centre wheel of his life was gone; he was at a standstill. He felt forsaken by the world, when, at last, something happened that changed the whole situation. He became a confidant. He was made to feel important and Miss Bohun, unexpectedly turning to him for sympathy, was revealed as nothing more monstrous than an unhappy old lady.

It was the first morning of spring sunshine when, with Faro on his shoulder, he was drawn out to the glitter of the open air. There was a bench under the mulberry tree. Despite the cold, he settled down to work there. When he heard someone crossing the garden he looked up to see Nikky, wearing a most elegant overcoat with an astrakhan collar. Nikky let it hang open so everyone could see the fur lining inside; it was so long, it tripped him several times as he walked, but he held his delicate, pale face aloof, apparently unaware of being tripped. Felix, awed and admiring, watched him as he went out through the back gate and crossed the stony wasteland beyond. Just as he was disappearing over the crest of the hill, Miss Bohun ran out, arms raised, and shouted: 'Has Nikky gone?'

'Yes.' Felix pointed after him but it was too late to catch him.

'Oh!' Miss Bohun flung down her fists in exasperation, 'I told him to clean the windows. He's supposed to do the windows once a week, but he does nothing, nothing. All he wants to do is dress up in his father's clothes and go out. It's too bad. It's so unfair to me.'

Her voice almost broke, so when Felix returned to the house at lunch-time he was less surprised than he might have been to find her crouched at the table with rounded shoulders and drooping head. He stood looking at her, feeling the change in her. It was not only that she had a deflated look, there was something tearful about her although her eyes were dry. If she had been crying Felix could have asked at once what was the matter. Instead he had to stand uncertainly by the garden window and pretend to be looking at his books.

Miss Bohun must have been conscious of him, for in a moment she sniffed and said: 'She told me I was a wicked woman. I'd just gone out to have a quiet word about Nikky's conduct when she flung at me – literally *flung* at me: "You could be an angel, but you're really a devil."'

It was her stunned manner rather than what had been said that conveyed to him her sense of shock. He felt shocked himself. How cruel to say that to Miss Bohun – Miss Bohun who had befriended the Lesznos and given a home to him and Mr Jewel! She had been an angel to everyone.

Miss Bohun sniffed again and continued: 'She doesn't mean it, of course; she *couldn't* mean it. It was just temper, but it hurt me that she could say it after all I've done for them.' She sat still again, brooding and silent, with Felix standing in sympathetic watchfulness, until Frau Leszno came in with the meal; then she jerked herself upright and looked as though nothing unusual had happened.

'Go on up now, Felix,' she said loudly and cheerfully, 'and wash your hands. I want to get luncheon over quickly. I've a pupil coming in twenty minutes.'

But as they ate, it was as though some barrier were down. Frau Leszno, coming in and out with a smirking look of guilt, seemed to sense this new relationship and slammed the door each time she left.

'Oh dear!' said Miss Bohun as it crashed a second time, 'and I've been so good to them. Well, *I* have nothing with which to reproach myself . . . but I must not lose heart. Whatever happens, I find I'm always rewarded in the end. When I make a gift to someone, it is returned to me a hundredfold. Does that happen to you, Felix?'

'I haven't noticed it.'

'Well, notice next time and you'll see.'

Felix, though he lacked other education, was deeply read in children's classics and he recognized here a true goodness. He was very impressed but, unable to think of anything adequate to say, remained silent.

'You know, Felix,' said Miss Bohun after a pause, 'I came out here when I was still a young woman. Yes, I was under forty when I came. It was just when I realized nobody was going to want to marry me that I felt drawn to come here and join the "Ever-Readies". My little income made it possible. By giving my heart and soul to the cause, I've worked my way to the top. Yes, it's my own little show now. I think – I think I can say I've not wasted my life?'

This, both statement and question, was spoken with so unexpected a tremulousness that Felix, although quite ignorant of the facts, felt bound to declare stoutly: 'Oh, I'm sure you're terrific, like a missionary, like Livingstone. Anyway, you've been jolly decent to me.'

'I try to do good. I'm only an old spinster. No one, except God, has chosen me.'

Miss Bohun's mood of humility discomforted Felix very much, but he recognized it as a part of virtue.

'I haven't a family. I have no children, but I have a whole circle of people who're indebted to me. I thought that meant something. I thought the Lesznos . . .' she broke off, swallowed, then continued in stronger tones: 'They've never *shown* much gratitude, it's true, but I always told myself that deep down they must be grateful. That's why I can't understand Frau Leszno saying that this morning. I *can't* understand it.'

'I think she's beastly,' said Felix with deeper feeling than he knew he possessed.

'Do you?' Miss Bohun glanced up with interest, 'you *really* think that, Felix?'

'I don't like her voice, and I think she's mean,' and for the first time he told Miss Bohun about the incident of the bath-boiler on the night of his arrival.

Miss Bohun was not, as he had hoped she would be, indignant over his failure to get a bath, but instead said in an elated and excited tone: 'There! I've always said it! Children's instincts are so acute, children's and dogs'. And she's always telling me she's a lady. She says she went to a boarding-school when she was a girl, and she says she's been used to every comfort money could buy. And she's always telling me how well servants are treated in Germany – like members of the family. That doesn't sound very German to me. After all, she and her husband had to do a bolt from the Germans; I've had to remind her of that more than once. Well, no one could have done more for anyone than I've done for her. That's the trouble, of course. Time was when she and Nikky were simply in possession here. They did what they liked. Nikky was getting so insolent, my students started to remark on it. I could see the danger. I've been forced to wean them from me. *Forced* – for their own sakes as well as mine. It's so bad spiritually, don't you think?'

Felix, baffled by this question, could do no more than make a sympathetic murmur. Miss Bohun now retired again into brooding quiet. She said nothing more at that meal, but there was more to be said. She had clearly decided to tell Felix the story of her relationship with the Lesznos, for during the next week each luncheon-time added to it.

Frau Leszno and her husband had arrived in Palestine some time before the war. Nikky had followed later. They had brought clothes and jewellery but only a little money. 'Frau Leszno,' said Miss Bohun, 'at once took this house and furnished it. She never stopped to think she'd need the money for other things; to her the most important possession was a home . . .'

'But this house?' Felix interrupted in his surprise, '*this* house?'

'Yes,' Miss Bohun seemed irritated by his surprise, 'the situation was quite absurd. Herr Leszno had married late. He was an old man and, to tell you the truth, he was dying before he left Germany. He had sclerosis. I prayed but nothing I did seemed to help him. He couldn't earn a penny. And as for Frau Leszno – you've seen for yourself what *she's* like. No one would employ her, except out of charity – yet she got the chance of this very nice house, which, mind you, belongs to an Arab. Yes, it belongs to an Imam at the big mosque. Well, they took it on. I'd been living at a *pension* but I wanted to move, *for a reason*. I began looking for something, rooms or something, in this quarter – my favourite; it's the most picturesque, I think, don't you? I happened to knock on this gate and Frau Leszno opened it – a poor, bedraggled, starved thing that started to cry before she'd said half-a-dozen words. They'd already sold part of the furniture at a loss to keep going. Well, I came in and took charge at once. I'm always looking for some way to be of use in the world and here was my chance – the sick old man, and Frau Leszno wailing and lamenting and wringing her hands. She showed me over the house – well, really, I showed her over it – and there were these simply splendid rooms, empty, just what I wanted. I told her I'd take two of the bedrooms. "Now," I said, "you're not to worry. I'll look after you." Ah, she told me I was her good angel, *then*! I furnished my own rooms myself. I gave English lessons to make extra money. I paid all the rent that was owing – a considerable sum! £25 as a matter of fact! – and I had the house put into my name to safeguard all of us. When Herr Leszno died, I promised him on his death-bed that while I had a roof to give her, his wife would never lack one. Oh, it was quite an undertaking for one lone woman. Mr Tadlow, who was assistant D.C. here at the time (such a nice man), said: "You're one of the bravest, Miss Bohun." Yes, he said that: "One of the bravest." And, I can tell you, Frau Leszno never let me forget my promise. Then Nikky turned up. She said she had a son who was trying to get out of Europe. She said the last she'd heard of him was he'd gone back to Poland to fight. I never thought he'd get here, but he managed it somehow. Trust Nikky Leszno!' She gloomed over this escape a while before adding: 'I had to go to Haifa to get him off one of those refugee coffin ships that came from Rumania. More trouble for me! He was in a state – thin and ghastly, dirty; ill, too – or, I mean, he thought he was ill. A mental condition, really, of course. Dear me, what a time that was.' Miss Bohun made a grimace and shook her head over her memories, but suddenly her voice rose loudly and cheerfully: 'Well, I did what I could for him. I introduced him into the "Ever-Readies" at once, and it made a power of difference. I'm sure if it hadn't been for the spiritual comfort he drew from our faith, he would have been dead long ago. Not that I got much gratitude from *him*. As soon as he was well again, he began to find distractions outside our circle. That sort of thing happens, I fear – but, there, he's a talented lad, a fey sort of creature. I always feel we mustn't impose on him. We mustn't complain.'

Felix said nothing. It would never have entered his head to complain about Nikky, whose good looks and aloof manner always made him feel his own insignificance. Reflecting upon it now, he waited in silence for Miss Bohun to continue her story.

In those days Frau Leszno had a bedroom on the first floor while Nikky slept in the attic. Miss Bohun earned the money as a sort of father of the family while Frau Leszno did the housework and cooking. Nikky, trained only as a gentleman, undertook a few odd jobs. They lived together on an equal footing.

'Not unhappily,' commented Miss Bohun with a sigh.

Change came when, during the war, she was asked if she would board an army officer 'at a generous rate'. It was then she realized how valuable her house could be. 'The only suitable room for letting was the one you now have,' she said, and Felix wondered why his was the only suitable room. What about the front room? Before he could ask this question, Miss Bohun continued: 'Well, Frau Leszno was installed in your room in those days. I had to persuade her to move out to the little room in the yard. I cannot *tell* you the trouble I had with her. That yard room is a nice little room, but she knew it had been designed for a servant – and that was enough! The wails, the obstinacy, the sitting at table with tears streaming down! Oh dear! But I had to steel myself. It was impossible for me to go on as I had been – working to keep both of them *and* the house going. I *had* to be firm for all our sakes. If I'd collapsed, where would they have been? In the end I got her out and the officer moved in. Then there was fresh trouble. He'd never heard of a servant eating at the same table as her employer. Poor man, he couldn't get used to Frau Leszno bringing in the food, then planting herself down beside him. I could see how it embarrassed him. He did not like her. He felt just as you did about her. She isn't a pleasant woman; and Nikky can be so boorish, too. And she neglects herself so – dear me! that smell of sweat in the hot weather. In the end I persuaded her to take her meals in the kitchen and suggested Nikky should eat with her, just for company. Again, what a struggle! Really! each time I suggested any small change, there was always a painful scene. She had to go, though. I insisted on it. But she's a foolish woman, incapable of facing facts. She pretended to herself that these new arrangements were only temporary – war-time measures, as you might say. She was sure when the officer went she'd be back in her old room and eating in here just as before. I said nothing, but I felt I simply could *not* have it all over again. So, as soon as the officer told me he'd been posted, I got him to recommend one of his friends, who moved in the day he moved out. I kept doing this all during the war and it worked very nicely until a few weeks before you arrived, when, with the officers all leaving, I was finding it a little difficult to get someone suitable. Then, of course, she started insisting that she must come back into the house. I was distracted! She's such an insistent person, you know. She wouldn't let the matter drop. I felt myself being battened down – then, as good luck would have it, I got a letter from Mr Shipton. About you. Just in time, you see! I was able to do you a good turn, and you, in a way, did me one. But before that, of course, Mr Jewel came. Oh dear, oh dear! That was another exhausting business. The poor old man was homeless. I felt I must take him in the attic. Months before, I'd suggested Nikky should find himself a job and pay a little towards his keep. After all there were two of them and only one of me. But he's bone-lazy. I'm fond enough of the boy, but I felt I owed it to myself not to let him take advantage. I gave him the alternative of finding himself a lodging elsewhere or taking himself down to the kitchen. I said I'd give him a mattress.'

'Does he sleep in the kitchen, then?' asked Felix, who knew that he did, yet somehow had never been able to absorb the fact.

'By his own choice,' said Miss Bohun gravely. She paused, her lips compressed, then sighed and said: 'Others have come to this country with no more to recommend them than Nikky has and yet they've worked and made some sort of position for themselves. Nikky has never done anything. He says he's a member of the intelligentsia, whatever that may mean. I suppose while there's someone to be imposed on, there'll be someone to do the imposing.' Another pause, then her voice lilted up strongly and happily: 'Well, there it is! And now, to keep Frau Leszno quiet, I've had to promise to get someone in to do the rough work. You see how I have to face up to one expense after another? Fortunately I've been able to find someone nice and cheap, an old

Armenian woman called Maria. She's arriving in a day or two. No doubt Frau Leszno will impose on the poor old soul, so we'll have to do what we can, you and I, Felix, to help, by not imposing on her ourselves. She may not be much use, but I feel it's one's duty to help support the aged.'

'Yes,' agreed Felix. In all he had heard he felt whole-heartedly on Miss Bohun's side. He could see, of course, the basis of Frau Leszno's grievance, but it lost significance in the light of his own dislike of her. How horrid, how really horrid, she had been to him! And he was sure she had been just as horrid to poor Miss Bohun. He could see clearly the point of Miss Bohun's wishing to get both the Lesznos out of the house and her wisdom in keeping them out. His mother would have hated them, too; she would have felt as revolted as he did by the thought of sharing the meal-table with anyone as stale-smelling and disagreeable as Frau Leszno. A wave of sympathy came from him towards Miss Bohun that gave her reality and humanity and made her seem to him almost lovable. He was her ally.

'I would like to ask you, Felix,' she said, '. . . of course you're still young and inexperienced, but when Frau Leszno said that terrible thing to me, I could not help wondering: "Have I treated them fairly?"'

'Of course you have. They're beastly. Frau Leszno must always have been beastly.'

'Well, perhaps. But Herr Leszno was a delightful old man – so handsome, so distinguished-looking. Nikky takes after him. I became quite attached to him. For the few months he was spared to me, we were real chums. I must admit I never felt quite the same for Frau Leszno.'

Felix said: 'I can't think why you ever took them on in the first place.'

She replied with quiet importance: 'You see, the situation is rather more complex than it appears.' As she paused, gazing down at her plate, Felix felt the whole mystery of the grown-up world behind her manner. He did not hope for an explanation, yet Miss Bohun seemed to try and give him one. 'Sometimes,' she said, 'you think God is telling you to do something – then, too late, you realize you're mistaken. I used to think God had led me to the Lesznos' door, now I'm not so sure. You see, apart from my promise . . .' she hesitated before repeating more firmly, 'apart from my promise, there is the religious question. Under my influence Frau Leszno joined the "Ever-Readies". Of course she's not the only person of Jewish blood in the "Ever-Readies" – dear me, no, there are a number – but she and Nikky are the only Orthodox Jews we've brought into the fold. I'm sure I could never had done it with Herr Leszno – he was such a strong character, such a patriarch. I had to respect his faith; I did all my praying for him in secret, which may be why it didn't do much good because God helps those who help themselves. But Frau Leszno was a different kettle of fish. She just wanted something to lean on . . . and Nikky, of course . . .'

'Nikky!'

'Certainly,' Miss Bohun sounded somewhat exasperated, 'I told you before that Nikky is a member. How could we have helped him otherwise? Anyway, it was all one to him – he's got no true religion. But with Frau Leszno it was different. It was a big change-over for her and it separated her from her own community. She'd been getting some assistance from a charity – well, that stopped, of couse. It meant she was thrown much more on me than she need be; and, of course, she's never let me forget my responsibility. You'd have thought she'd done me a favour. They couldn't see it as I did; they couldn't see that I was saving their souls alive. I keep telling her she'll be among the elect when the Day arrives.'

'What day?' Felix managed to ask quickly.

'Judgment Day, of course,' Miss Bohun said casually and went on: 'No, she thought she was doing me a favour by joining. Really, it was just as though she imagined she was repaying me for all I'd done for them, and, at the same time, increasing my responsibility towards them. I didn't like it. I've often regretted her conversion. It's been a nuisance.'

'Do you think perhaps if Frau Leszno didn't work for you she'd leave the "Ever-Readies"?'

'She might. I must say it would be the best thing. She could drift back to her own people and get *them* to help her for a change. Still, I'd be sorry to lose Nikky; he's our only young blood.'

'Does he go to the meetings?'

'Yes,' Miss Bohun replied irritably, then, on second thoughts: 'Well, not to the meetings exactly, but he still comes to the entertainments.'

The entertainments! The word echoed and re-echoed in Felix's mind and he wondered why, if the 'Ever-Readies' needed young blood, Miss Bohun did not invite him in straight away. Perhaps his eagerness was conveyed to Miss Bohun, for she gave him a reflective glance, then said: 'I'm afraid my experience with the Lesznos has made me think twice of introducing people who might . . . well, who might prove a responsibility.'

Felix, subdued by the implication of this remark, stared down at the tablecloth and began to draw on it with his finger-nail.

'Don't do that, there's a good boy!'

Felix let his hand drop to his lap. In the silence that followed, as Miss Bohun carefully folded her napkin and put it into an olive-wood ring, Felix remembered again the question he wanted to ask, and asked it:

'Miss Bohun, couldn't Frau Leszno have had the room at the front? The one you were preparing?'

Miss Bohun held her mouth very firm for several moments before replying with withdrawn quiet: 'I would rather you did not question me about the front room, Felix.'

Felix murmured an apology. There was silence again. The spate of Miss Bohun's confidences had passed and the air had cooled between them. Suddenly Miss Bohun shook off her quiet and, giving a quick look round at the alarm-clock on the dresser, said: 'Well, Felix, time for bed.'

3

Felix was doing his best to study, but as the days became brighter and the garden greener, his ability to concentrate grew weaker. If he sat in the garden everything and anything distracted him. He could bear the confinement of his room only if he had Faro in with him, but she was the worst distraction of the lot.

It was late January; the coldest time of the year. Felix was allowed to have an oil-stove upstairs on condition he cleaned it himself and filled it from the kerosene drum in the kitchen. The stove gave off more smell than warmth, so on grey days he shivered at his desk; when the sun did appear, sliding round the room in a great, shield-shaped block of light, it was surprisingly hot. Faro would leave Felix's knee and follow the sunlight from the bed to the floor, from the floor to the basket-chair, from the chair to the desk.

One afternoon when he came up from luncheon, Felix found her sprawled across his open books, her fur hot with sun, her paws limp and tender with sleep. He sat and looked at her for a while, then said: 'How do you expect me to work while you're on top of my books?' She lifted an ear at his voice but did not move. At last he made a half-hearted attempt to push her to one side, but when she murmured complainingly in her throat, he said with mock-resignation: 'Oh, all right,' and, glad of any excuse to delay the moment of settling to work, tickled the very soft fur at the base of her ears. Her eyes opened, a flicker of blue; she gave a token purr of recognition, then, stretching her chocolate-coloured paws to their full length, rolled over into a ball, uncovering his Hall & Knight's *Algebra*.

The sight of the plum-coloured binding was enough to set him yawning. Slowly and extremely unwillingly, he forced his attention on to the three problems set him that morning by Mr Posthorn. When he looked at the back of the book and found that, somehow, he had got two correct answers, he regarded his day's work as done. He picked up Faro's toy, a rabbit's paw, and threw it across the room. Faro, who would scarcely have bothered to move if Felix had dropped a shoe, heard the soft, familiar fall and awoke, alert.

'Get it,' urged Felix, and Faro, sailing like a flying-fox off the table, retrieved the paw. While this game was going on, Felix stumbled against and overturned the basket-chair, the only 'easy' chair in the room, and looked with surprise at the heavy folds of cobwebs inside. This made him gaze up at the ceiling-corners, as he had seen his mother do, and he realized how dirty the house was. His mother, who described the thinnest film of dust as 'squalor', would have been shocked. Felix supposed this dirt was shocking, but to him it was merely another proof of how the Lesznos were imposing upon Miss Bohun.

At that moment he heard her voice as she opened the dining-room door on to the garden and emerged just below his window: 'Oh, I do love the sun,' she was saying, 'and a walk round the garden will do us both good.'

Felix, glad of a new distraction, crossed to the window and saw her hurrying out across the grass with her pupil following her. She was wearing her electric blue dress. She apparently had only two, one blue and one rust-coloured. Each was short and cut straight from shoulder to hem, with sleeves that ended at the elbow. The rust dress was decorated with fringe; the blue embroidered with wool. Today she was wearing a large straw hat which Felix had seen for the first time last week. She had said to him: 'I call it my "cartwheel". It's such a nice hat, such an old friend! And this scarf is genuine batik. I made it myself years ago. Very valuable.' Because his mother had always spent more than she could afford on clothes, he supposed the age and limitations of Miss Bohun's wardrobe must result from poverty.

Now, watching her, he wished he had not given all his mother's dresses to Mrs Shipton but had saved some of them for poor Miss Bohun.

'This is a leaf. L-E-A-F, leaf,' she started her lesson by raising her voice to a high, clear sing-song, then she darted over to a low stone wall where some sheltered geranium bushes were still hung with autumn leaves. 'This is a *dead* leaf. A dead – D-E-A-D –

leaf,' her tone changed suddenly to normal as she said: 'Perhaps, Mr Liftshitz, you'd be good enough to help me pluck off these dead leaves – *these-dead-leaves. Pick-them-off.* That's right. They do so disfigure the plant.'

Felix settled himself comfortably, feet up on the window-ledge, to watch Miss Bohun and Mr Liftshitz in the garden. He had watched them before – she darting about like a very active insect, almost a flying insect, while Mr Liftshitz, fat, unhappy, soon shiny with sweat, did his best to keep up with her. Felix thought Mr Liftshitz in his skin-tight, dark suit extremely funny, but Miss Bohun, because he was her friend and ally, he did not find funny at all. Today he could not see her face; only the cart-wheel hat which almost hid her body. Indeed, at times, the hat seemed to be moving by itself from one geranium bush to another.

Felix's mother had been tall. She had said sometimes: 'With my figure, I could earn a fortune as a model girl in Mayfair,' yet something about her had made Felix feel at times the elder, the more responsible. Miss Bohun, tiny as she was, so impressed Felix with her authority that he often forgot he was no longer a small boy. His mother, of course, had had no faults; but she had not shared with Miss Bohun such obvious virtues. With Miss Bohun, listening to her talk, he was always reflecting how honest she was, how good to people, how right in her judgment. It did not seem to him possible she could be anything but right, even in her disapproval of Mr Jewel, whom Felix liked in spite of every-thing. There must be a reason for this disapproval. After all, she knew Mr Jewel very well; Felix did not . . .

She called from under her hat: 'Pick, Mr Liftshitz, pick with a will.'

Mr Liftshitz slowly picked a leaf here and a leaf there until he had made a neat bunch of half-a-dozen leaves. This he offered to Miss Bohun.

'No, no,' she brushed him off irritably, 'don't hand them to me. Scatter them. *Scatter them*, as you would scatter your boun-ty.'

'Please?' asked Mr Liftshitz frowning, his body tense with effort to catch a familiar word.

Miss Bohun ignored him. She passed rapidly to some potted

plants that stood in the shade of the wood-shed. Felix recognized her as being what older people called 'active'. She was much more active than his mother, who had always said things like: 'Don't ask me to climb up there, Felix darling,' or 'My dear boy, I can't possibly go out in this heat,' and had always rested in the afternoons.

Sometimes Miss Bohun's arms and legs shot out from under the hat. Despite the cold, these were bare; they looked no more than bones covered with skin as brown as roasted chicken-skin. Her elbows were sharply pointed and when straightened they disappeared into whirlpools of wrinkles. In dry weather she always wore camel-hide sandals that had grown too big with age so that her thin, mummy-brown feet slid about inside them. She did not seem to mind the water in the grass, but Mr Liftshitz kept looking down miserably at the neat, pointed toes of his black shoes. Miss Bohun was now bending over some pots. She stuck a finger into the earth of each in turn.

'Come over here,' she sang to Mr Liftshitz. He trotted over, panting a little, and gazed with her at the largest flower-pot. 'Here,' she said, 'is a plant that had been put into too small a pot. It was wilting and dying, so I bought it cheap. I said to myself: "I will put it into a larger pot and see how it will reward me." Now you can see what a fine plant it has become. I hope, Mr Liftshitz, if God is ever good enough to put you into a larger pot, you'll reward Him in the same way.'

'Please?' Mr Liftshitz moved troubled hands.

'Now, perhaps we'd better go in and do some dictation.'

Miss Bohun's hat crossed the lawn to the house. It disappeared under Felix's eyes; Mr Liftshitz behind it. For the next half an hour her voice came up through the floor droning simple sentences with the most exact intonation. Felix, deciding that no one could concentrate against such a noise, picked up Faro's rabbit's paw and offered to throw it for her again. She got up reluctantly, yawning and stretching herself, and he went out of the room to give her a long run down the passage. He swung his arm and sent the paw flying towards the front bedroom door; before it landed, Faro was off the table and after it. Speeding with a furious scuffling noise, she seized the paw in her mouth, brought it back and dropped it at Felix's feet. When he had thrown it three times,

Miss Bohun gave a long-drawn, wavering call from the bottom of the stairs: 'F-e-e-l-iks!'

'Yes, Miss Bohun?' He bent down over the stairs so that he could see her standing at the bottom.

'Please don't make that noise, there's a good boy. Teaching, you know, calls for so much concentration. The least sound is distracting.'

'I'm sorry, Miss Bohun.'

'Shouldn't you be at your studies?'

'I've finished them.'

'Well, try and be quiet until tea-time.'

Standing in the passage, wondering what he could do next, he looked at the door of the front bedroom and saw the key was in the lock. Once or twice during his first weeks in the house he had tried the door and found it locked; now he tiptoed towards it, turned the key and entered. He felt a slight, immediate shock at the change in the light. His own bedroom was full of sunlight. This room, running the length of the house-front and having three windows, was filled with cold, blue shadow. It was much longer than its width; in it stood a single bed, made up and covered with a white counterpane, a wooden chair and a little desk on which stood a bible. The room, narrow and chill, looked like a hospital ward. It touched Felix with a desolating sense of emptiness; he left it at once and locked it in on itself.

Then, from sheer boredom, he decided to take a look in Miss Bohun's bedroom. It was, he knew, as bare as his own had been on his arrival, but the time he had seen it – on his second day, when Miss Bohun had called him in and suggested in an undertone that it would be seemly were he to pay his rent in advance – he had noticed a fretwork book-shelf hanging on the wall. While Miss Bohun was talking he read the titles of the books: *The Golden Treasury*, *The Broken Halo*, *The Fountain*, *If Winter Comes*, *The Story of San Michele* and all the works of C. S. Lewis, also a large black book called *Control of the Flesh*.

Felix had said: 'I suppose you haven't any books by Rider Haggard. I read one at the Shiptons' and it was super.'

'No. And I'm afraid *my* books are a bit above your head. Anyway, I never lend books on principle.'

'My mother used to read C. S. Lewis.'

'Indeed! I believe he's quite widely *read*; whether he's understood or not is another matter.'

'Is he hard to understand?'

'Now, Felix, I can't discuss these deep matters with you,' she had dismissed him – quite unlike his mother, who would put down anything she was doing, at any time, to discuss any matter, the deeper the better.

Rapidly, alert to any sound outside, Felix now went to the shelf and, taking down the C. S. Lewis books one after the other, moved his hand across the cover of each. He thought sadly of those evenings when he had sat with his mother in the *pension* garden and gazed towards the red, satin-surfaced Tigris, talking, talking, talking. As he took down the last book he heard steps on the stair and instantly, with the preternatural speed of guilt, he replaced it and got himself safely outside the door again. Then he realized the steps were not ascending but descending. Someone was coming down from the attic. Felix stood against the wall as Mr Jewel, in an old brown suit from which his body had shrunk away, crossed the passage and went on down to the sitting-room. He was too absorbed in his own progress to notice Felix.

There was silence downstairs. Mr Liftshitz must have gone, but Miss Bohun was still there, for as soon as Mr Jewel got down Felix heard voices. He wondered if Mr Jewel were going out. If so, this would be a heaven-sent opportunity to satisfy his curiosity about the attic. He made no attempt to overhear the conversation below, but waited impatiently for it to stop. At last the door opened on to the garden and Mr Jewel came out to cross the lawn. Felix watched him through the passage window. Although the old man was cautious on the stairs, he walked briskly enough on level ground. He straightened his shoulders, shot his wrists out of his sleeves, and went off with the alert air of an old soldier. As soon as he was through the garden gate, Felix made his way silently up the attic stair. He held his breath as he went. At the top the sudden, under-roof chill made him sneeze. He paused, heard the tea-things chink below, then edged round the torn, heavy, dusty curtain and entered the attic. Inside there was the smell of an oil-stove but no warmth. Under the oil-stove was the smell of Mr Jewel – a combination of strong, stale tobacco and the odour of ear-wax. The room was no more than a space under the roof. There was a dormer window and six square foot of floor-boards with a surround of bare rafters. On the island of floor there was a camp-bed, neatly made, a kitchen table and a chair. On the table were little pots of household paint and a bunch of brushes stuck into a jam-jar. Again holding his breath, Felix moved over a pathway of boards to the table and looked at the pieces of cardboard and plywood on which Mr Jewel worked.

There were only three pictures on the table, but there were dozens more stacked under it.

'Pictures of flowers,' Felix said aloud. He bent over them while Faro, who had come up with him, sniffed at Mr Jewel's spare pair of boots, then passed to the slop-bucket. Mr Jewel had painted, no doubt from memory, primroses and violets, a large pink rose, primroses and moss surrounding a nest in which lay three speckled blue eggs.

'How wonderful,' thought Felix, who could not draw anything himself. His admiration for Mr Jewel quite transcended Miss Bohun's disapproval of the old man. To think that Mr Jewel, working up here alone in the cold, was an artist! Perhaps a *great* artist!

He was startled from his thoughts by Miss Bohun's singing from below: 'F-e-e-l-iks!'

Felix slid round the curtain and got down the stairs in a flash, Faro, infected by his panic, close at his heels. He gathered her up and got her into his room, then shouted: 'Coming.' He washed his hands. When he reached the sitting-room he had regained his breath.

Miss Bohun was sitting at the table. Felix's tea looked as though it had been poured out some time, but she did not ask what had kept him. She seemed preoccupied. He felt that some new confidence was behind her silence and as soon as he had taken a piece of bread, she said in an aggrieved way:

'Mr Jewel wants to bring a visitor in to dinner to-night. He knows it's unfair on the servants, and I get the backwash. Frau Leszno is so bad-tempered when she has to cook an extra meal.' After she had sipped her tea for a while, she said: 'Heigh-ho!' (Felix had never before heard anyone say the words exactly as they were written) then brightened as she often did: 'But I suppose it's my own fault. I said when he came first: "I want you to regard this as your own home, Mr Jewel, and if you ever want to invite a friend in for a meal, you have only to let me know." You see, I used to let the officers bring in a friend occasionally, but then they often went out for meals themselves and they were most generous about getting food from the Naafi. All that made up for the trouble. With Mr Jewel, of course, I was unwise. I said it on an impulse; out of kindness. It never entered my head he knew anyone to ask. Besides, Frau Leszno can't bear her.'

'Is Mr Jewel's friend a lady, then?'

'Of sorts,' Miss Bohun replied with a twist of the mouth, but suddenly she lifted her eyes, looked at Felix and smiled: 'You know,' she said, 'I'm not in the habit of judging people. No doubt Frau Wagner is a very nice sort of person. I don't know her well enough to say – but there is something about her. For one thing, she's Austrian! They say the German Jews are the worst of the lot – very rude and pushing when they can get away with it and very subservient when they can't. That's because they're Germans, of course, not because they're Jews. I would never say anything against anyone for being a Jew; dear me, no. I'm not an anti-Semite; and I've some very nice Jewish pupils. Look at Mr Liftshitz, a perfect gentleman. Well, the Eastern Jews don't like the German Jews, and Frau Leszno thinks she's an Eastern Jew because she was born in Poland, so she doesn't like Frau Wagner.'

'But I thought you said . . .'

'Yes, as I said, Frau Wagner is an Austrian. She came from Vienna, as a matter of fact. But I must say I dislike the Austrians even more than the Germans. They're so deceitful and so ingratiating and so . . . That "charm" of theirs is quite sickening. Well, you'll see for yourself. Frau Leszno disliked Frau Wagner on sight. After Frau Wagner came here the first time, Frau Leszno made a scene. She said she wasn't a servant and she wasn't going to wait on other servants, especially women like Frau Wagner. She said Frau Wagner was often seen sitting alone in the King David Hotel, and she said Mr Jewel visited her in her room. You're old enough, Felix, to understand what I mean.'

Felix, with his mouth slightly open, blushed and lowered his head.

'Frau Wagner is a sort of cook-housekeeper. I went round to

where she works and asked her employer if she thought it nice that gentlemen should visit Frau Wagner in her room. Her employer, a Frau Doctor Zimmerman, a very nice person in a way, showed me the room. It *was* quite definitely a bed-sitting-room – it had a wireless set and Frau Zimmerman said that anyway it was so difficult to get good servants, she could not interfere with Frau Wagner's private life. I had to sympathize. Well, Mr Jewel knows he must not take lady visitors upstairs so he goes round occasionally and sees Frau Wagner. I'm sure it's all quite respectable,' Miss Bohun made a slight click with her tongue against her upper teeth, 'but it's not quite nice, not quite *healthy*. He brought her here to supper last summer and I had to give my whole evening to entertaining her. To-night is my "Ever-Ready" night – perhaps that's as well. I don't suppose Mr Jewel remembered it was "Ever-Ready" night, still – I don't like it. *And* the waste of electricity.' She paused, then said: 'I want you to promise me something, Felix.'

'Yes,' Felix looked up, willing to be helpful.

'I want you to promise not to leave Frau Wagner and Mr Jewel alone together in the house to-night.'

'Why?' he asked from surprise.

'Because,' Miss Bohun spoke with a sudden aggravated clarity, 'it would not be nice. Now, I want you to give me your promise.'

'All right,' Felix was annoyed to feel his cheeks grow hot again, 'I wasn't going out anyway.' Because of his embarrassment he started washing down the last of his bread with his tea in haste to get away. Perhaps Miss Bohun felt his distaste for she said:

'You know, Felix, I keep Mr Jewel for practically nothing.'

'Hasn't he any money?'

'Not much. He left the Merchant Service before his time was up.'

'Why did he leave?' asked Felix.

Miss Bohun drew down her mouth into a small half-hoop. For some moments Felix feared she was going to answer, as she had done once before: 'I have not asked him,' but she seemed to remember in time that she had admitted him to a friendlier footing now and she said: 'Well, as he told me quite openly – not in confidence, you know – I don't see why I shouldn't tell you. When his boat was at Alexandria he had a fall and hurt his head.

45

He had to be taken to hospital and the boat went without him; he was in hospital a long time and when he came out his Company told him to join another ship, but he wouldn't. He'd taken a fancy to Egypt and he said he wouldn't go home again. He's been hanging around ever since.'

'Why didn't he want to go home again?'

'My dear child, how do I know?' Talking about something other than the Lesznos, Miss Bohun seemed always to be discouraging. 'I can only tell you what he told me. He got himself a little job in the passport office at the British Consulate. Very pleasant, I'm told. They used to spend the summer in Alexandria and the winter in Cairo. Well, he gets a small allowance from the Consulate; a ridiculous amount, really. I can tell you, if he were in England, he'd be in the workhouse. He must have outlived his usefulness in Cairo – anyway, when they evacuated the city they took the chance to get rid of him. He came up here. A lot of very odd people came here at that time – those who had money went to hotels and *pensions*, and the rest were packed into a barracks in Bethlehem. I'd never seen anything like it. I went down to distribute some tracts. I saw the poor old soul, he seemed lost among that mob – mostly foreigners they were. Well, we got talking, I felt it was my duty to offer him a home. I've always said we're put into this world to help one another. And I had to get Nikky out of the house. I felt I owed it to myself. I said to Mr Jewel: "This is an occasion when we can do each other a good turn. I want to let my attic, but it's not everyone who'd take it; you need a home and you won't be too particular – so, it's mutual aid." He was very grateful and I must say, on the whole, he's been no trouble – but this Frau Wagner – it's taking advantage.'

'Yes,' agreed Felix, indignant on Miss Bohun's behalf.

'Well, I don't know,' Miss Bohun muttered and sighed to herself, then raised her voice to include Felix, 'perhaps the time has come to make a change.'

When Felix went up to his room after tea he found his oil-stove already lit. For this he had to thank the new servant Maria, the Armenian woman. He wondered if she would light the bath-boiler for him, too, and make his bed properly. He had never really complained about this work, but he had at first mentioned to Miss Bohun that Frau Leszno threw the bedclothes back on his bed so carelessly that they always fell off during the night. 'Oh dear,' said Miss Bohun, 'I must speak to Frau Leszno, but you know, Felix, with the cooking and so on, there *is* a lot to be done in this house; I don't like to overwork servants, and I'm told that in England even the *best* people have to do their own chores these days.'

Now, if Maria were going to do all these jobs, Felix could not help feeling, in a slightly guilty way, that life would be much pleasanter. He had never been able to make his bed properly himself and when he awoke in the middle of the night to find the bedclothes on the floor and Faro crouching against him for warmth, he had felt a genuine hatred of the Lesznos while his sympathy with Miss Bohun became intense.

Although Miss Bohun had kindly said: 'Don't forget, Felix, the sitting-room is as much yours as mine,' Felix usually stayed in his own room when indoors. The sitting-room had a desolate air of shabby discomfort and, with the stairs leading into it and doors leading directly to garden and courtyard, it was very draughty. The single-bar electric fire was switched on, if at all, by Miss Bohun herself just before dinner began. Felix had been worried each evening by the sight of Mr Jewel's very cold, old hands, until at last, he had run down one evening and switched the fire on at about six o'clock. It was no good; before he got back to the top of the stairs he heard Miss Bohun's entry, her exasperated exclamation and then the ping of the fire being switched off.

When Felix came down to dinner that evening he found Mr Jewel and Frau Wagner already seated at the table. The fly-blown, solitary bulb in its age-yellowed shade threw down a circle of light; the rim of this cut across their faces. Their shoulders were hunched forward with cold, but they communicated to Felix less a physical than a mental discomfort. Mr Jewel introduced Frau Wagner, who pursed up her mouth to smile and nodded her head in a grand way. 'How do you do?' she said. A very refined English accent – almost, Felix thought, a joke accent, a 'plum-in-the-mouth' accent – lay over her Austrian accent like jam spread on butter. Mr Jewel sat grinning at Felix, but at the same time, somehow, he looked guilty and unhappy. Felix also felt guilty and unhappy because he felt bound to disapprove as much as Miss Bohun did of Mr Jewel's bringing in Frau Wagner. That made it impossible for him to appear as friendly as politeness demanded.

Mr Jewel, usually silent, had suddenly become talkative and joking.

'You ought to sit next to the lady,' he said when Felix took the chair opposite her.

Felix blushed miserably, but stayed where he was.

'He's shy,' said Mr Jewel.

Frau Wagner smiled.

'He is so nice a boy,' she said, 'I like such fair hair.'

Frau Wagner sat stiffly upright and seemed very high above the table. She wore a dark green velvet frock trimmed with gold. The sleeves were wide and fell back when she raised her hands to show her gaunt pink arms. She had large aquiline features covered with a skin so thin it had the high mauve-pink tint of an albino. Felix could see she had tried to hide it beneath a coating of white powder. She was quite old, of course – fifty or more, but her long-bob hair, lint-white, made her look ancient.

Mr Jewel rubbed his hands together and said: 'Do you think we could light the fire, eh? Do you think we dare?' Felix, who could hear the dry, old skin crackling with cold, got up and switched on the fire.

'You're a brave boy!' said Mr Jewel.

'Ah, Alfred, it is not kind. Perhaps the boy will be blamed.'

'No, I won't,' said Felix, his voice high with embarrassment. 'I can put the fire on if I like.'

'That's right,' said Mr Jewel, 'the boy pays enough for what he gets.'

'It's not that,' said Felix miserably.

Frau Wagner, smiling, her manners more elegant than before, cut across something Mr Jewel was about to say and asked: 'And how do you like Jerusalem, Feelix?'

'It's all right,' said Felix, staring over to one side of the room.

'Not much fun here, eh? No English boys, no football, no cricket. What do you do all day?'

'Nothing much. I'm studying for matric.'

'Perhaps soon they will send you home?'

'There's a long waiting list.'

'They should send such a boy home first, I think.'

'Oh, no. First there are ladies with babies, and troops.'

Mr Jewel and Frau Wagner laughed together as though Felix had said something funny. They stopped abruptly. The door from the courtyard opened, then they gave another laugh when it was only Nikky who entered. He carried in the soup when it was too heavy for his mother. Now, holding the battered metal tureen in his hands, he kicked the door closed behind him and trailed across the room in his black coat with the astrakhan collar. Frau Wagner fixed on him and followed him with eyes of brilliant, inhuman blue. When he had put down the tureen, he glanced round the table with a look of insolent amusement and went.

'But what a handsome butler!'

'That's Nikky,' said Felix.

'So? I have seen him, of course, at the King David and the Innsbruck café. They tell me he is a Polish Count.'

Felix was rather puzzled. 'He is Polish,' he said, 'but I don't think he can be a Count. His father was *Herr* Leszno.' But Felix's doubts were lost to the world because as he spoke them the door opened again and Miss Bohun entered. She had on her lamb-skin coat, a scarf bound in a turban round her head. 'So sorry,' she said. 'One of my flock needed advice. I hope you're not waiting for me.'

'But of course,' cried Frau Wagner. 'We must await our hostess.'

Miss Bohun hung up her coat and hurriedly unwound the scarf from her head so that her hair stood out in wisps. She came to the table holding knitted gloves and kept them on her knees during the meal.

She took no notice of Frau Wagner's polite remark, but feeling the fire on her legs she jerked round and looked at it: 'So glad you did not fail to light the fire,' she said, 'I am fortunate in never feeling the cold myself, but they *say* the winters here are chilly. Well, let us have some nice hot soup.'

She served the soup in a rapid, businesslike way, keeping her eyes off Frau Wagner. It was pale soup and no longer hot.

'I see,' Frau Wagner leant smiling towards Miss Bohun, 'you have a Count for a butler! But how chic!'

Miss Bohun, surprised now into looking at her, frowned,

49

as bewildered as Felix had been: 'We haven't got a butler,' she said.

'Frau Wagner means Nikky,' said Felix. 'He brought in the soup.'

'Oh!' Miss Bohun made no other comment, but said: 'Excuse me if I eat quickly; I've got to go out.'

'But how extraordinary to find a Polish Count who will work, I have never known it.' Frau Wagner laughed and gave Miss Bohun a sidelong glance. 'He must do it for love, I think.'

Miss Bohun put down her spoon and compressed her lips. She rang the bell.

Frau Wagner gave an exaggerated sigh, saying: 'Ah-ha,' as she did so. 'I, too, must work. In Vienna how different! My husband had a great factory. We had such a house, such a park – the Nazis took all, they took my husband, too, and now I must work. I am a cook. To think! Once I could not make water, now I make all.'

Mr Jewel guffawed and Felix began to giggle in spite of himself. Frau Wagner cocked an eye at them with the humorous sternness of a pantomime dame, revealing that she had had success before with that one. Miss Bohun, looking from one to the other of them, seemed bewildered, but when no one explained the joke, she became irritated and gave the bell a second ring. The others subsided under the noise. There was silence.

'Really!' Miss Bohun burst out. 'What has happened to Frau Leszno?' She was about to get up when Maria, wraith-thin, bent, her face dark and wrinkled as a prune, came in. Miss Bohun asked sharply: 'Where is Frau Leszno?'

'She sick.'

'Sick!' Miss Bohun spoke less with concern than with disgust. Maria picked up the empty tureen and as she went out with it Miss Bohun called after her: 'Tell Frau Leszno to come here.'

Everyone was silenced by Miss Bohun's annoyance. They scarcely breathed until Maria returned with the second course.

'Frau Leszno in bed,' she said.

'What's the matter with her?'

'She got headache.'

'But she *can't* have a headache.' Miss Bohun spoke with such decision that, looking round at the others, she felt forced to explain. 'Frau Leszno is a member of the "Ever-Readies". We don't believe in illness.'

'So?' Frau Wagner made an elegant move of interest.

'Frau Leszno say light in kitchen very bad and give her a headache.' Maria left the room.

Miss Bohun clicked her tongue.

Frau Wagner asked in a tone high with interest: 'Please to tell me, what is this "Ever-Readies"? It is like a trade name, is it not?'

'"The Ever-Ready Group of Wise Virgins" existed long before trade names.'

'How interesting, but please to tell me about it. I am greatly curious.'

Miss Bohun stood up to carve the meat. 'I have no time now, I fear, to satisfy anyone's curiosity.'

'What a pity! But another time, yes?'

'I cannot promise, Frau Wagner. We make a point of revealing our creed only to a select few. Please pass this to Frau Wagner.' Miss Bohun gave to Felix on her left a plate which she might as easily have placed before Frau Wagner on her right. It held a sliver of meat so small that Felix felt compelled to say as he handed it over the table:

'Are you sure you won't have more than that?'

'Oh no, oh no,' said Frau Wagner, 'I could not possibly eat more.'

Miss Bohun made no comment on this exchange. She cut off a meat sliver for each of the three remaining plates, then rang the bell and told Maria to take the joint away.

'We have meat only once a week,' she said to the table as the plates were passed, 'so we must make it stretch. And we must think of the servants. Both the Lesznos and Maria are allowed their share. It pays to treat one's servants well.'

'Indeed yes,' said Frau Wagner with feeling.

'Also I make a point of never buying on the black market.'

'*Never*? How then do you live?' Frau Wagner's surprise had in it admiration.

'One can always make up with potatoes.' Miss Bohun pushed the dish towards her.

'Ah, your English boiled potatoes,' Frau Wagner exclaimed

with delight. She put on her plate two potatoes that seemed to be made of soap. 'How clever a housewife you must be! My employer, Dr Zimmerman, buys meat every day (except, of course, Friday, when we have fish). He sees to the matter himself, personally; and *always* on the black market.'

'I've no doubt. Even some English Government officials are remiss enough to encourage the black market. I buy nothing; except sometimes eggs. When they're plentiful, they are cheaper on the black market – so it's different.'

'That is true,' agreed Frau Wagner enthusiastically.

'I don't like boiled potatoes,' Felix suddenly announced. 'I like chips.'

Miss Bohun looked at him sharply and said:

'Chips take too much cooking-oil.' She had been eating at a great pace; now, the second course finished, she rose, holding her gloves in her hand. 'You must excuse me. Felix will act as host. Here is the bell, Felix; ring it when you are ready.' She rebound her head in her scarf. As she put on the sheepskin coat, Frau Wagner, who had been watching her with glittering eyes, exclaimed wildly: 'What a lovely coat!'

This seemed to Felix most blatant flattery, but for some reason it made Miss Bohun unbend. She passed a hand over the dirty skin, then turned up a corner to look at the shaggy inside hair and said complacently: 'It's all right. It keeps me warm. But I'm afraid these coats are very common.'

'Oh,' breathed Frau Wagner, 'last year they were common, yes. But not *this* year.'

'Well, I must be off. I'll say "good-night" Frau Wagner, you'll be gone before I get back.'

As the door closed after Miss Bohun, Frau Wagner covered her mouth with her hand and laughed silently. Mr Jewel seemed to be trying not to laugh. Felix looked at the plates – all empty, except for a solitary cold potato which Frau Wagner and Mr Jewel refused in turn. He rang the bell. Maria brought in small plates, three dates on each. She took from the dresser some brass finger-bowls and filled them with water.

'Very nice,' she announced and, smiling round at them, she went.

When Frau Wagner and Felix had each eaten their dates, Mr

Jewel offered them Miss Bohun's share, but neither wanted them.

'It's too late for dates,' said Felix, 'they're slimy and too sweet.'

'Ah, Felix, you are a connoisseur!' said Frau Wagner. 'You know what is good.'

Felix smiled uncomfortably. He did not think Frau Wagner was laughing at him; he would have felt happier if she had been.

'Tell me,' she said to Mr Jewel, 'where has our hostess gone so quickly?'

'Don't you know? She's gone to see the other Wise Virgins.'

Frau Wagner gave a hoot of laughter and Felix laughed too, but he flushed slightly, still discomforted, scarcely knowing why. For moments, when there was a gleam of humour about her, Felix had thought Frau Wagner 'great fun', but all the time he could not help feeling in her the quality that Miss Bohun did not like. Like the lion in the puzzle picture, once seen it was difficult to see anything else.

Mr Jewel seemed to feel Felix's discomfort. He rubbed his hands together between his knees and grinned at Felix. As though they were boys of the same age, he said: 'I wonder if we could get some coffee?'

'But we never have coffee at night.'

'This is a special occasion. I bet Nikky's making some for himself – he always does; I've *smelt* it. If Frau Leszno is in bed, he might make us some. You go, Felix, you can get round him.'

Felix, startled and yet flattered by this mis-statement, whispered: 'Oh, he wouldn't let me have any.'

'Go on,' said Mr Jewel. 'He's not a bad sort.'

Against his own judgment Felix went out to the kitchen. Before he reached the kitchen door he heard Miss Bohun's voice coming from Frau Leszno's room and he paused, on the point of escape. Miss Bohun was speaking sternly, '. . . whatever the excuse, Frau Leszno, never – I repeat, *never* – again send in and say in front of visitors you are unwell. It's letting the side down.'

Then came Frau Leszno's high whine, but Felix could not hear what she said. 'As far as the attic is concerned,' Miss Bohun replied: 'I can't make any promises, but I'll think about it. I'll *think* about it.' The door opened. Miss Bohun hurried off without seeing Felix. He put his head in the kitchen. Only Maria was there, washing the dishes.

'Where's Nikky?' he asked.

'Gone out a long time,' she replied.

'Mr Jewel would like some coffee.'

'Coffee!' repeated Maria, willing enough, too new to know the regulations. She looked round the dark, dingy kitchen and fixed her eyes on a cupboard. 'No key. Coffee, tea, rice, sugar – all locked up.'

'Oh, thank you,' Felix replied politely and went back, glad he had done what he had been asked to do.

'Humph,' said Mr Jewel, 'that's that. Anyway, let's sit somewhere a bit more comfortable.'

He and Frau Wagner took seats at either end of the horsehair sofa. Felix sat in one of the arm-chairs with wooden arms. They were near the fire now and Mr Jewel shook himself with a noisy shiver as he felt the heat.

'Like an ice-box over there,' he said.

Frau Wagner made no reply to him, but turned to Felix with an air of great interest and asked: 'Tell me, what will you do when you grow up?'

'I don't know. I've got to go into the army.'

'But the war will be over first, surely?'

'I might go in, anyway. I want to be a veterinary surgeon. I'll have to pass exams, of course.'

'So? In England veterinary surgeons are gentlemens, perhaps?'

'I suppose so. My uncle's a vet.'

'So?'

Since Miss Bohun left, Felix had felt a tension in the room. Perhaps for no reason other than that he had promised to stay in, he wanted to go out. Frau Wagner seemed to have nothing more to say but she smiled whenever he glanced at her. Mr Jewel was occupied with his pipe that he held in two pieces in his hand. He put a pipe-cleaner through the stem. The cleaner went in white and came out brown, then he blew through the stem, joined the two pieces together and blew again. When he was satisfied, he got out an old tobacco pouch and started to fill the pipe. It all took a long time. Felix looked at the clock. It was only half-past seven and Miss Bohun would not be back for two hours or more. He moved restlessly in his seat, feeling like a prisoner.

'Before you came here, you lived in Baghdad?' inquired Frau Wagner. 'Perhaps you had a nice home there?'

'We only lived in a *pension*.'

'Ah, a *pension*, but that is nice. And have you lived all the war in Baghdad?'

'Yes. At first we had a house of our own, but when my father was killed, my mother could not afford it, so we went to a *pension*.'

'He was killed!' Frau Wagner shook her head in regretful sympathy. 'Such a bad thing! How came it so?'

'The Iraqis shot him,' said Felix, gazing intently at a piece of string he had found in his pocket. He started tying knots in it. There was a lot to tell about his father's death but his whole attitude expressed unwillingness to tell it. How could he tell anyone who looked as German as did Frau Wagner that the rising in which his father had been killed was a German-inspired rising? His restraint communicated itself to the others and even Frau Wagner gave up trying.

At last the clock struck a quarter to eight. Mr Jewel was smoking at his pipe as though it were the most engrossing thing in the room. Frau Wagner sat upright with her clasped hands on her knees. When she caught Felix's glance she made one last attempt and, smiling, she pursed up her mouth and told him the spring would soon be coming. 'You will like that, Felix.'

After that the silence went on as though no one had the strength to stop it.

There was something about the two of them sitting there apart on the sofa that touched Felix painfully. He fidgeted in his chair. Because Miss Bohun had said it would be wrong to leave them, he was obsessed by the sense that they wanted him to go; he felt it like a physical force impelling him to bolt from the room. He would not have minded could he have been sure, as Miss Bohun was, of their wickedness. The trouble was that he wasn't at all sure, and on top of his uncertainty he was beset by something he could not bear. He did not know what it was. Suddenly he jumped up and said: 'I'm going to the pictures.'

Frau Wagner let her breath out as though it had been pent up for some time.

Felix, without another word, ran upstairs for his coat. When he returned, he said good-bye and shook Frau Wagner's hand with the enthusiasm of relief. Frau Wagner seemed relieved, too, and said happily: 'Ah, at the Zion there is a so funny film.'

Out in the courtyard, Felix felt like a genie that had been let out of a bottle. He started to laugh at the idea, then, almost at once, remembered he had broken his promise to Miss Bohun. He stood still, wretchedly uncertain what to do, but knowing that whatever he did, he could not go back to the sitting-room. As he stood, he stared through the dirty lace curtains that covered Frau Leszno's little window and saw Frau Leszno lying in bed. She had her back to him – her backside made a large curve in the bedclothes, her shoulders a smaller one, and at the top was the greasy knot of her hair. She held a book in one hand and was reading by the light of an oil-lamp. Above the bed a heart made of pink sugar dangled from a ribbon. The room had been meant for an Arab servant and was no more than a white-washed cell to hold a mattress. Frau Leszno had somehow got into it not only her bed and chair, but a large wardrobe. This furniture was stuck together like objects packed into a box. When he realized he was doing a quite inexcusable thing – staring into a lady's bedroom – Felix made off at once.

In the street, he again did not know what to do. It was near the end of the month and he had no money for the cinema. His mother, who had lived on an allowance that died with her, had left a few hundred pounds that the British Consul in Baghdad, acting as executor, was doling out to Felix at the rate of £22 a month.

When the Consul heard that Miss Bohun was charging Felix £21 a month, he wrote to someone he knew at the YMCA and discovered that Felix could live there for £4 less. He then wrote to Felix: 'You would have your own room, with central heating and hot running water and I'm told the food is excellent. I advise you to put your name down at once.'

Felix tore up this letter in small pieces and burnt each separately, afraid Miss Bohun might see it and think that, after all her kindness, he was planning to leave for the sake of £4. But now he could not help thinking that an extra £4 a month would be jolly useful.

At Herod's Gate he turned right and went uphill beside the long, dark city wall to the Jaffa Road. The Jaffa Road was the centre of life in Jerusalem, but after dark it looked like everywhere else, shut and deserted. A strict black-out was imposed on everything, except, of course, military headquarters. The only sign of life appeared when someone opened a café door; with the momentary flash of light, there came a smell of fried food that made Felix realize he was still hungry. Indeed, at Miss Bohun's he was always more or less hungry, but there was nothing to be done about it. Miss Bohun would never buy on the black market and there was very little food anywhere else.

As he passed the Jaffa Road cafés, he occasionally heard from behind the black-out curtains the sound of voices; in one café the wireless was repeating some Arab saga, in another someone was playing a kanoon. He, out in the cold, dark street, felt lost and without destination in the world. He went over the people he knew here – Miss Bohun and Mr Posthorn, Mr Jewel and Frau Wagner, Frau Leszno, Nikky and Maria. The only one who did not enhance the isolation of his youth was Mr Jewel, and Mr Jewel had Frau Wagner. Felix came to the first cinema and stood a long time staring at the 'stills' pinned into cases behind wire mesh and lit by small blue bulbs. They were pictures of a cowboy film he had seen in Istanbul months before. They were familiar but, because of the strange, inadequate light, they looked mysterious and exciting, and for some reason they reminded him of the dream he had had on the aeroplane.

He had never dreamt of his mother again. He might dream of Mr Posthorn or of Maria or of a camel he had seen pass the house, but he did not dream of his mother, who was the person most in his waking dreams. Now as he thought of her, he was filled with a longing for her so profound, his eyes swam with tears.

He went on down the street till he came to Zion Circus and the cinema with the funny film that Frau Wagner had mentioned. This was the film he most wanted to see and he was able to put in a lot of time looking at the stills. He took out his money and recounted it, but he had not enough. Cinemas were expensive here; last week he had gone twice, for now the only place in which he was happy was the cinema; the world to which it gave him access was as much his as anyone's. When the cold drove him on, he took a roundabout walk through the side-streets to look at two more cinemas he had discovered during his early days in Jerusalem. One had the stills inside a passageway that was warm and well lit, with basket-chairs and a palm or two. By pretending to be waiting for someone he was able to spend half an hour there. Sometimes he pulled aside his cuff a little as though glancing at a wrist-watch and sometimes he stared with an anxious, grown-up frown at the clock inside the paybox, but however long he stayed no one would come to say: 'Hello Felix, darling, so sorry I'm late. I can't think what kept me.' (His mother was always late and never knew why.) He had to go in the end.

Twice, as he wandered about, he passed the post-office to see the time. He was afraid of returning too soon, but he arranged things so well that when he reached the gate of the house from one direction, Miss Bohun was coming towards it from the other. They met on the step. She peered at him through the darkness: 'Is that you, Felix? You went out? You left them alone? After you *promised* me!'

He had expected her to be hurt, but because she was merely indignant, he did not mind so much. He said: 'I couldn't stay. They didn't want me to. I thought perhaps you'd understand.'

'Couldn't stay? My dear boy, that's exactly why I wanted you to stay.'

He hurried ahead with some idea of warning Mr Jewel and Frau Wagner that Miss Bohun was behind him, but he found the sitting-room dark and empty. As Miss Bohun crossed the yard, he ran up the stairs and managed to get out of sight before she switched on the light.

4

On Sunday morning Felix was hanging around the kitchen door. He was unencouraged but gained from the nearness of Nikky and Maria a sense of being in company. Ten minutes before he had watched Miss Bohun go off to the 'Ever-Readies', with Frau Leszno half a step behind. Miss Bohun, wearing her 'cartwheel', was giving instructions or advice, and this was met every few moments by Frau Leszno's subservient whine: 'Yes, Miss Bohun.' 'No, Miss Bohun.' 'Yes, Miss Bohun.' The two women seemed now to be on better terms, a condition made more obvious to Felix by the fact that Miss Bohun had scarcely noticed him since his defection. He felt very low, very much in the wrong, and the cathedral bells with their repeated frill of noise seemed to him to be mapping out the monotony of the friendless days to come.

He leant against the kitchen door-frame and gazed fixedly at Nikky and Maria. Neither noticed him. Nikky was sitting on the kitchen table smoking a chocolate-coloured cigarette, and Maria, as slowly as a slow-motion film, was drying the breakfast dishes.

Maria was telling Nikky how, on her afternoon off, she had helped her son kill two tame pigeons at his place of employment.

'My son,' she was saying, 'took the first and I held the second, so, so,' she put down the tea-towel and cupped her two dark claws tenderly over nothing, 'the first moved – ah, very much, but my son with a strike, so, cut off its head. And when the second one saw what had happened to her friend – ah, her little heart failed and her head drooped so, so –' Maria's head fell slowly to her shoulder, 'and I called to my son: "Quickly kill this one or it will die," and quickly, before it could die of fright, while I held it fainting so, he cut off its head.'

Nikky was not watching the old woman's actions but staring

out through the kitchen window. He smiled distantly and ac-
knowledged the story with a down-twist of the lips.

Maria put the tip of her finger to a tear that lay in the wrinkle
by her nose and trailed it off the edge of her face. 'I have wept
since.'

'The old weep easily.' Nikky took a slow, elegant pull at his
cigarette and narrowed his eyes at the distance. His face was
touched with amusement as he saw Mr Jewel go into the bathroom opposite with his slop-basin. He nodded towards the closing bathroom door:

'We're getting rid of that one,' he said.

'What? What?' Maria turned quickly to look. 'He is going, the
old man upstairs?'

'Yes. She has said to him: "Please Mr Jewel, take up your bed
and walk." To-morrow, he walks.'

'You say!' Maria breathed, then pursed her lips and shook her
head slowly with surprise.

Felix was surprised, too. He had, it was true, overheard Miss
Bohun promise Frau Leszno to 'think about the attic', but that
had seemed to him no more than a formula putting things off
indefinitely – but now, suddenly, it was all accomplished; and
behind his back. All the week Mr Jewel had been as silent as
ever. Miss Bohun had been preoccupied, but when Felix spoke,
she had answered with bright, aloof efficiency, forestalling the
possibility of the suggestion that there was anything wrong anywhere. Yet, at some time, Miss Bohun had seen and spoken to
Mr Jewel: everyone – Miss Bohun, Mr Jewel, Frau Leszno and
Nikky – had known of the change coming in the house: Felix
alone had known nothing. Used to his mother's habit of discussing with him every move for days before making it, and used
also to her inability to keep up a quarrel, he was startled by Miss
Bohun's withdrawal. Also the swiftness with which she had acted
against Mr Jewel seemed to him ruthless and frightening. To
feel contact with someone, he spoke to Nikky, knowing as he
spoke, he'd be snubbed for it.

'But what will happen to Mr Jewel?'

Nikky slid his eyes round to look at Felix, then, without turning, twisted his mouth so that the smoke he blew out went in
Felix's direction. 'This is a kitchen,' he said. 'A kitchen is for

servants, not for little gentlemens. Now, be so kind and hop it.'

Felix went off slowly. He wandered down the passage to the garden. It was a bright morning. Osman, the gardener, stout and slow-moving, was bending awkwardly to pluck the new grass up from the gravel path. On seeing Felix, he straightened himself with relief, grinned and gave a greeting, touching his brow and heart. As all the language they had in common were the words similar in Palestinian and Iraqi colloquial Arabics, Felix knew from experience that it was not much use trying to talk to Osman; besides, Miss Bohun had told him that Osman was paid by the hour so was not there to waste time in talk. Osman seemed only too happy to waste it. He made a long speech with gestures towards the sky and the grass. Felix smiled and nodded and replied, from habit, in Iraqi-Arabic; then began calling: 'Faro, Faro.'

'Faro heneh,' said the gardener and, delighted by this own perception and helpfulness, pointed to Faro asleep along a limb of the mulberry tree. She half-opened her eyes when Felix called her, but would not come down. Felix wandered off, disconsolately kicking a stone, and made his way round the wood-shed, in which Maria now slept. He had seen her go in and come out and had wondered how such a place could be combined into wood-shed, tool-shed, bedroom. On the side away from the house he noticed a small, unglazed window cut high in the wooden wall of the hut. He caught its edge and jumped. With his elbows gripping his waist he managed to hold his weight long enough to see stacked in one corner the gardening gear; and in another the wood; and in another an old mattress heaped with ragged covers. Above it was a hook from which hung Maria's other dress. The air smelt stale. He dropped back to the ground.

At last Mr Posthorn arrived. Occasionally on Sunday mornings Mr Posthorn, who attended the English cathedral, would drop in on his way back to look through Felix's week-end exercises. He had suggested, which Miss Bohun never did, that Felix should attend the cathedral and walk back with him, but Felix said: 'I couldn't do that. My mother did not believe in organized religion.'

'Indeed,' said Mr Posthorn, 'and what about your father?'

'He was an atheist.'

Mr Posthorn made no comment, but screwed his face as though he smelt something unpleasant. He was a very tall, narrow-shouldered man, who, at the end of an undistinguished career, took pride in the one thing that set him apart from his fellows – his learning.

He told Felix once: 'Latin makes the gentleman. You'll have to mug it up, my boy. You'll get into no sort of nice society without it.' While Felix was with him in his office, Mr Posthorn often had to speak on the telephone to other Government officials, and sometimes, not knowing Felix was there, one of them would look into Mr Posthorn's office to discuss some small matter. The officials of his own age, many of whom had fought their way up to Jerusalem in the Allenby Campaign and been rewarded with Government appointments, accorded him a sort of N.C.O.'s respect for book-learning: to these he spoke with a half-sneering smile, in an elaborate phraseology that hid his unease of the world; to the younger men, who saw him as a joke, he had nothing to say at all. It seemed that what friends he had were among the boys he had tutored, and when one of these rang him up, a mild humorousness seemed to come over him and, forgetting Felix's presence, he would talk and laugh with a natural sweetness. Sometimes Felix would picture to himself the day when Mr Posthorn would admit him into this select group of his friends, but he knew it to be far distant. At the moment Felix's ignorance forced Mr Posthorn to treat him as though he were a senior Government official.

Mr Posthorn sighed now as, sitting on the garden wall in the sunlight, he went through Felix's exercise books. 'I despair of you, Latimer,' he said in his thin, genteel voice, 'I despair of you.'

Felix, restless, bored and getting hungry, watched for Miss Bohun's return across the wasteland. He had determined that at luncheon-time he would break through all barriers and ask her about Mr Jewel's departure.

At last Frau Leszno appeared, trotting ahead to attend to the meal. Seeing Mr Posthorn, who did not see her, she looked down with humility and hurried through the gate. Miss Bohun, who now rose over the crest, was talking with loud good-fellowship to a companion, a soldier.

'Ah!' she cried, 'how nice! There is my young friend Felix of whom I told you, and he's with his tutor.' As she drew near she said: 'Good-morning, Mr Posthorn. Now, Felix, here is a lonely young warrior who wandered into our "Ever-Ready" Meeting. I hope you'll be great friends. And you, Mr Posthorn, I know, are fond of the young. If you could see the gratitude of these poor boys, separated from home and loved ones, when we offer them spiritual refreshment and, indeed, *physical*, for I never begrudge a meal in a good cause – I think it would warm your heart.'

Mr Posthorn flicked his book impatiently so that it closed itself and he looked, with his discouraging smile, from Miss Bohun to the soldier. The soldier stood a step behind Miss Bohun, his head hanging.

'His name is Marshall,' said Miss Bohun, as though the soldier were too young to speak for himself. 'Now sit down on the wall, Marshall, and make friends, while I go in and see about the luncheon.'

Miss Bohun hurried away across the lawn, her batik scarf floating after her. Marshall edged himself uncomfortably on to the wall. Felix expected Mr Posthorn to rise at once and abandon the pair of them, but instead, with his mouth askew, he fixed his eyes on Marshall's large, unshinable boots and offered him a cigarette. Marshall, his red hands hanging between his knees, in an attitude of crouching meekness, looked up without raising his head and smiled weakly: 'Oh no, sir,' he said, 'I don't indulge. Don't smoke. Don't drink. I promised my mum.'

'Oh!'

Marshall kept his head down while Mr Posthorn lit a cigarette for himself, then shook out the match and put it back dead into the box. 'Been here long?' Mr Posthorn asked stiffly.

'Three months. Getting a bit homesick.' Marshall began fumbling in his shirt pocket. 'Got a photograph of my mum here.' His red, square fingers with nails so bitten down they had become no more than dents in the flesh brought out a wad of dog-eared letters and photographs. 'That's her,' he said.

Mr Posthorn gave the photograph a glance: 'Very charming face,' he said and passed it to Felix. Felix, gazing into the small brown square, saw someone that might have been Marshall had Marshall worn his hair bobbed.

'This one's my sister Glad, only the sun got in the camera; and here's our little Bethesda, West Hartlepool Road. I'm Little Bethesda myself at home, but,' he added quickly, 'I take my hat off to the "Ever-Readies". Can't say a thing against them.' Marshall's voice, that had been, at first, thin and nasal with respect, now took on a deeper note of confidence.

'Indeed?' sounded Mr Posthorn, stiffer than before. Another pause, then he asked: 'Have you done any sight-seeing here?'

'Yes,' said Marshall. 'The Colonel laid on the Holy Places when our draft came out.'

'What did you think of them?'

'Well,' Marshall wriggled slightly, obviously trying to suppress his sense of superiority. 'What I says is: All that's all right for show, like, but it's not religion. Now religion – this is only my idea, mind, and I don't say you haven't got a right to question it, but what I always says is . . .'

As Marshall was speaking, a clock in the distance struck one and Mr Posthorn got abruptly to his feet: 'Must be going,' he said and walked out through the gate.

Marshall stopped speaking, but his mouth remained open. Humble again, he glanced round to see if Felix were still there.

'I say,' said Felix, 'do tell me about the "Ever-Readies". What do they *do*?' But he was also interrupted, for Miss Bohun came out to the door, waving to them in a light-hearted way, shouting: 'Now you two, come on, come on,' and ringing the bell at the same time.

On the table there was a mound of mashed beans. Marshall, as he seated himself, stared at it in a disturbed way. When Miss Bohun put a wodge on his plate, he hung his head over it, but his eyes wandered over the rest of the table. Seeing nothing but the dark Palestinian bread, the pepper, salt and a jug of water, he slowly lifted his knife and fork.

'Bread?' said Miss Bohun. 'I don't eat bread myself. The millers here grind up stone with the corn to make the flour weigh heavier – so bad for the intestines.'

Marshall ignored the bread. 'Is this all you folk get to eat of a Sunday?' he asked, his humility ebbing again and a sort of sullen aggressiveness taking its place.

Miss Bohun seemed not to notice the change; her voice still

rang out happily: 'We civilians have got no Naafi, you know –
but this is wholesome food. It'll do you good. Don't cut it with a
knife, just use your fork as we do.'

But Marshall cut off a cube of the bean-mash with his knife
and put it in his mouth. He chewed slowly, a dark and swindled
look on his face.

Miss Bohun talked on: 'I'm sure you'll agree it's a good thing
you boys should experience civilian conditions here. The army do
themselves very well – they just requisition civilian supplies on
the frontier. I'm told they don't know what to do with the stuff.
Half of it's wasted. Of course we don't begrudge you boys your
food, but I'm sure you've never been so well fed in your lives
before . . .'

'That's a lie.' Marshall stared angrily at Miss Bohun. 'My mum
never stinted us. On Sundays we'd have a proper blow-out –
roast beef and Yorkshire, and roast potatoes and cabbage, and
apple pie and custard and tea. None of this muck.'

'My dear boy,' Miss Bohun's tones grew hushed and refined in
rebuke, 'there's no need to bawl. I'm quite sure you were ade-
quately fed at home, but conditions out here are different. Besides, I believe in the virtue of vegetables. Some of the great
thinkers and mystics of India ate nothing else. As for this excellent
bean-mash – it may taste different, but it's quite as *strength-
ening* as meat. At school our teacher used to set light to a bean to
show us how it burnt with a blue flame – that meant it was full of
protein.'

'Maybe it was,' said Marshall. 'But you'd need ten times as
much.'

'I don't understand.'

Marshall let his voice rise again with a harsh superiority. 'I'm
not denying there's protein in them beans, but you'd have to eat
ten times as much of 'em as meat – that's what I mean. I know.
I've taken the "Health and Hygiene" course.'

'Well –' Miss Bohun seemed at a loss. 'You're welcome to a
second course.'

'Can't eat this lot,' he gave his plate a pettish push. 'My mum
never gave me mash – she knew it made me puke.'

'Have some bread then . . .?'

'What, with stones in it? No thanks.' A new derisive note came into his voice and he lumbered to his feet. 'I'll shove off. I can get my Sunday dinner at the barracks.' He glanced over the table once more with a wry, disillusioned smile, then made a large patronizing gesture with one hand: 'Day to you,' he said and went with a trampling of feet.

Miss Bohun looked after him, an unnatural pink tinging her cheeks: 'Well!' she shook her head, for some moments seeming quite crushed. 'How hard it is to help some people! And he was so respectful at first.'

Felix, although his imagination had been swept away by Marshall's description of Sunday dinner at home, felt sorry for Miss Bohun. He also realized that his own discontent with the food (mild, of course, compared with Marshall's) was something he would now have to leave unexpressed. He tried to think of something comforting to say, but Miss Bohun recovered before he could speak.

'Oh well,' she said, 'the more for us. Now, Felix, eat up and have a second helping. I often say, the diet may not be rich but at my table everyone is welcome to a second helping. You won't get that in restaurants.'

Felix, out of sympathy for Miss Bohun, poured himself a glass of water with which to wash down the bean-mash. Now feeling himself restored to the position of Miss Bohun's friend and ally, he took the opportunity to say: 'Nikky says Mr Jewel is leaving.'

'Oh,' said Miss Bohun. Despite everything, she did not sound encouraging; there was a long pause before she said: 'Well, the truth is, I don't think it's quite the right thing, not quite nice, having Mr Jewel in the house – it's not as though either of us were married – and you're only a child really. Besides, I need the room.'

'For Frau Leszno?' Felix asked unwarily.

'Ah! so Nikky told you that, did he?'

Felix hid his hot cheeks, not daring to vindicate Nikky.

'I must say, Felix,' said Miss Bohun, 'I'd much prefer you didn't discuss these matters with the servants – not that Nikky sees himself in that class, but he gets pocket money from me for cleaning the knives and the windows and other odd jobs, and I can tell you if he were dependent on himself he'd be destitute.' Miss Bohun rose with some dignity and went over to her writing-desk to telephone someone. 'If you want coffee, ring the bell. I must soon hurry off. It's my turn to distribute tracts at the hospital.'

Perhaps because it was no longer a secret from Felix, Miss Bohun spoke to Mr Jewel that evening about his departure: 'I suppose,' she said, sounding brightly interested, 'you've got everything packed up?'

'No.' Mr Jewel seemed to be trying to make a joke of his answer. Miss Bohun, however, did not respond in the same spirit.

'But you're going to-morrow morning.'

Mr Jewel shook his head. 'Got nowhere to go.'

Miss Bohun raised her eyelids and fixed on him an exasperated stare. Mr Jewel did not look up to meet it. She said: 'You can go back to the refugee centre at Bethlehem.'

'They're closing it down.'

Miss Bohun drew in her breath. Felix, looking at her apprehensively, expected her anger to be terrible; instead she seemed suddenly to be deflated. 'But I gave you a week's notice,' she said, with weaker peevishness.

Mr Jewel was eating furtively. He tried to swallow before replying and his words came muffled by his food: 'Where can I go?' He swallowed successfully this time, then added in a mild humorous way: 'You'll have to put me on the street.'

Miss Bohun sighed. Nothing more was said until their plates were empty, then she rang the bell and spoke sharply: 'You're taking advantage.'

Felix, who had been mazed by compassion for Mr Jewel, was relieved to have the situation clearly revealed from Miss Bohun's viewpoint. It really was too bad that everyone took advantage of Miss Bohun.

Mr Jewel's only defence was to shake his head again.

'I suppose it's my own fault,' Miss Bohun sighed, 'I should have made it clear from the first that the arrangement was temporary, but you should have realized it. Surely you didn't think I could go on keeping you indefinitely for . . . for a mere pittance. But that's always the way when one tries to do good. And on top of it all, you brought that woman here.'

There was a pause as Maria entered with some sardines split and fried. There were two each and half a one each left for a 'second helping'. Mr Jewel's hand was trembling as he lifted his fork. He mumbled: 'If it's Frau Wagner, I won't ask her again.'

'Of course it's not Frau Wagner.' Miss Bohun was still exasperated but her tone softened a little: 'I've got nothing against her. It's just that I want to make changes. You've been here all winter. It's given you a chance to find your feet, and now, well, people are likely to talk. I owe it to myself not to give rise to gossip – and, besides, I want the attic for a particular reason and I really must have it.'

In her agitation Miss Bohun was cutting her fish, putting down her knife and fork, lifting them and cutting it again. Felix, watching Mr Jewel, who troubled him very much, saw the old man raise his eyes and give her a pitying look.

'You'll just have to look for somewhere. Seriously,' she said.

'I have looked, but there's such a lot of refugees here. People can ask any price for a room.'

'Exactly!' Miss Bohun significantly agreed.

On Saturday Felix saw Mr Jewel knocking at doors in the Old City and the poverty of the quarter made Mr Jewel's poverty evident. Perhaps he was not taking advantage of Miss Bohun. Perhaps he was as helpless and alone as he looked. Felix felt he ought to go to Mr Jewel and offer him help of some kind, but he had nothing to offer, so, instead, he hurried out of sight. He began to wish that Mr Jewel would go away and release them all from the embarrassment suffered each evening at the dinner-table, especially that suffered by Mr Jewel himself.

Miss Bohun said nothing more about the matter, but her silence spoke. Then, one evening, the old man did not come down when the bell rang. Miss Bohun 'tutted' to herself and gave the bell another ring, then she said: 'Mr Jewel again. He might at least spare us his ill-breeding. Well, we can't let the soup get cold.'

Felix and Miss Bohun had their soup; when Maria entered, Miss Bohun said: 'Go upstairs, Maria, and ask Mr Jewel if he has heard the bell.'

Maria ascended slowly to the attic and as slowly descended while Miss Bohun sat in restless silence.

'Well?'

'Mr Jewel sick.'

'No!' Miss Bohun turned sharply in her chair and her long period of exasperation crystallized suddenly into militant anger: 'This is the last straw. What does he say is the matter with him?'

Maria spread her hands: 'Don't know.'

'Really! It's too bad.' Miss Bohun turned to Felix, 'Felix, you go up.'

Felix went up almost as slowly as Maria had done. He was certain Mr Jewel was dead, but when he whispered: 'Mr Jewel,' into the dark, icy attic, the old man murmured hoarsely.

'What's the matter?' asked Felix.

'Light the lamp, there's a lad,' said Mr Jewel. 'Matches in the saucer.'

Felix put back the curtain to get a glimmer from the landing and found and lit the lamp. 'I'll light the oil-stove, too.'

'No kerosene,' croaked Mr Jewel, 'used it all last week. No more coming up.'

'I'll get you some.'

'No, no. Don't ask her. Quite warm in here. Be all right in the morning. Bit of a chill like.'

'Can I get you anything?'

'Drink of water.'

There was an Arab water-cooler and glass on the floor by the bed. Felix, feeling efficient and useful, filled the glass and held it for Mr Jewel. The old man's face shone with sweat. The skin of his neck felt very hot as Felix propped him up.

'I'll bring up your soup,' said Felix.

Mr Jewel shook his head: 'Don't ask her. Don't want it. Be all right to-morrow.'

'Shall I leave the lamp?'

'Better not. Don't need it. She wouldn't like it.'

When Felix went downstairs he said with some importance: 'He's got a temperature.'

'Oh, dear! Now what are we supposed to do?' She was silent through the rest of the meal, but at the end she said in sudden, cheerful decision: 'But he must see a doctor. I know the hospital doctors so well – they've always been so kind to me.'

She went over to the writing-desk where the telephone stood. After a long delay, during which she remained unperturbed, she got on to the sister on duty at the English Hospital: 'Sister

Smart? Ah, how good to hear your voice. I am so worried . . . No, it's my lodger, Mr Jewel. I don't know what's the matter, but I suspect pneumonia, always a serious business in the very old. If someone could come over to Herod's Gate . . . No. I understand. But I think it would be very dangerous to delay. Another night – the crisis – you know – and I feel so responsible. He has no friends. He came up here as a refugee and I took him in. It seems to me *vital* that he get attention to-night . . . Well, yes, that would indeed be the best thing. Thank you. Thank you so much.' When she put down the receiver she sat some moments smiling gratefully before she said: 'How good of Sister Smart. How very kind.'

'Is a doctor coming?'

'No, but she's sending the ambulance. She, too, suspects pneumonia. Mr Jewel will get the very best of attention at the English Hospital.'

'Poor Mr Jewel,' said Felix, 'I wonder how long he'll have to stay there?'

'I don't know,' Miss Bohun lifted her chin with a movement of tranquil and gracious decision. 'But he's not coming back here.'

Next morning, as Felix was struggling to write an essay on 'The Animal World', he heard a ceaseless coming and going on the stairs. When he put his head out, he saw that under Nikky's direction Maria and the gardener were moving everything out of the attic. As Maria passed down with a bundle of Mr Jewel's paintings under her arm, Felix asked Nikky anxiously: 'You're not going to burn them, are you?'

Nikky answered: 'Not yet,' and shouted after Maria: 'Put them in the wood-shed.' He turned his back on Felix to prevent further questions and Felix went back to his room to write slowly, in a childish forward-sloping hand:

'Faro is a little cat, but being a Siamese she is not an ordinary cat. She has some toys of her own and the one she loves best is her rabbit's paw. She brings it and places it on my lap and waits for me to throw it. When I throw it . . .' Felix paused, sucking his pencil-end and cogitating how he could describe the flurry and pin-pricking of claws with which Faro went off his knee, leaping, flying – like a leaping frog, perhaps he could say, but it reminded him also of the pictures he had seen of the fruit-bat; her brown velvet toes stretched, stretched in excitement, looking webbed as they stretched, she would pounce on the rabbit's paw – then back she would bring it to be thrown again with all the flurry of before. After a long pause he started to write again: 'She sails through the air like a frog and lands on the paw, then she brings it back for me to throw again.' Another pause – now he had to describe how, when she got tired of playing with the rabbit's paw, she would continue to jump down after it, just to show her appreciation, but slowly and more slowly, and then, in the end, she would place it, not on his knee, but out of reach somewhere, perhaps on the window-sill or the bed. Then she would settle herself beside it with paws curved in beneath curved breast – he could see the dark paws neatly placed beneath the white swansdown curve of fur, her head half up, erect but dreaming, and that lioness poise, that unselfconscious dignity of a queen! The picture hung on his mind as on a cinema screen, but how could he put it into words? He sighed and wrote:

'When she is tired . . .' and suddenly there was an uproar of sawing and banging from upstairs. His door fell open and Miss Bohun appeared, cheeks pink, voice high: 'I hope this isn't disturbing your studies, Felix, but the work *must* be done. The sooner it's started, the sooner it will be finished.'

'Yes,' Felix began packing up his books.

'Oh, I'm so excited,' she brought her hands together in a single clap. 'I've wanted to do things in the attic, but with Mr Jewel there I couldn't get in. I had a little spare cash and I asked myself: "What shall I do with it? I know," I said, "I'll make the attic a *den*, a positive den."'

'For Frau Leszno?' Felix was surprised.

'Oh no. I've been thinking of moving up there myself. It's so quiet and away from the traffic of the house. I'm having a door put on, too. I can shut myself up there with my thoughts and compose my sermons. Oh, I *do* look forward to it.'

Miss Bohun seemed unusually happy, but Felix was wondering if he very much wanted Frau Leszno in the room just across the passage. He decided he did not and gloomed a little over the idea until at luncheon-time, as he was about to descend the stairs, he heard a new uproar break out, this time from the room below.

'What then is it for me,' Frau Leszno somehow wailed and raged at the same time, 'to spend my life in this so little box, like a prisoner? Am I a bad that I spend my life so? How is my son, a black-beetle, that he must in the kitchen sleep? Is this the roof you put upon my head and the head of my child? And here mine own furnitures – mine six dining-chairs, mine table, mine horse-hair sofa? For what? That I may not sit at mine own table, that my child may not sit at mine own table? Then I go. Then I find myself such a big job as is fitting . . .'

'That,' Miss Bohun's voice broke in quietly, 'is for you to decide, Frau Leszno. If you insist on going, of course, I cannot . . .'

'So!' screamed Frau Leszno, 'now I am to go! Such is the great promise of the death-bed of Herr Leszno. Always a roof I have – and now to go. Now I, a lady, who had been to boarding-school, must make herself a servant in another's house.' Frau Leszno's voice was pitched on a note of self-pity and self-righteousness and accusation that roused in a listener neither remorse nor compassion, but rather a murderous irritation of the nerves. Miss Bohun's voice, breaking in, was in comparison reasonable and dignified:

'But you always tell me the Germans treat their servants very well. You might get an *au pair* job in a German-Jewish household . . .'

'Never,' screamed Frau Leszno. 'Never do I leave my home –'

Miss Bohun again interrupted, speaking with decision: 'I really think, now you have suggested it, that you had better go, Frau Leszno. These scenes are exhausting me. They break into my contemplative life and I owe it to my nephew to give him a tranquil home in which to pursue his studies. You are not happy here. You could do better elsewhere.' She picked up the bell, rang it loudly, but called 'Felix' as though she knew him to be within hearing. He began to descend the stairs. Frau Leszno gave him a look of distracted disgust, then went out, crashing the door behind her.

The meal was served. Felix ate his, but Miss Bohun sat for some time with her right hand shading her eyes. After a long pause, she said: 'Frau Leszno is leaving. I have broken my promise. Do you think I have done wrong?'

'No,' said Felix, who could not feel sentimental about a promise that had proved so troublesome to all concerned.

There was another long pause, then Miss Bohun said: 'I like you, Felix, I think you're a very nice, well brought-up boy; but you are, after all, very young and a member of the opposite sex, so I hope you won't feel hurt if I feel – have indeed felt for some time – that I owe it to myself to have someone here who will be my friend. You *do* understand?'

'Oh yes,' said Felix, not knowing whether he was hurt or not.

Miss Bohun continued: 'I have met a young widow, a Mrs Ellis, who would like to come to me. Mr Posthorn put me in touch, as a matter of fact; he met her at the Hendersons'. She's a quiet little thing – simple perhaps, but there's something so nice about her, so trusting. I'm sure you'll like her.'

'Yes,' said Felix again, rather coldly, already dissociating himself from this female partnership. In his mind he said: 'I've always got Faro,' and at the same time he began to think he must go and inquire about Mr Jewel. He felt now that Mr Jewel was out of the house there could be no disloyalty to Miss Bohun in visiting him.

Miss Bohun suddenly gave a sigh and said: 'Of course, in a way, I don't like to see the household breaking up. The Lesznos have been with me for nearly five years.'

'Is Nikky going too?' asked Felix.

'I don't know. We haven't discussed it. I am quite willing to let him stay; he reminds me so of his father – such a handsome, charming old man. A very beautiful sort of friendship existed between Herr Leszno and me. I'm fond of Nikky, too, in a way. I could never feel quite the same about Frau Leszno.'

'When she goes, will she take all this furniture?'

'What furniture?'

'Oh, I thought I heard her say that the table and chairs and the sofa were hers . . .'

'In a way they are; *in a way*. Our first arrangement was that we held everything in common. She supplied some pieces of furniture, it is true, and I supplied others. But if she chooses to be petty and lay claim to the things she provided – well, she must just take them with her. I don't doubt something can be found to take their place,' Miss Bohun's voice became cheerful as she talked. 'I find that my troubles always sort themselves out. You can't do better than trust in the Lord. I don't know of any occasion when God has failed to look after me. Faith is a wonderful thing. Since I've found it, I've never had a day's illness, and as for money – well, money seems to grow on trees. And I used to be such a nervous ailing sort of girl! I used to dread the future with nothing but my own little private income – a mere two hundred pound a year – but how wonderfully things have worked out for me.' There was in Miss Bohun's tone something exultant that held Felix amazed. She raised her face with her eyelids shut and smiled a rather knowing smile: 'But I'm afraid Frau Leszno was not over-pleased when I read her Mr Shipton's letter about you. Dear me, no. She thought that time she'd worn me down at last. When I pointed out to her that it was my duty to offer my orphaned nephew a home, she said – well, I won't tell you what she said, but I'm afraid she thought God had let *her* down.'

'I suppose He had rather.'

'My dear boy,' said Miss Bohun briskly, 'the ways of the Lord are beyond our understanding. Now, if you don't mind, I have Madame Babayannis in a few minutes.'

That afternoon Felix went to inquire after Mr Jewel. The English Hospital, surrounded by a walled garden, stood in a square known as the Russian Compound. It was a bare, gravelled space, like a barracks square, and enclosed also the Arab Hospital and the Law Courts. In the afternoon warmth Felix made his way through crowds of Arabs who mingled gossiping and squabbling as they waited to get into either building. The stone-built English Hospital was as cool as a cellar. A nurse, an Armenian girl, stood in the doorway, her face dark against her white tunic and the white-washed walls: when Felix asked after Mr Jewel, she said indifferently: 'You can run up if you like.'

'But isn't he very ill?' Felix hesitated, unprepared to visit Mr Jewel so soon.

''Flu, and undernourishment,' said the nurse. 'He is in no danger.'

Mr Jewel was sitting up in bed in a small ward. There were five other beds, but only two were occupied, both by young English policemen, who called Mr Jewel 'dad' or 'granddad'.

'Hello, young fella-me-lad,' he shouted to Felix, 'I was expecting you.' He looked as though he had been enjoying himself. He was no longer the repressed, head-hanging Mr Jewel of the supper-table, but a gay old boy, a man popular among men. 'I'm all right. You'll have me back in no time.'

'But do you want to come back?'

'Can't stay here for ever, y'know.' He didn't add 'worse luck', or 'wish I could'. Felix was surprised, then, and at other times – for he started to drop into the hospital twice or three times a week – that there was in Mr Jewel no rancour against Miss Bohun. He had come to think everyone must be ungrateful to poor Miss Bohun, but now, when he secretly felt that there might be cause for ingratitude, he found none.

On his way to the hospital he had supposed he would have to withstand some criticism of her. He could not, of course, stop Mr Jewel saying things against her, but he would say nothing himself, so Mr Jewel would understand that he was Miss Bohun's friend. But the situation proved to be quite different. Indeed at the back of Felix's mind there was a certain guilt as though Mr Jewel were championing Miss Bohun against a doubt in Felix's own mind. The doubt, indeed, had spoken when Felix with surprise asked Mr Jewel if he wanted to go back. Mr Jewel laughed.

'She's an old skinflint,' he said, 'I'll hand you that. She got the last piastre off of me. I had to think twice about putting me nose out of doors – not a penny in me pocket for a bit of baccy or tea, but she's all right at bottom. She took me in. There I was in that place at Bethlehem. Ever been there? Proper Bedlam, it was. Looked like a prison and sounded like a looney-bin; all packed together, foreigners and all sorts; kids yelling, women squabbling – and the rows! One man got knifed; yes, he did. Well, foreigners, you know, they're used to being pushed around; it happens all their lives; they know how to look after themselves; but if you're British, you're used to something different. That's right, ain't it? I'm not as young as I was; I felt I needed a bit of quiet; place of me own; no one touching me things. H.M. Government give you a cot and your grub, no more. Then Miss Bohun turned up and we hit it off and next time she came she offered me her attic. "Just what you can afford, Mr Jewel," she said, but when I was inside it, it was: "What have you got, Mr Jewel? All right that'll do,"' Mr Jewel laughed heartily at this. 'I do a bit of

75

painting, you know!' He lowered his voice confidentially and Felix, restraining himself from answering: 'I know,' said: 'Do you really, Mr Jewel?' Mr Jewel assured him. 'Used to paint at sea; helped to get the time in. The fellows said I'd quite a turn for it – but you need a table, a bit of space. Well, nothing like that here no more than at Bethlehem.'

'After you moved in, did you go on being friends with Miss Bohun?' asked Felix.

'In a way. She talked, I listened. Everything all right at first. Trouble was, she didn't like me picking up Frau Wagner.'

'No,' agreed Felix.

'Ah!' Mr Jewel gave him a significant nod. 'You noticed that, too? Perhaps I oughtn't to have brought her in, but the girl needed a change. Social life. I felt sorry for her. There was nothing more to it than that. I happened to meet her in the street. She'd got a basket of stuff; I said: 'Give you a hand?' and we got talking. She's all right; she just likes a bit of fun. Can't blame her. I wasn't much good to her without any cash. But, then again, you can't blame Miss Bohun. Women aren't made to get on together. She's not got anyone else in the attic, has she?'

'No.'

'Ah! She won't get anyone. No one'd want it. She didn't want me to go, y'know. She was just warning me.'

That evening Felix in a mild, small voice asked Miss Bohun: 'Did you tell Mr Jewel he couldn't come back to the attic?'

'No, but I told Sister Smart. I've left it for her to tell him when she thinks fit,' Miss Bohun sighed. 'Someone else *must* shoulder the responsibility now. I have done my share.'

'But what will he do? Where will he go?'

'Oh, they'll keep him there for a bit,' and as she made a movement that threw the idea of Mr Jewel off for ever, Felix knew he must not speak of him again.

While Felix was worrying about Mr Jewel's future, Miss Bohun apparently had her mind upon nearer matters. She said with slight melancholy: 'I saw Mrs Ellis today. I wanted her to come in and meet you, but she's off to Egypt on the night train. She's getting some baggage there out of store. Dear me, she might have waited until after she'd moved in; so many little things to arrange. You ought to have met her *before* – for one thing, I'd like your opinion of her. This time I wasn't sure I hadn't been perhaps rather precipitate . . . She has suffered, of course, but there's something *hard* about her. And I'm not sure you'll like her. I feel I owe it to you to have someone you'll like.'

Felix said not to worry. After all, Mrs Ellis was to be Miss Bohun's friend: but Miss Bohun seemed worried despite his reassurance, and during the warm spring afternoons, when the windows were open, Felix in his room or in the garden could hear Miss Bohun telephoning likely acquaintances: 'How strange, one is always hearing of people desperate for accommodation, but when one has the most charming room to offer, there is no one . . . Ah, yes . . . well, of course, I can't wait till the summer. This girl means to come here with all this baggage straight from the station. She's given up her hotel room, but if she had to, she'd find another all right. It means I must have someone who'll move in *at once:* a *fait accompli,* if you get my meaning . . . No, I'd have no objection to an officer. Yes, it's nice getting things from the Naafi, but then one has to offer to pay for them. With that tinned stuff we might get a slightly *richer* diet, but I am sure it could not be more *nourishing* than I provide already.'

To Felix she said: 'Oh dear, oh dear, I've been so foolish – *jumping* at this young woman. But then, there was no knowing with Mr Jewel! I told her I was moving up to the attic; but I feel now I need my own room. I'm a pastor, Felix; I have to interview those that come unto me; I have to create my sermons. Congenial surroundings are all-important.'

'Perhaps she wouldn't mind,' said Felix, 'if you put her in the attic.'

'Oh no, I couldn't do that. I *agreed* to let her have my room; but I thought if she were dropping in and out this week, I could show her the attic and just *hint*. After all, she might *prefer* it – it looks very nice now it's finished: quite chintzy. The trouble is you can only see the sky. I had hoped with one thing and another I could suggest doing a swop. But now, she'll walk straight in and expect to find my room ready for her.'

'You could tell her you'd let it,' suggested Felix.

'My dear boy, that would be dishonest. Besides, I can't afford to keep rooms empty.'

Felix moved uncomfortably, feeling he ought to offer to move into the attic himself, but before he reached the point of doing so, Miss Bohun's manner changed and she said brightly: 'Well, we must make the best of it. Mrs Ellis arrives to-morrow and she must have the room she has been promised. That is only fair. The attic can be made quite cosy for the summer months – after that we shall see. Whatever happens, Felix, I am determined you won't have to move. You need a properly lighted room for your studies.'

That afternoon, when he went upstairs, he stood for a long time looking into the garden. The lawn was deep in the green of spring. Miniature leaves, buff-green, transparent and edged with brown, covered the mulberry tree like a glow. The summer was coming and somehow that made everything seem different. As he watched, Maria came out of her shed carrying a square wire cage in which something moved. He leant from the window and called to her: 'What have you got?'

She shaded her eyes to see him and answered: 'Rats. I catch them in my bedroom,' she held up the cage so that he could see the dark-furred rats with their undulating bodies and their small, brilliant eyes. They did not look vicious or unfriendly.

'What are you going to do with them?' he called, but she did not understand and merely waved her hand in reply and went off round the side of the house. He tried to settle down to work, but for some reason he was worried by the memory of the rats turning about in the small cage, their muzzles twitching as much with interest as with suspicion. Uneasy because he did not know what was being done with them, he felt forced at last to go downstairs and ask Maria again. Frau Leszno was in the sitting-room putting the tea-things ready on the table. She turned her back to him. The door into the courtyard lay open and Felix went to it, oddly apprehensive. The cage stood on the ground and the rats within it were darting about in terror, their fur on fire. Maria stood watching them with the kerosene can still in her hand. The smoke that arose filled the air with an acrid stench of burning fur.

Felix shouted at Maria: 'What are you doing? How could you do it? Stop it. Stop it at once.'

She lifted a bewildered and simple face: 'Good to kill them,' she said.

'But not like that. How beastly, how cruel! We must stop it.'
He ran to the kitchen to get water, but Maria caught his arm.

'See, already dead. Very quick, this.'

It was true the rats had toppled over, dead or overcome by smoke. They lay motionless, letting the fire consume them. Felix, in a panic of disgust and horror, wrenched his arm free and ran back into the room. He demanded, breathless with indignation: 'Where is Miss Bohun?'

Frau Leszno turned slowly and regarded him with a sullen distaste: 'Must I be addressed so? Such manners I never have.'

'*Please*, where is Miss Bohun?'

Frau Leszno looked at him from head to foot and back again, then, turning away, said frigidly: 'She prepares the room.'

'Which room?'

'The room. The room.'

He realized and ran upstairs; without knocking, he burst into the front bedroom that was, as he had seen it before, severely tidy and severely cold. The only difference was that there was a smell of burning from the yard. Some cleaning materials lay by the door. Miss Bohun was kneeling in prayer before the Bible on the little yellow-wood desk. Hearing Felix enter she raised a sleepy face, then, when she saw him, she gave her exasperated frown. He was too distracted to apologize:

'Oh, Miss Bohun, such a beastly thing – Maria put paraffin on the rats and set them alight. Please tell her she mustn't do it again. Please, Miss Bohun . . .'

Miss Bohun got slowly to her feet. His state apparently gave her patience with him, for she said: 'Really, Felix, you must control yourself. It's nothing to get excited about. Arabs always kill animals that way. They do it even if they want to destroy cats and dogs . . .'

'*Cats and dogs!*'

'Yes, it's nothing to get excited about. I'm sure such a death is just as quick and painless as drowning.'

'But it can't be,' Felix broke in, his voice raised. 'They were so terrified . . .'

Miss Bohun was cool and sensible. 'It's the way the Arabs do it and you can't stop them, so don't be silly. And don't burst in here like that. This room is strictly private.'

'I'm sorry.' Felix went off, the smell of burning fur still in his nostrils. It seemed to him he could smell it all over the house. In his room he picked up Faro, who was asleep in the sunlight, and whispered: 'Never leave me. Never. If anyone tries to hurt you, I'll murder them.'

Faro, unaware she existed in a world of enemies, stretched out her paws and yawned luxuriously in his face.

Frau Leszno was due to leave at the end of the month. Miss Bohun told Felix that she had found a very nice job in a Tel-Aviv hotel and had nothing to grumble about at all.

'She's to have a considerable salary, *very* considerable. Twenty pounds a month or more. I don't know what she has to do for it, but dear me, I wish I could earn money so easily. I think when she discovered how much she could earn, she began to see things differently. Anyway, she's very pleased with herself, but I've had scarcely a word of gratitude. Heigh-ho, such is life.'

'And Nikky's staying?'

Miss Bohun nodded: 'He's useful in small ways – and it's nice to feel he wants to stay. The last of our little family circle! Dead or dispersed.'

This puzzled Felix for a while until, after reflection, he supposed she referred to Herr Leszno dead and Frau Leszno dispersed.

'And she's leaving the furniture?' he said in a way that implied congratulation, but Miss Bohun seemed to see it differently.

She clicked her tongue slightly and said: 'Yes, indeed. I've had to agree to store it for her – but I'll never know when she'll be disorganizing the whole house by asking for it.'

5

Frau Wagner's promise that Felix would enjoy the Palestine spring was fulfilled. He had known springs in Iraq, of course, but there the season was so brief that one was likely to miss it. A shower of rain would fall over desert country and flowers would form suddenly as a mirage, but their lives were as brief as the mirage. By the time someone, having crossed the desert at the right moment, came into town exclaiming, it was all over. Here the rains, following one another at intervals through the winter, carpeted the naked spring earth with a green as vivid as light. Later the grasses were enriched by the intricate leaves of trefoils, ranunculuses, anemones and vetches, and the spears of the bulb and tuber plants. Shortly before Mr Jewel was taken ill Felix saw the green cyclamen buds open, each dropping a screw of petals like a wrung-out cloth. In a day these had become flowers, alert and delicate as the ears of a gazelle. Suddenly Felix became very excited about the flowers. To his mother flowers had been something to help decorate a room and Felix had seen them, like her embroideries or her perfumes, as a part of her which he did not analyse. But now he saw them quite separate from her – growing from the earth, budding and flowering. When the anemones started to appear everywhere – mostly scarlet, but some mauve or white, and others, transplanted into Jerusalem gardens from remote parts of Palestine, deep purple or the colour of biscuits – he was carried away by them. The first February anemones opening in the grass, satin-surfaced and flawless, looked to him like jewels. He planned to list all the flowers in Palestine and describe them minutely. Each morning he went round the garden in a business-like way to see what new flowers had appeared. The morning Mrs Ellis was due, she was put out of his mind by the discovery of the garden's first irises. They were almost lost in the grass, stalkless, gauzy things, two of them silver-white and the other a saffron yellow, all sheened so that they seemed radiant. He had expected to find nothing in this corner, and as he came upon them he was startled a moment, then felt – amazingly – as happy as he had been before his mother died. Holding Faro safe on his shoulder, he bent over the irises, wondering that they were there, as complete, as carefully hidden, as a nest of young birds.

He heard the sitting-room door open and glanced up. As he looked across the lawn and through the cage-shaped branches of the mulberry tree clouded with their sheen of leaves, he realized that the season had changed. The cold had gone. The air was softer than silk. There was an extraordinary delicacy about everything. Here was a quality he had seen before only as a sort of effusion of his mother – and now, seeing it apart from her, he was amazed by the beauty of the visible world.

Miss Bohun's voice rang through the air as she stepped into the garden. She looked back and pointed dramatically, excitedly, at an old, striped rug that lay just inside the door.

'I do hate this rug. I bought it out of kindness for a pound. But, oh, how thankful I have been to have it.'

She crossed the grass with a movement that was almost a waltz; her face was lit by an eager and happy expression that made it seem – what? Felix could only think of the word 'generous'. She called out: 'Feel-ix. Come and meet Mrs Ellis.'

Then Mrs Ellis stepped into the garden. Felix stood where he was, watching her. Miss Bohun had spoken of her as 'young', but he had not expected anyone really young. He had heard quite old women of thirty or forty called 'young'. But Mrs Ellis was young. She was wearing a navy-blue jersey and trousers, and her hair was cut off. She was very slender. She would have looked like a boy of Felix's own age had it not been for the jewellery and the red on her lips and finger-nails. That made her a young lady – a grown-up, a sophisticated person. For some reason, Felix suddenly blushed to the roots of his hair and he pretended to be absorbed again by the irises.

'There he is,' sang Miss Bohun, no trace of her usual irritation in her voice. It was as though she, too, had felt the spring and, with it, wonder and excitement. 'What's the matter with the boy? Is he deaf? F-e-e-l-iks!'

Felix raised his hot pink face and saw Miss Bohun aglitter,

with Mrs Ellis behind her. Mrs Ellis was sauntering casually across the grass. To Felix she would have been the picture of self-sufficient indifference to himself and everything else had she not as she approached lifted her right hand with a rattle of bracelets and touched the corner of her mouth. Despite the magnificence of its scarlet, spiked finger-nails, and its great square topaz ring, her hand was trembling.

When Miss Bohun introduced them, Mrs Ellis said a casual 'Hello.' Felix tried to say 'Hello' in reply, but his mouth was dry and he found it difficult to speak.

'What have you chanced upon?' Miss Bohun asked excitedly. 'What are they? Oh! Irises! Such interesting flowers.' She stared blindly at them for a moment, then swinging quickly round she all but trampled them under her feet. 'I've all *sorts* of rare irises in the garden,' she said. 'A young botanist planted them here. He was caught in the Middle East at the outbreak of war. He'd been everywhere getting these bulbs – Mount Tabor, Djebel Druse, the Lebanon – I don't know where not. He was going to Cairo to join up and he didn't know what to do with all these valuable bulbs – so I offered him a home for them.'

'Has he never been back for them?' asked Mrs Ellis in a husky voice.

'No – but he did write from Tunisia and ask me to dig them up and post them to him. As though I knew where they all were! Some people have no scruples at all about putting others to trouble. I didn't reply and I hope I shall hear nothing more.'

'Won't he be sad about losing them?' asked Felix.

'No doubt – but I rather suspected he intended smuggling these bulbs into England and it's forbidden, you know. They carry plant diseases.'

'I didn't know.' Felix appreciated Miss Bohun's scruples, but he could not help feeling sorry for the young man. Mrs Ellis, however, appeared indifferent to the story. Her face was turned aside and Felix, glancing furtively at her, noticed the even china-white of her skin and her delicate, regular features. Her hair, a light chestnut, was completely smooth. Felix had always regarded his mother's blonde fluffy-haired prettiness as the ideal of feminine beauty, but now he looked at Mrs Ellis as though he were seeing beauty for the first time. Miss Bohun, also looking at her, said: 'You're admiring my potted plants, I see. I got them from an old Armenian woman down the road. She had them on a balcony and every time I passed I could see them wilting away. At last I knocked on her door and said: "Why don't you water your plants?" She said they'd belonged to a lodger who had gone to Aleppo, so I said I'd take them and look after them. One day she came down the lane and saw how fine they'd grown and, if you can credit it, she asked for them back again.'

Mrs Ellis smiled, then, turning with a sudden, quick movement and seeing Felix watching her, her smile widened and she said: 'I like your cat.'

'She's called "Faro".' Felix blushed again, this time with pure pleasure.

He lifted Faro down from his shoulder and held her in his hands thinking Mrs Ellis might want to take her, but Mrs Ellis merely put out a white, claw-thin hand and gave her a chuck under the chin. Felix realized that, to her, Faro, who for weeks had been his companion, talking, feeling and thinking exactly as Felix did himself, was only a little animal. Felix, looking into Faro's eyes, seemed to see them blank and unthinking and, as he watched her, she turned her gaze entranced upon the movements of a fly. Of course she was not a human being like Mrs Ellis, but a cat whose reactions were to warmth, mice, birds and flies. As this thought passed through his mind, Faro wriggled and jumped to the ground, where she lifted one of her front paws so that she could stab at her creamy front with her pink, darting tongue.

When Felix looked up he found that Miss Bohun was watching him; she looked cross and, catching his eye, said:

'As a matter of fact she's my cat.'

'She's a beauty,' said Mrs Ellis politely.

Miss Bohun made a movement as though offering to conduct Mrs Ellis away, but instead she walked off, saying: 'Well, I'll leave you two to get to know one another while I order luncheon.'

As Miss Bohun disappeared into the house, Mrs Ellis gave a laugh: 'She's a joke, isn't she?'

Felix looked in surprise towards the door, then laughed himself. Suddenly it seemed that that was, of course, the explanation of Miss Bohun. She was a joke.

'But she's quite clever, really,' he said quickly, 'she teaches English.'

'Oh, she's all right.' Mrs Ellis paused, her hands in her pockets, looking down at her feet, then she added in an aside and in a tone different from any she had used before: 'She rang me up and said she wanted to offer me a home. I should be grateful. It's more than anyone else has done.'

'She offered me a home, too,' said Felix, 'I had nowhere else to go.'

'Haven't you any relations out here?'

'Only Miss Bohun, and she isn't really a relation. You see, when she was a little girl she was an orphan. Well, not an ordinary orphan; she had some money left her, but she hadn't a mother or a father. My grandfather gave her a home, the same as she's given me. But his wife died and he got married again and he had some real children – I mean, they belonged to him, and, of course, Miss Bohun didn't, and she was a lot older by that time. My mother thinks she wasn't happy and it made her funny. My mother said: "It's given her an inferiority thing" – do you know what that means?'

'Oh, yes.' Mrs Ellis laughed in at herself.

'But I don't think she feels inferior.'

'Neither do I. Rather the reverse.'

They stood silent a moment; then she jerked her hand nervously, her bracelets rattled, and she said: 'I must go and unpack.' Without glancing at him again, she returned to the house.

Felix wandered around, troubled, the garden and the spring no longer beautiful in themselves but somehow now oddly related to his own disturbance. He disliked this disturbance and when he saw Faro sitting alone on the garden seat, he was swept with remorse that put everything else from his mind. He crossed to her and started to stroke her, but she turned her head and bit his hand with quiet decision. The bite did not hurt; it was no more than a warning; not understanding, he tried to lift her and in one instantaneous movement she caught his wrist between her paws and bit him sharply. He drew his hand away with a cry, and she stared at him with a sort of defiance. Looking into her eyes he seemed to see her retreat into cold, animal independence, but behind this there was resentment.

'Faro,' he said, 'I'm sorry,' but as he put out his hand again she backed from him, and as he rose she ran up the mulberry tree out of his reach.

He stood under the tree thinking Mrs Ellis must be noticing him from her window, but when he caught a glimpse of her through the glass she was absorbed in putting her frocks into the wardrobe. With a pang such as he had never felt before in his life, he knew she had not seen him at all.

Miss Bohun, sitting with a piece of cold meat before her, kept one hand on the bell that she had now rung twice. She glanced towards the stairs as though she could better hear Mrs Ellis's descent if she looked in that direction, but there was no sound. She clicked her tongue.

'Dear me,' she said, 'I hope we're not going to have this sort of thing. I don't like to ring three times. I don't want her to think I'm annoyed,' but she gave the bell a little shake and at once, as though as a result, Mrs Ellis's door could be heard opening and Miss Bohun at once became quite cheerful.

'Ah, *here* you are,' she said as Mrs Ellis appeared, 'I always like to get the luncheon over in good time. I never know when one of my pupils may turn up early. They're so eager, you know, and I don't think it does to have food on the table when they arrive.'

Mrs Ellis smiled as she sat down, obviously not relating Miss Bohun's ideas to herself.

Miss Bohun, as she sliced the meat, talked loudly and with a wild gaiety. Felix could not keep his eyes off her. He had never seen her so animated, so – yes, happy. He realized that Miss Bohun was happy. Little pink patches glowed on her cheek-bones; her eyes were not half-shut now but open and shining.

Felix glanced at Mrs Ellis to see if she were as surprised as he was, but Mrs Ellis, staring over his shoulder at the garden behind his head, was obviously far away in her own thoughts. And why, after all, should she be surprised? She did not know Miss Bohun.

As Miss Bohun sliced the meat, her voice rose higher and higher in a sort of exaltation of gaiety: 'I do hope you'll be comfortable in my room. It gets the morning sun which I always enjoyed so much, but you must not worry about me. I shall be very happy in the attic. Very happy. The carpenters have done a wonderful job, and – this is important – I shall be nicely tucked away up there. I shall have *quiet*. I cannot tell you what that means to me! You must realize, when I'm seeking inspiration for my sermons – the voice is so thin, the thread that carries it so very, very thin, and the birth-pangs so terrific, that the slightest sound can disturb it; the slightest jar.' She touched Mrs Ellis's arm confidentially, causing her to turn in a startled way: 'I must tell you about that one day.'

'About what?' Mrs Ellis asked.

'My religion. It is something only for chosen spirits, but I shall tell you.'

Felix looked up to see if he were included, but Miss Bohun was looking only at Mrs Ellis. Mrs Ellis, lifting her last scrap of meat to her mouth, murmured a vague interest.

'Will you have another piece of meat, Mrs Ellis?' Miss Bohun asked, almost eagerly.

'No, thank you.'

'Nor I. I find I am happier and healthier, and my brain is clearer, on vegetables.' Miss Bohun rang the bell, then noticed Felix: 'Oh, what about you, Felix? You're always hungry.'

'No, thank you.' Felix had lost his appetite, but Miss Bohun did not notice; she chattered on:

'Now, don't forget, Mrs Ellis, I want you to feel free to bring in a guest if you wish. There's room at the table. I can always poke myself in the corner.' Mrs Ellis looked up as though startled. 'I'm just a little wisp of a thing,' went on Miss Bohun, 'no flesh on my bones, but you're a hundred per cent feminine and fully-fashioned. I used to be so sorry for myself being so flat-chested, but now I know things like that don't matter. I'm very wiry.'

'Oh!' Mrs Ellis made no attempt to appear interested. A long silence followed.

Maria had brought in the joint, but it was Frau Leszno who entered to take it away. Apparently she had come with a purpose, for, as she trudged round the table she fixed on the new lodger such an expression of suffering resentment, Mrs Ellis, suddenly seeing it, opened her mouth with surprise. Frau Leszno, going off with the meat dish, seemed satisfied.

'Is she annoyed about something?' Mrs Ellis asked.

Miss Bohun nodded darkly: 'She's under notice. She goes at the end of the week, but she has nothing to complain about. I've found her another position and I'm letting her son remain, although, goodness knows, he does little enough for his keep.'

'Is that the handsome young man I saw in the yard?'

'Handsome? I suppose he is handsome, although he hasn't half his father's looks. I've had to promise to let him have his mother's room when she goes although it's Maria's by rights. Still, Maria is a good creature; she doesn't complain, and after all, she's never had much better than she's got.'

The door opened again; Miss Bohun whispered: 'This is Maria.'

Maria, coming in with a rice pudding, smiled in a pleasant, motherly way at Mrs Ellis, who smiled back. Miss Bohun seeing this exchange, smiled herself and gave her hands a clap of delight. 'Isn't this nice! I'm sure we're going to be just one big happy family.'

Mrs Ellis looked a little startled, but Miss Bohun did not notice. 'I know what we'll do,' she said in the manner of someone promising a treat to children, 'to-morrow we'll all go together and pay the rent.' This time she did notice Mrs Ellis's expression, and she explained: 'Oh, perhaps you think that's not amusing. Actually, it's quite an expedition. The landlord is an Imam at the big mosque. I have to go early, when the mosque is open to Christians, and present my salaams and so on. Dear me, I do feel so sorry for landlords; they are not allowed to raise their rents, you know, and rents here are so small. This house, for instance, is controlled at £60 a year. My landlord would be much worse off if I had not voluntarily – voluntarily, mind you! – offered to pay him more.'

'Oh, do you pay more now?' exclaimed Felix.

'Well, not at this very moment – but I've written to let him know that next quarter I intend to start paying £65 a year.'

Mrs Ellis yawned so that tears stood in her eyes. She refused coffee, saying she was going to lie down. 'I could not get a sleeper on the train. The army had all of them,' she explained as she went upstairs.

Felix when he went up himself could hear no sound of her. Faro was not lying as she usually was in the sunlight on his desk.

It was clear to him that Mrs Ellis was not the sort of person to give much time to a schoolboy – or to Miss Bohun either, he was sure – yet for her sake he had upset Faro. Feeling foolish and deserted, he opened his desk. Almost at once he heard Faro jump from a mulberry branch on to the ledge above the door, then come along to his window-sill. Making no move that might discourage her, he pretended to be absorbed in his books. In a moment she was on his knee. He looked down at her and met her steady glance of reconciliation. He slid his hand round her silken neck and she licked him with a tongue as rough as emery paper.

6

At supper Mrs Ellis looked very tired; her pallor had a blue tinge; she wore no lipstick and her lips were as white as her face. She seemed to have nothing to say. Miss Bohun kept glancing at her, but received no answering glance. At the end of the meal Miss Bohun put her hand on Mrs Ellis's arm and said as though on the spur of the moment: 'Come up to my room for a chat!'

'I'm sorry,' said Mrs Ellis, 'but really I feel too tired to-night.'

Miss Bohun drew in her lips a moment, then said quietly: 'Oh, I do sympathize. I often get so tired myself – so very tired,' she broke off, studied Mrs Ellis's face a moment, then added: 'Get to bed early and have a nice, long sleep.'

Mrs Ellis shook her head: 'I don't sleep very well, but I'll have a good read.'

'In bed!' Miss Bohun clicked her tongue. 'Oh, dear, what a waste of electricity.'

Mrs Ellis, already on her way upstairs, said nothing but 'Good-night.'

At breakfast it again seemed she was not going to appear.

'Dear me,' said Miss Bohun, 'I do hope Mrs Ellis won't make a habit of this. I don't like to see food wasted – not that it *will* be wasted, of course.'

At that moment Mrs Ellis could be heard on the stairs and both Miss Bohun and Felix turned to look at her. Felix caught his breath, for now, rested after her journey, there was behind her pallor a glow of energy and health as though a pink globe were lighted within an alabaster vase.

Miss Bohun, her manner abruptly changing, sang out happily: 'Come along now, we must start early for the mosque.'

'Oh, yes, the mosque,' Mrs Ellis sounded at once contrite and offhand. 'I wish I could come, but I cannot. I have an appointment.'

'Oh!' Miss Bohun dropped her eyelids over her eyes, and asked: 'Do you take milk and sugar in your tea?'

'I wonder – could I have coffee?'

'No,' Miss Bohun spoke rather brusquely; 'we can't run to both tea and coffee for breakfast, so I'm afraid it has to be tea.'

Mrs Ellis did not ask why it had to be tea, but a slight frown ruffled for the first time the placidity of her expression. She took the cup of tea as though it were a little distasteful to her. Miss Bohun jumped up, jerking the table as she did so, and said to Felix in a very gay voice: 'Now, Felix, off we go,' and Felix, without courage to say he no longer wanted to go, was led off before Mrs Ellis had started to eat her very small piece of breakfast bacon.

It was a brilliant spring morning, but Miss Bohun did not mention it. As soon as they had shut the gate and were in Sulaiman Road, she said: 'I must say, I'm afraid Mrs Ellis may prove rather a trying person to have in the house. She seems to me a bit of a *poseur* – you know what I mean – actressy. And those fingernails! Dear me! I did so hope she would fit in and we'd be just a jolly little family.' After a reflective pause, she said half to herself: 'She *is* an odd girl.'

Felix's heart thumped in apprehension that these remarks should prove for Mrs Ellis what similar remarks had proved for Mr Jewel, but Miss Bohun made no threats and Felix reflected with relief that Mrs Ellis probably paid much more than Mr Jewel. When they turned into the main road, Miss Bohun, the question of Mrs Ellis apparently forgotten, said in a high, excited tone: 'Let's go in by the Damascus Gate. It's *much* more fun.'

As they passed through the great medieval gate, around which lay a litter of paper and orange-peel, Felix threw off the first nervousness of his infatuation with Mrs Ellis and began to think the expedition was fun. The covered lane called 'King Solomon's Street', made narrower by the display of fruit, vegetables, and sweetstuffs, and café chairs, was packed with people and donkeys. Almost as soon as they entered, a woman beggar, wrapped in black, touched Miss Bohun's arm. Miss Bohun, looking at the oval where the face should be and seeing only the stretched black and white patterned veil that made its wearer seem faceless as a leper, cried: 'Dear me! Poor creature. How disgusting!' and shook her off.

Miss Bohun had not much to say, but she occasionally and with determination distracted Felix from something that interested him to show him something that did not.

'There!' she caught his shoulder as he was watching a sudden flare-up between two Arab tradesmen who, without actually touching one another, were producing all the uproar and excitement of a fight – 'There!' she made him face a heap of onions, 'look at the price of those! Four piastres a kilo and I paid five in the Nablus Road.'

Felix murmured something, but by the time he could look round again at the fight, a third Arab, ostentatiously and with an eye on the audience, had come between the combatants and was making peace.

'One has to pay so much for food,' Miss Bohun said. 'And the English are cheated all the time. Someone like Mrs Ellis, for instance, can have no idea how difficult it is. I am sure she was annoyed because we don't have coffee for breakfast, but I prefer tea and you prefer tea.'

'Oh, I don't mind,' Felix said, 'I used to have coffee.'

'Tea is better for you. I wish I could afford to give you milk, but it's out of the question. Perhaps one month Mrs Ellis will take over the housekeeping and *then* she'll understand.'

When they were brought up by the wall and gateway of the mosque a small Arab boy ran at them shouting: 'Mamnû Ekfel.'

Miss Bohun stopped with her mouth open: 'What,' she said, 'is it Friday?' But it was not Friday. She looked very cross and brushed the small boy aside. He at once flung after her a stone he had been holding in his hand. When she had spoken to an Arab inside the gate, she beckoned commandingly to Felix: 'Come on,' she called and as they passed through the archway she smiled happily and said: 'Sucks to the little boy.'

After the confined and shadowed lanes of the Old City, the great area of the mosque opening before them seemed adazzle in the early sunlight. There had been a shower in the night and the slabs of white paving-stone had a scrubbed and powdery look. Between the stones, here and there, the jewel-green grass had pushed up as fine as hair. On the courtyard the tiled mosque with

92

its dome, the rows of pillars, the little Dome of the Chain, the place of ablution and the single cypresses black as rook feathers stood isolated each over a distance that had a dream-like immensity.

Gazing around him, Felix whispered: 'Oh!'

'Haven't you been here before?'

'No.' Felix had been nowhere.

'I keep forgetting,' Miss Bohun murmured, 'we must do something about your sightseeing, but another day. Now, we go over here. Shoulders back, head up, walk slowly – make a good impression.'

Felix glanced sideways at Miss Bohun and modelled his movement on hers. Together they did a dead march towards a doorway in the wall through which an old Imam could be seen sitting cross-legged on a rug. The walk was a long one. Miss Bohun had time to say: 'I remember our Major Joffey who preceded me as pastor of the "Ever-Readies". He was such a wonderful man, such an organizer! Before we entered a meeting he would take a duster out of his pocket and polish my shoes, and polish his own shoes, and then he'd say: "Head back, shoulders square," and we would march together into the hall. How right he was! How very right! It is so necessary to make a good impression.'

As they drew near, the old man could be seen gazing through the doorway as though completely unaware that two persons were advancing at a crawl upon him. It seemed that only when their shadows fell across his rug did they become visible for him. He made no move, but looked up and smiled broadly. Miss Bohun gave her greetings very competently in Arabic.

'. . . and this is my young friend and lodger Mr Latimer,' she said.

The Imam nodded to Felix and waved towards a stone ledge that ran round the wall of the bare little room. Two or three hangers-on of the mosque, who were sprawling on this, shifted as Miss Bohun and Felix sat down. One of these was sent for coffee; the others watched the money pass with eager, interested eyes. Felix felt rather embarrassed when Miss Bohun put down, separately and with a flourish, the one pound and twenty-five piastres that she was voluntarily adding to the quarter's rent; it seemed such a small sum, but the Imam expressed delight and Miss

Bohun flushed with pleasure at his appreciation and her own liberality. When the coffee pan appeared with three set in brass egg-cups, Miss Bohun seemed to be carried away: 'It is a long time,' she said, 'since I have received a visit from the ladies of your family.'

The Imam, who understood but could not speak English, made a pleased gesture with his hands and replied: 'Bukra.'

'Ah!' Miss Bohun nodded, her cheeks pink: 'Bukra fil mish-mish,' and the Arabs roared with laughter.

Felix watched the exchange with admiration so that even Mrs Ellis passed from his mind. As they walked back Miss Bohun seemed equally admiring of the way she had carried off the visit to her landlord: 'But English women are highly respected here,' she said. 'Of course we have Lady Hester Stanhope and people like that to thank, but, apart from that, I think the Arabs appreciate our spirit. I'm told that an English woman is the only sort of person that can travel in safety from one end to the other of the Levant. That is one of the things that draws me to this country. As an Englishwoman, one has standing,' and she smoothed the front of her dress with satisfaction. 'And then,' she continued as they passed out into the dark lanes full of smells of fruit, wine, drains and stale meat, 'there is their wonderful, old-world feeling for hospitality. We understand it; we appreciate it. And in return, of course, you need only make a gesture – like my inviting his wives and daughters to come and see me. They won't come, of course. I don't suppose the older ladies ever leave the house.'

At the Jaffa Gate, where there was a perpetual noisy traffic of men and beasts in the spring sunlight, they stopped at a small fish-shop and Miss Bohun bought sardines. The man tried to add another to make the half kilo but she would not take it. 'They're really quite expensive,' she explained to Felix, 'and two-and-a-half of them make a good meal for anyone.' At another shop she bought cabbage and then all the way to Fullworth's she talked about the price of vegetables until Felix felt guilty at being part of the cause that involved her in so much expense. If it had not been so near to luncheon and he could have thought of any excuse to go off, he would have gone, but as they returned through the Russian Compound he was rewarded for staying.

'Look, look,' Miss Bohun touched his arm. 'Can that be Mrs Ellis?'

'Yes, it is Mrs Ellis.'

'Coming out of the Government Hospital! How very odd!'

'Perhaps she's been to see someone.'

'Yes,' murmured Miss Bohun with a deep and speculative frown, 'perhaps she has.'

Frau Leszno left a few days later. Felix did not see her go: as far as he was concerned, she simply ceased to be there. Miss Bohun never mentioned her again, nor did she replace her. Everything was done now by Maria, who cooked neither better nor worse than Frau Leszno and who did her work much more willingly. Felix noticed it was she who now cleaned the windows and knives, but he was much too wrapped up in his admiration of Mrs Ellis to reflect on the possibility of Maria's being overworked.

The next time he went to see Mr Jewel, he longed to talk about Mrs Ellis and only Mrs Ellis, but he was forced to avoid mentioning her for fear Mr Jewel would guess the attic was now occupied.

Mr Jewel was sitting on a bench in the garden, a blanket over his knees, and as he lifted his faded, blue-white eyes to the sky he said: 'The sun – that's what a feller needs.' Behind his head bloomed a little jacaranda tree, a delicate branch of colour feathering out violet against the pallid stonework of the wall. He lifted his face round to smile at it: 'And flowers,' he said. 'Sun and flowers.'

'Don't you ever want to go back to England?' asked Felix, who privately thought England might be the best place for Mr Jewel.

'No. When I came to Alex, I had an accident and in hospital they used to wheel me out every day on to the balcony, and there I lay in the sun and I thought: "This is the stuff – this is what I've always wanted. No grey skies, no rain, no cold – people in England don't know what they're missing."'

'But haven't you any relatives there?'

'Only my brother Samson, and I doubt he's forgotten me now. Lord, no!' Mr Jewel brooded a while, then shook his head: 'An English winter'd do for me.'

Mr Jewel had always been a frail old man, but there was about him now a rustling, silvery dryness like that of a skeleton leaf.

Felix, sitting on the grass that was already turning yellow in the sun, gazed at Mr Jewel's bone-thin, dry, old hands spread on the blanket; he supposed Mr Jewel was better off in this part of the world where, however poor a man might be, he was more often hot than cold; but Mr Jewel twitched inside his clothes and shuddered down his spine: 'This has been a chilly spring,' he said. 'And it was a cold winter. A cold winter!' Suddenly something seemed to strike him: 'Has she said anything about the rent?'

'The rent?' Felix thought of the visit to the mosque.

'The rent of the attic. Does she think I ought to be paying?'

'Oh, no. No, I'm sure she doesn't.'

Mr Jewel was not listening to Felix's reassurances.

'Wonder she hasn't been in for it. She's religious, y'know,' he said in a cracked, humorous whisper. 'Where I came from it's all religion; keep the Sabbath like anything they do – lot of Holy Joes but wouldn't give you what dropped off their finger. D'you think you'd better take her this quid,' he began fumbling in his breast pocket. 'Wouldn't like her letting it over m'head.'

'I'm sure it's all right; wait till she asks you.'

'Ah, well,' Mr Jewel let his hand drop, 'I've got to give a bit here, y'see, not being a Government official. It doesn't leave much.'

Felix, brooding over Mr Jewel's condition, decided the thing to do was to find someone who would help the old man. This brother Samson was the best bet. In his mind, Felix began to formulate an anonymous letter modelled on some he had met in his reading: '*To Mr Samson Jewel: Sir, Are you aware that your brother is lying penniless in . . .*' In his efforts to discover more about Samson Jewel, Felix sent Mr Jewel's mind back to very early days when he had just left home and set out to see the world.

'Samson! I met a Falmouth man once who told me Samson became an alderman.'

'D'you think he's rich?' Felix cunningly asked.

'Maybe. We were both left a bit,' said Mr Jewel. 'I remember I lent mine to poor Eli Frobisher. Eli owed money to everyone. It just slipped through his fingers. One day he borrowed twenty pound from a money-lender, had a good binge and shot himself. The only feller I knew that ever got the better of a money-lender.' Mr Jewel cackled to himself.

'And what about Samson?'

'He had a headpiece, Samson. He invested his bit in a business. Sent lobsters and crayfish and such to big London hotels. Did very well, they say. *And* they made him an alderman.'

'*Alderman Samson Jewel, The Town Hall, Falmouth. Sir, Are you aware . . .*'

'Did you come from Falmouth, Mr Jewel?'

'Near enough. Our old dad was a coastguard. Funny thing your asking all this now, for sometimes lately my mind's gone back there so I think I'm a lad again. Yes, it's a funny thing when you imagine you're only a lad and then you look down and see your own hands like this,' he fixed his eyes on his hands and murmured: 'Deary me!' then, quite suddenly forgetting his hands, he said: 'The coastguard station was out on a headland. To get to it, I mind, you'd walk a double hedge for two miles with the wind blowing a gale over you.'

'What! Always?'

'In the winter anyway. It'd come across there so strong the birds 'd drop exhausted from the sky. Some of them died, too. I remember I found a guillemot once – dead, without a mark on it. I can see that bird lying on the sand now; I can see every feather – the breast so white and silky, the wings folded, the little feet clenched under it and the beak lifted as if it were still driving against the wind. As clear as clear. I've wondered often since at God who made these birds so perfect to fly, and the wind too strong for them.'

'Yes,' murmured Felix, much affected by the bird that had fallen before the wind perhaps fifty years before he was born.

'Ah,' said Mr Jewel. 'In my head here I can walk again over the cliff-top and see every leaf and stone. And there's a cove there, the most beautiful in the world, and I've seen the world, you know. I don't speak from ignorance. No, I've seen nothing like it, with great caves in the green rock and the sand as smooth as a ballroom floor. The sand went right into the caves – like a carpet fitted everywhere – and when you walked alone, everything was silent, except the sea.'

'Where was that?' Felix asked eagerly. 'What was it called?'

The old man shook his head as though puzzled by the question.

'What was the name of the cave?' Felix persisted.

After a pause Mr Jewel shook his head as though he had lost interest: 'I can't remember.' The conversation was at an end.

Mr Jewel shivered a little and, suddenly petulant, said: 'They're leaving me out here too long.'

Felix said: 'Shall I help you in?'

'No, no. They said stay in the sun until tea-time. But it must be tea-time. I'm getting hungry.'

Felix was getting hungry, too. When Mr Jewel shut his eyes and sat for several minutes as though asleep, Felix got to his feet and whispered quietly: 'Good-bye, Mr Jewel.'

Mr Jewel answered in a surprisingly firm voice: 'Good-bye, good-bye. Come again,' but did not open his eyes.

While his mind was alight with the idea, Felix went over to the post-office and bought an airgraph. He went into a corner to write to Samson Jewel. At the top a line demanded his name and address – and of course some sort of address must be given. Weeks would pass before a reply came and meanwhile Mr Jewel might leave the hospital. After some consideration he wrote: *'From: "X", c/o Miss Bohun, Herod's Gate, Jerusalem. To: Alderman Samson Jewel, Falmouth, Devon. Dear Sir, Are you aware that your brother Mr Jewel is in desperate straits without home or money here in Jerusalem? Drop a line to "X" if you can help. Yours faithfully, A Friend.'* When he handed in the airgraph he was relieved that the girl behind the counter glanced neither at it nor at him.

7

Felix had been afraid that by some super-subtle instinct Faro would know that, despite his reconciliation with her, his mind was still occupied by Mrs Ellis: but Faro still came to lie in the sunlight in his room and at night would push her way in between the covers as soon as he was in bed. He was surprised, and perhaps as much hurt as relieved that the secret workings of his emotions made no difference to her. He accused her: 'You're only a little cat. You only want to be warm and fed and made a fuss of. You don't care for anything else,' and she yawned enormously, showing the corrugated roof of her pink mouth.

Whenever he was working in his room he was alert for the footsteps of Mrs Ellis, who was more often out of the house than in it, more often out for meals than in. Even Miss Bohun had ceased to complain that Mrs Ellis regarded the house merely as a *pension* and could not be controlled. At meal-times she would look at the empty chair and say: 'I wonder if our young lady is coming in or not?' but there was a strain about her forbearance that was less irritated than disappointed. Felix reflected that, after all, Miss Bohun had more to be disappointed about than he had. She had discovered Mrs Ellis and had planned to make her a friend, while Felix had expected nothing until he met her. Then he had been startled delightedly by the sight of her, and by the luck that brought her to live in the same house and share four meals a day; he could scarcely complain when it became clear that Mrs Ellis intended to share very few meals with them. Her life was lived in some independent way, mysteriously and out of their reach. Miss Bohun's cheerfulness became subdued. The relationship was clearly at a standstill.

Mrs Ellis was out of the house when, a few days after the visit to the mosque, Felix sat in his room unwillingly overhearing Miss Bohun giving a lesson to Mr Liftshitz. Now that the windows were open, he could hear every word she said. He recognized the exercise as one from the Russian grammar.

'There are weasels in the palace of the Czar . . . Weasels, weasels,' she repeated impatiently, then was forced to spell the word: 'W-e-a-s-e-l-s, Mr Liftshitz . . . Yes, weasels . . . Oh, something like rats. Now, *do* let us get on. Coachman, bring your drosky nearer . . . Drosky, d-r-o-s-k-y. What is a drosky? I've no idea. Now . . . Tell me a queer story . . . a *queer* story . . .'

A door opened. Suddenly (it seemed to Felix) the dictation lesson was lost in a babble of voices. The noise grew rapidly. Laughter rose. It was as though an endless stream of persons was pouring into the room below. Faro pricked her ears and sat alert on Felix's lap. Felix listened intently, but could make nothing of it. Whoever had arrived had evidently settled down to stay. At last, consumed by curiosity, he sorted out what excuse he could give for going down. Miss Bohun had said: 'Please, Felix, try not to pass through the room when I'm giving a lesson,' but there were some excuses that had to be accepted. He decided to go to the privy in the yard.

He shut Faro into the room behind him and quietly, unobtrusively, started down the stairs.

As soon as he had descended half-a-dozen steps, he could see into the room. It was full of women. They were all dressed in black. Some, very old, wrinkled and dark-skinned, were wrapped in black robes from head to foot; but the girls – some lovely girls, pale-skinned, black-eyed, smiling – wore short skirts and silk stockings. Each one, as soon as she glimpsed him, raised a hand to her veil, but seeing at once that he was not a Moslem, she let the hand fall again. All of them, young and old, seemed to be excited and shy; and each, even the oldest, as she caught Felix's eye, began to giggle.

Miss Bohun was still sitting at the table with Mr Liftshitz; her face had the blankness of someone too lost to express anything. Seeing the others look at Felix, she looked up herself and in her helplessness seemed to snatch at him:

'Why, Felix, there you are. Isn't this nice! The ladies of the Imam's family have paid us a visit. Could anything be nicer? What on earth – I mean, what can we do?' her voice dropped and she repeated: 'What *can* we do?'

The visitors – Felix by now had counted them and found there were only thirteen – were sitting wherever possible. A few of the younger girls were forced to stand, but Mr Liftshitz, understanding nothing, remained in his seat like someone stunned by shock, and stared about him with owlish eyes.

The women were grouped round the table like an audience. They were chattering in hushed tones among themselves, the younger ones going off at times into fits of giggles, but all the time they were conscious of Miss Bohun, alert to be silent should the party begin. Felix felt her dismay; it was painful. Then, suddenly, some solution presented itself. Her face lit up and she brought her hands together: 'I know,' she called happily and in a few moments she had hurried from the room and returned again with a piece of halvas on a plate.

'The very thing,' she kept saying. 'The *very* thing. Felix, get a knife from the dresser. Now, cut the halvas into – How many?' she stood in the middle of the room and turned round as she counted her guests, pointing a finger at each as though they were children. The guests expressed delight and amusement at this behaviour, so Miss Bohun let her voice rise higher and higher as a form of entertainment: 'Thirteen,' she concluded, 'cut it into fifteen pieces, there's a good boy. You and Mr Liftshitz must share in. How fortunate I noticed this in the kitchen this morning. I think it belongs to Nikky; I will have to pay him for it, still it was a very lucky thing.'

Felix cut the halvas into small cubes and offered the plate round the room. Each of the visitors took a piece and sat holding it until everyone was served. When the plate with two remaining pieces was presented to Mr Liftshitz, he seemed overwhelmed and stammered his refusal, his hands moving, his face twitching in worried nervousness.

'Oh, well, I'll have it then,' said Miss Bohun, and, every piece delivered, they were eaten in unison.

This accomplished, Miss Bohun seemed quite at her ease and she gave her attention to the eldest lady in the room and talked at her fluently in Arabic. The lady smiled broadly, her hand raised to hide her toothless mouth, but she did not seem to understand what was being said to her. The others kept up their own conversations but their eyes seldom left Miss Bohun. Half an hour must have passed before the eldest lady rose, rather abruptly, and held out a hand to Miss Bohun. Miss Bohun looked disconcerted; she stopped talking, then remembered to rise and shake hands. The others, nudging one another to attention, rose too, and Miss Bohun, moving in a circle round the room, shook hands with each of them. Then they adjusted their veils and, all black except for the silken legs of the girls, filed out through the door into the yard. Miss Bohun, with Felix and Mr Liftshitz following at a discreet distance, saw them into the taxis that awaited them. As they went off waving through the windows, she turned back into the yard and let her breath out with relief: '*What* an invasion! When they came in my first thought was: "How can we possibly spare coffee for all these . . ." Poor Nikky's halvas!' Then she noticed Mr Liftshitz. 'Dear me, Mr Liftshitz, your hour is nearly up. Today was not exactly a lesson, I'm afraid, but an interesting experience nevertheless. I hope you profited by it.' She looked at her watch pinned to her dress and exclaimed: 'Ten minutes left – now then, let us see how much we can get done. To work, Mr Liftshitz, *to work*.'

She motioned Mr Liftshitz back to the room as though the whole delay had been caused by his folly, and as Felix returned upstairs he heard Miss Bohun dictating at top speed: '"Coachman, the postillion has been struck by lightning." Postillion? Oh, a sort of man-servant. Really, Mr Liftshitz, we'll get nowhere if you keep interrupting with these questions.'

8

Although the spring was bright and dry, the night cold held a long time that year. At supper Miss Bohun would say: 'I usually put the fire away in the spring, but if you *still* feel the cold . . .' Felix did feel the cold, so also did Mrs Ellis. She said: 'I've never lived in a house as cold as this; it's like living in a vault.' One evening when she came down from the attic, Miss Bohun found Mrs Ellis holding her hands to the bar of the fire, her fingers dark with cold.

'Haven't you any gloves?' asked Miss Bohun.

'No thick ones. I can't find any here.'

Miss Bohun started her meal, but suddenly, as she was lifting a fork to her mouth, she exclaimed: 'Oh, I know!' and, dropping the fork with the food still on it, she rose and ran upstairs. When she came back she was holding a pair of fur-lined leather gloves.

'Now,' she announced impressively, 'these are for you. I'm going to make you a present of them. They were given to me one Christmas by an officer friend who lived here, but I've never had occasion to wear them. They're too good – so you must wear them for me.'

Mrs Ellis frowned at the gloves, then shook her head: 'It is very kind of you but I could not possibly accept them.'

'But you must,' Miss Bohun looked surprised at this refusal, 'I want you to have them.'

'No. I couldn't take them.' Her refusal was coldly decided: it was clear that nothing would persuade her to take the gloves.

Miss Bohun still stood holding them towards Mrs Ellis. Felix, seeing Miss Bohun's hurt and confusion, wished that Mrs Ellis would anyway reach out, take the gloves into her hands, and perhaps admire them or make some alleviating comment before returning them. But Mrs Ellis did nothing.

Miss Bohun at last put them down on a corner of the table, where they lay throughout the meal with a forlorn, repudiated look. She ate in silence: the others had nothing to say. Mrs Ellis sat with a cross little frown as though there had been in the incident some insult to herself. Felix, unable to understand her annoyance, felt her remote now, a disturbing and frightening person. Her behaviour was to him different from the behaviour of anyone he had known before; this greatly increased her attraction for him.

Mrs Ellis was the first to speak. After the last course, she turned her chair to be nearer the fire and suddenly smiled at Felix: 'Look who's here,' she said and Felix saw that Faro was curled on her lap. At that moment Miss Bohun, as she often did, threw off her depression and said loudly and cheerfully: 'How nice! How nice! To-night we really are a happy family. What a pity I have to dash away again. And Faro, too . . .' she put out her dry, yellow hand and gave Faro a touch: 'How thick their fur is!' she said. 'How easily they grow it! When you think of a bald-headed man – he'd pay thousands to be able to produce what kittens and puppies sprout so luxuriously.'

Mrs Ellis gave a small, distant smile and ran her finger-tips over Faro's head, outlining the base of the seal-dark ears that fitted like wings on to pale fur of the brow. Miss Bohun went on talking, but in the middle of a sentence she broke off to ask: '*Must* I go on calling you Mrs Ellis?'

Mrs Ellis raised her face with a surprised look, but, after a moment, said: 'My first name is Jane.'

'And mine is Ethel,' said Miss Bohun. 'Now this would have been an *ideal* night for our cosy chat, but, alas! I'm away to my "Ever-Readies".' She was putting on her coat and winding her scarf into a turban. With a wild, uncertain laugh and a wave of her hand, she went out, shouting: 'It'll be splendid when we can go hand-in-hand.'

Mrs Ellis, occupied with lighting a cigarette, made no reply. Felix crossed over to stroke Faro, who awoke, yawned, purred a moment, then recurled herself and slept again. Felix, feeling a sort of electricity come from Mrs Ellis's nearness, could not speak. He had to move away. He returned to his seat at the table and said hoarsely: 'Faro likes you.'

'And I like her.' Mrs Ellis stretched and yawned: 'Didn't I see you leaving the hospital today?'

'Yes. Were you there?' and as she nodded he found himself able to ask: 'But you aren't ill, are you?'

'No. I'm going to have a baby.'

It was as well that Felix, at the table, could keep his face hidden, for he was appalled by this revelation. He sat for several moments, dizzy as though he had been struck a blow, then said with anguished quiet: 'But Miss Bohun said you were a widow.'

'I am a widow. I've been a widow for three months. My husband never knew we were going to have this baby.'

'Oh! Have you told Miss Bohun?'

'No.'

'Will she mind – I mean, having a baby in the house. She's a bit funny.'

'It won't affect her. I'm taking the house over in the autumn. She heard I wanted to rent a house and offered me this one. That's why I'm here.'

'Really?' He swung round in his surprise and asked: 'But what is Miss Bohun going to do?'

'I don't know. She told me she wanted to spend one more summer here because of her beloved garden, then she wanted to throw off "the care of housewifery". I said that suited me; I don't need a house before the autumn. Then she said she had a room to let and whoever rented the room would get first chance of the house, so I had no choice but to move in. It's not for long. I can bear it.'

'What about Faro?'

'She can stay with me.'

'Well, that's something.'

Felix moved the napkin rings about on the table. Nervously and disconsolately, he considered the break-up of this house that was, he supposed, his home. Probably it was because of this Miss Bohun had wanted to throw off the responsibility of Frau Leszno. After a long pause, he said:

'I hope I get a passage to England before then.'

'If you don't, you can stay on here.'

'Really!' he swung round again, very excited: 'Don't you mind?'

105

'There's plenty of room.'

'Yes,' he agreed eagerly, 'you know, there's another big bedroom at the front.'

'I know,' Mrs Ellis smiled with bewildered interest, 'why does she keep it empty?'

'I don't know, but she keeps getting it ready for someone.' Felix described how he had heard her brushing the room on the day he arrived. They smiled at one another in the understanding and comradeship of their frank curiosity.

Mrs Ellis stretched herself again, then put Faro carefully down in front of the fire. She sat up as though preparing to leave, but said: 'What do you do here at night?'

'At night?' Felix looked uncertainly about him. 'Nothing.'

'Nothing. Surely you don't just sit around this gloomy room?'

'Oh, you mean if I go out? Sometimes I go to the pictures.'

'The pictures?' said Mrs Ellis as though she did not regard them as a form of entertainment. 'What about all those cafés? Which are the best of those?'

'I don't know.'

'Let's go and find out. Get ready.'

With a sense of unbearable excitement Felix followed her upstairs. While he was putting his coat on, Mrs Ellis, who had thrown round her shoulders a loose coat the colour of her fingernails, sauntered through his half-open door. A cigarette drooped from her lips and she kept her eyes narrowed and tilted back from the smoke. She moved round, glancing at the embroideries and the lamp beside his bed.

'Does all this stuff belong to you?' she asked, keeping the cigarette in her mouth as she talked.

'Yes. It was my mother's.'

Mrs Ellis peered in a short-sighted way at things, but made no comment. Felix waited for her to speak. Her voice was quite different from his mother's. He remembered an American saying in their Istanbul *pension*: 'These English ladies are so soprano! There's Mrs Latimer now, her voice just seems to come tinkling down from the top of a high mountain.' But Mrs Ellis's voice, naturally low, was husky with chain-smoking; its quality seemed to give wit and significance to everything she said.

Now she crossed to the window and, peering out into the dark garden, said vaguely: 'Shall we ask old what's-it to come with us?'

'Who?' Felix asked, unable to guess.

She agitated her fingers as though to draw the name from the air, then said: 'Nikky Leszno.'

'Oh, no,' gasped Felix, startled by the audacity of the suggestion and by fear that she might carry it out. 'He wouldn't come. Besides...' Felix was suddenly elevated by inspiration, 'he's probably gone with Miss Bohun to the "Ever-Readies".'

'What! He goes in for that religious business?'

Felix nodded: 'Yes. Miss Bohun says she's saved his soul alive.'

'Really!' Mrs Ellis blew her cigarette smoke out in a long exclamatory stream. 'I can scarcely believe it. Who are these "Ever-Readies" the old girl's always trotting off to see?'

Felix began to giggle. When Mrs Ellis swung round on her heel and raised her eyebrows at him, his giggles became uncontrollable. She caught his arm and ushered him out with comic sternness: 'You're a naughty boy,' she said, 'you're laughing at the poor old girl. It's too bad! Somewhere, probably, she's got a heart of gold.'

Even while he was helpless with giggles, he felt some relief at this reassurance of Miss Bohun's fundamental goodness. It was a relief, too, that the reassurance came from Mrs Ellis, who was, he was sure, not to be easily deceived.

When they reached the sitting-room he had sobered enough to notice the fire was still burning, Faro curled like a shrimp before it. 'We're supposed to switch it off if we go out,' he said.

'And leave poor Faro alone in the cold? How could you?'

Mrs Ellis swept Felix out with a gesture that infected him with her own recklessness. As they passed through the gate to the street, he raised his face to the sky. He had never before seen such enormous stars – and the sky's colour, too, was changing from its winter dinginess to the grape-blue of spring. His heart seemed to swell within him. He felt if he jumped into the air, he would not come down again. He wanted to spread his arms and pretend to fly – but now he was too old to behave like that. He was growing up. He was going out on a grown-up expedition. He could scarcely breathe at the realization. It was as though the gates of the world were slowly opening for him and he was dazzled by the light he saw beyond.

'Where shall we go?' Mrs Ellis asked when they came into Allenby Square. 'Let's go to the Innsbruck; I've never been there at night.'

The Innsbruck café was quite dark outside. Its lights were hidden away behind heavy black-out curtains. Inside the air was stifling and heavy with smoke. Felix started to cough. The room was half-empty. At some of the occupied tables there were chess players, middle-aged exiles from Central Europe who bent silently over their boards, each player keeping safely within sight a chessman-box on which his name was printed in large letters. Some people were reading newspapers attached to cane holders. Some were talking, but most sat staring in a melancholy way at nothing at all. Very few were drinking wine and laughing; there was no music; no one was wearing evening dress; there were no ladies in ostrich feathers dancing in a row on the floor.

'Don't you like this place?' Mrs Ellis asked when she saw Felix's disappointment.

'Cafés are different on the films.'

'Are they? I expect you're thinking of night clubs. Such goings-on are forbidden in the Holy City – but you wouldn't be allowed into one anyway. You're much too young. What will you have? Lemonade? I need coffee.'

As Felix sat silent, depressed by his own youth, Mrs Ellis smiled at him, and with the most flattering implication that Felix knew everything and could be infinitely entertaining in his knowledge, she said: 'Now, tell me all about Miss Bohun.'

Felix shook his head, unnerved now he was actually sitting alone with Mrs Ellis at a table in a café.

'Well, then,' said Mrs Ellis, content to change the subject, 'tell me about yourself – or about your mother.'

'Oh.' Felix had to face the fact that he had scarcely thought of his mother since Mrs Ellis arrived. He said: 'My mother was terribly pretty and terribly clever. She died of typhoid. Everyone said: "I'm sure she'll get better," but she hadn't had her typhoid injections. She said: "I think I'll skip a year because they make me feel so ill," and then she died.'

'I'm sorry.'

'I saw her when she was dead. She had on her best night-dress. It was grey crêpe-de-chine. She looked . . . she looked . . .' Felix bent over his lemonade but, in spite of his efforts to control them, the tears welled into his eyes and a sob broke from his throat. Mrs Ellis slid a hand round the nape of his neck and patted his shoulder. He was too desolated to wonder at her kindness: he felt nothing but gratitude.

'And where is your father? In the army?'

Felix shook his head. 'No. He's dead. He was killed.'

Mrs Ellis, seeing that his eyes dried as he remembered his father, asked with sympathetic interest: 'How long ago was that?'

'About a year. He was sent to Mosul because there was some trouble. There were German agitators, you know, and the Iraqis were all shouting round the house. The man who lived there said: "Better stay inside," but my father was terribly brave. He thought if he went out and faced them they'd respect him – perhaps they did, but they shot him just the same.'

Mrs Ellis shook her head slowly over this tragedy. Felix said: 'Your husband was shot, wasn't he?'

After a pause Mrs Ellis said: 'Shot down in flames.'

'In the RAF! Really! A pilot?'

'No, only a rear-gunner. I used to think it was lucky, his being in the Air Force. He could fly into Cairo sometimes. I saw him only two days before.'

'Were you married a long time?'

'Four months and five days.'

Felix nodded in what he felt was a grown-up way. He stared reflectively over Mrs Ellis's shoulder until suddenly, jolted unpleasantly, by the sight of Nikky trailing his furlined coat in through the black-out curtain. Felix looked away at once, shrinking within himself and changing back to an insignificant little boy. He hoped if he could not see Nikky, Nikky would not see him. He heard Nikky being greeted by a party of young men – the noisiest in the room – and, unfortunately, these loud greetings caused Mrs Ellis to turn.

'There's Nikky Leszno.'

'He's horrid,' said Felix. 'He's terribly conceited and he's rude,' but Nikky had seen them and was coming over. He did

109

not seem his usual aloof self, he moved his hands nervously as he looked at Mrs Ellis and said: 'May I join you, madam?'

Mrs Ellis, strangely enough, did not seem displeased by his request. 'What about your friends?' she said.

Nikky shrugged his shoulders and, taking her question as permission, he said: 'I see them too often; here, at the Cultural Mission, at the Library . . . Sometimes they bore me.'

'What is the Cultural Mission?' asked Mrs Ellis.

'You do not know it, the Cultural Mission?' Nikky jerked up his head in surprise, and sat down without further question. 'It is a very important thing. I go in the afternoons, sometimes the evenings. We learn English; study literature and such. We hope to get scholarships and go to London.'

'Do you think you'll get a scholarship?'

'Yes.' Nikky looked down modestly, but with quiet confidence.

'And what about the others?'

He shrugged his shoulders and gave them a glance. 'What are they? There are some Poles – and there are two Arabs, three Jews – and the young man in the green shirt, he is an Armenian who has been to Europe. They think they are intellectuals of Palestine – very tolerant, meeting here Arabs and Jews to talk about art – but how different, eh? from such intellectual life in Warsaw, or Berlin, or London? What talk there must be in the cafés of Piccadilly!'

Mrs Ellis said without much interest: 'I've only been to London once and then I was taken to see *Peter Pan*.'

'*Peter Pan!* Very original book!' Nikky commented gravely.

Felix sat back, sipping his lemonade, concentrating his attention upon it, supposing he could not now hope to be included in the conversation.

'What do you drink?' asked Nikky, 'coffee? How about some wine?'

'Why? Are you feeling very rich?' Mrs Ellis watched him with a cool and critical smile.

'Rich! Is it so likely? when I am – what? A servant? and in such a house?' Nikky laughed glumly.

'Have some coffee?'

'If you like,' he frowned, but apparently his displeasure was against Miss Bohun for he said with sudden vehemence: 'What food, eh? Never before have I eaten it. But we can do nothing.

She does the shopping, keeps all the money, so,' he held up his delicate white hand with fingers clenched. 'Even when my mother would ask for such a thing – pepper at one piastre, a piece of sage, a lemon – always, "I will buy it myself". No Arab would touch this job – and no Jew. The Histadruth see that servants are well paid. No, it is for some poor beggar like me who has suffered and says now "I have anyway the roof above my head".'

Felix, forgetting his lemonade, listened, fascinated by this new aspect of Nikky. Nikky's pathos touched him in spite of himself, and when he glanced at Mrs Ellis to confirm his sympathy, he could scarcely believe in the smile of mockery that touched her lips.

'Still,' she said, 'Miss Bohun "saved your soul alive".'

Nikky parted his lips, momentarily at a loss, then, like a clever acrobat, at once regaining his footing, he exclaimed: 'Ach!' He raised his hands to his head with a gesture of disgust and frantic humour that revealed him to Felix as someone not aloof and contemptuous, but really deliciously droll. Felix gave a sudden yelp of laughter that startled the whole café and made Nikky look at him as though the revelation were mutual.

'But . . .' Nikky protested elaborately at the impression he had made; he caught his breath as though words would not come, then sighed: 'These "Ever-Readies"! What can I do? How am I to escape? I was so innocent when I came, and ill, and without friends. My mother, too, she had no idea – and then, alone here, strangers!'

'But Jerusalem is full of Poles,' said Mrs Ellis. 'I should have thought you would have lots of friends.'

'There are Poles and Poles,' said Nikky and hurried on before this statement could be discussed. 'But – but these "Ever-Readies"!' he covered his face and laughed into his hands.

'How often do you go to meetings?' asked Mrs Ellis.

'How often? I . . . Do not ask me. I am not the most ardent worshipper. *No.*'

'But what is it all about? What are they "ever ready" for?'

Felix leant forward, holding his breath at Mrs Ellis's question. Nikky looked at Mrs Ellis, at Felix, then back at Mrs Ellis, and answered quietly: 'For the Second Coming.' With the suddenness of a dramatic actor, he shot out his arm and raised his voice: 'It

111

will happen here – today, to-morrow, next month, next year? Who knows? And Miss Bohun is Chairman of the Reception Committee. She has a room ready...'

'The front room?' cried Felix, '*the front room!*'

Nikky nodded with dignity and echoed in deep, hollow tones: 'The front room!' He slid his large, dark eyes round on to Mrs Ellis and said in the same tone: 'You have seen it, madam?'

Mrs Ellis shook her head and laughed so she could scarcely light her cigarette.

'It's empty, the front room,' said Felix, 'why is it always empty?'

'It is empty,' agreed Nikky, 'but it is *prepared*.'

'For the Second Coming?' asked Mrs Ellis as she shook out her match. 'And who believes in all this?'

'Not I, for one,' said Nikky with sombre decision, 'but there *are* believers... And for this our house was stolen from us. When they knew the war would start, they said: "This is, of course, Armageddon. We must have a room prepared." (The last war was Armageddon, too, but no matter.) So, to find a room, Miss Bohun enters our house, hires two rooms from my silly mother – and in no time, what? She has the whole house. But that is another thing. I am not here to pity myself. You ask about these "Ever-Readies"! There used to be many such. You must have noticed how many places here are called "colony"? – the American Colony, the Germany Colony, the Swedish, the Greek, and so on! Well, at a time – perhaps forty, fifty years ago – all those people came to see the Second Coming. Some have lived here since, very old now, but most are dead. The "Ever-Readies" are one such.'

'But what sort of people belong?' asked Mrs Ellis.

'Oh, there are Christian Arabs, a few convert Jews – all women, need I say, like my silly mother. For them, it makes a nice club. And then there are a few old English women, and a few old men – very prized, those few old gentlemen. I, I am the baby and so I am privileged.'

'Does Mr Jewel belong?' Felix asked eagerly.

'No, no.' Nikky, with a gesture, brushed aside such an idea. 'Here there are such old gentlemen, such old ladies... *such* a sort! Ach!' Nikky turned sideways in his chair and, covering his eyes with one hand, threw up his other hand in appreciation of their fantastic quality.

'And they really believe the Second Coming will be any day now?'

'How can I say? But there is money in it. Indeed, yes, money comes from America. In America there is a big "Ever-Ready" organization. Very rich, very important. At a sign from the Jerusalem end, the big American airliners rise into the sky to bring here the Wise Virgins prepared for the Coming. Miss Bohun preaches very nicely on this subject.'

'I see,' said Mrs Ellis quietly. 'So Miss Bohun is not an unpaid pastor.'

Nikky gave a laugh and in a voice humorously and pertinently deep said: 'What do you think?'

'Well!' Mrs Ellis stubbed out her cigarette, 'we're learning things! And what about the room? Is she paid rent for that?'

Nikky shrugged his shoulders. He and Mrs Ellis smiled at one another in a contempt of Miss Bohun that Felix could not quite understand. Perhaps it was not so much contempt as resentment, or even pure dislike. And yet Miss Bohun had looked after the Lesznos and saved Nikky's life: and Mrs Ellis herself had said on the day she arrived that Miss Bohun alone had been kind to her. Although he could not understand their condemnation of her, yet he found himself sharing it.

'At the meetings?' asked Mrs Ellis. 'What happens at the meetings?'

'Ach!' Nikky, with a grimace, with a sudden skilful movement of the wrist, seemed to place the nullity of the meetings before them on the palm of his hand: 'What can happen? What can they think of that was not thought of a thousand years before? They pray, they sing psalms, they read from the Bible . . .' as he listed these activities he made them absurd by swaying his head from side to side, 'and then . . .' Nikky paused; he threw up a ridiculous finger; his face sprang into delighted life, he looked at Mrs Ellis, at Felix, back again at Mrs Ellis, keeping them breathless. . . . Felix watched entranced; he could not even glance aside at Mrs Ellis, so held was he by this manifestation of Nikky. Indeed, he was not certain that Nikky was not a greater wonder than Mrs Ellis.

113

'And then, Miss Bohun gives the sermon.'

'Really! Does she preach a sermon at every meeting?'

'No. There are visiting preachers. There are "Ever-Readies" in Beirut, in Cyprus, in Cairo . . . Sometimes they come here for the entertainments.'

'The entertainments?' breathed Mrs Ellis.

'Oh!' Nikky made a gesture that exceeded all his others in the expression of the inexpressible. 'The entertainments! Last year there was a play which she wrote herself.'

'No!'

'Indeed, yes; and she played the chief part – a man!'

'I don't believe it.'

'Yes. She fancies herself in male costume, you know. In all her plays there is a chief part, a man in an historical dress, and she is it!'

'Oh! And what was her play about?'

'Ask another person – not me. It was very symbolical; full of ambiguities. Poetry today must be full of ambiguities.'

'But surely it wasn't written in poetry?'

'There, dear lady, you say it – but Miss Bohun, *she* said it was poetry. And this play was about a mysterious stranger who visits the court of the King of Spain. Who is this stranger? Ah, who knows! But the King of Spain – our own Miss Bohun – he knows. And see our Miss Bohun in a black velvet suit – so!' Nikky indicated balloon sleeves, 'pearls – so! A great cross here,' Nikky swung a hand in front of his chest. 'Magnificent! And the stranger – that is old Mr Buffey who has a beard – has just a white robe and sandals. A small part. He comes – and then he goes.'

'But where did the costumes come from?'

'The YMCA wardrobe. Pre-war. Very good. Oh, yes, very good! And every time the King of Spain spoke he marched to the footlight, threw out his chest, so! Threw out his hand, so! and shouted to the back . . .' Nikky raised his voice and again the café was startled. Felix pushed aside his lemonade so that he could prop his head up to laugh; tears ran down his cheeks. He had never dreamt Nikky could be so funny, but Nikky was going to be much funnier. Suddenly he rolled his eyes from Felix to Mrs Ellis, and whispered:

'Then someone laughed. Hey!' he threw out a hand like a policeman stopping the traffic and imitated Miss Bohun's voice: '"Stop the play! Stop! Stop, at once! Now, who laughed?" No one replies. So! She shouts:

'"Put the lights on!" and someone in the dark puts out the footlights. "No, no, put on the lights! In the hall! In the hall!" Off goes all the lights on the stage – on go the hall lights, off go the hall lights, on go the stage lights – "No, no, no. Put off the lights – put on the lights – put off the lights . . ."'

Felix was convulsed: he leant weakly on his hands, sobbing and near hysteria. Mrs Ellis had tears in her eyes, her cigarette burnt forgotten in her hand.

'"At last! All light on. Now, who laughed? I won't go on until the one who did it owns up. Now, who laughed? Out with it! We'll be here all night!" And so, at last, a soldier – there are always, I should tell you, one or two lonely soldiers who wander in – a soldier put up his hand. "You should be ashamed," says Miss Bohun, "would you behave so in your own home town?" The soldier mumbles, head hanging . . . "All right, now we go on . . ."'

Felix sighed, almost sobered into coldness, incapable of laughing any more; he wiped his eyes.

'And then it is all over and Miss Bohun says: "Hands up all those who would like us to do it again. No one? – Now, come on. Hands up! Is it this, the gratitude of the 'Ever-Readies' for all our work? Hands up at once. Ach, a hand! Loyal Gertie Goldberg . . . and Mrs Putkin . . . and chivalrous Captain Jenkins. Now, come on! If we get four hands we'll do it again. Ach, one more hand! That makes three, now we only want a fourth. Come now! Be sports, girls of the 'Ever-Readies'! You want us to do it again, don't you? At last, a fourth hand." Miss Bohun does, so!' Nikky slapped his thigh: 'A splendid show!'

Felix, who had started laughing again, was shaking weakly, a sharp pain across his waist. He felt he could scarcely bear any more, but there was more to come –

'And, the year before,' said Nikky, 'when she played Romeo . . .'

'Oh, no. She did not play Romeo?'

'Yes, in the same black velvet – and the balcony broke down.'

'No?'

'Look,' said Nikky, 'we must have wine.' He dug into the pocket of his coat that hung about him like a black tent, and brought out a handful of small, dirty notes. Felix felt it impossible to let Nikky spend this money when he had so little, but Mrs Ellis said nothing. In a grand way, opening the sticky notes as he spoke, Nikky ordered three glasses of red wine.

'Oh, not for Felix,' said Mrs Ellis.

'It will do him no harm.'

Felix, pushing aside his empty lemonade glass to take on the large, globular glass of cheap red wine, felt this the crown of the evening. Exhausted from laughing and sleepy because it was past his bedtime, he found as he drank the wine that his hold upon the conversation was slipping. When the wine was drunk, Mrs Ellis ordered three more glasses. Felix kept laughing weakly because now everything Nikky said seemed funny, but at one point, when he shook himself awake, he found he was no longer in the café, but had somehow been transported to Mrs Ellis's room. He was sprawling on her bed, his shoulders propped against the wall, and Nikky was sitting at the end of it, drooping over the dark iron rail. Mrs Ellis was in the one comfortable chair. The fun seemed to have stopped at some time, for Mrs Ellis was talking seriously and Nikky was watching her with a serious, intent face. There was between them some sort of understanding from which Felix felt himself excluded. Except that the books and bookcase were gone, the room was furnished just as it had been when Miss Bohun slept here, but both the centre light and the reading lamp were lit, which made it seem quite different. On the table were cosmetic bottles and powder boxes such as his mother had had. There were some red rose-buds drooping like the heads of chickens whose necks have been wrung. The air was full of a heavy, unusual scent.

'French scent,' thought Felix. His mother used to send to Cairo for it and it got dearer and dearer as the war went on. Thinking of her, he was filled, not with the old despairing emptiness, but with a gentle sadness. Mrs Ellis, who was the most beautiful person in the world, had said he could stay on when she took over the house: and Nikky, who had been his enemy, was now his friend. He lay in a haze of delicious, melancholy peace through which he listened to Mrs Ellis's voice:

'. . . it would have been better if I'd been in England, thousands of miles away. I'd have known less about it – at least, that's what I feel now. I did not know what to do, where to go – Then the doctor sent me up here. Cairo is a bad place for babies.'

Nikky nodded gently: 'But in England, you have a home, you have parents. You are not a refugee.'

Mrs Ellis shrugged her shoulders: 'I haven't anything much. No home anyway. My father is in the regular army. My mother died years ago in India. The summer before the war my father was in Alex. He couldn't get home so he arranged for me to come out to Egypt by boat. It was great fun. The boat was full of school children going out to their parents; it used to be called "the children's boat". We had the time of our lives. The grown-ups must have been driven mad by us. I loved Alex. I was fifteen and I met officers who were not much older than myself. I began to think I was grown-up. Then the war broke out and father was afraid to send me home, so I went to a finishing school full of Greeks and Egyptians – all stiff and correct and trying to be French. I loathed it. Two years later father was transferred to the Sudan; he's there now. At that time things weren't looking too good in the Middle East. There was one of those evacuations and father thought I'd better go home. It was fairly safe going round the Cape. I was given a passage straight away – another "children's boat", but I counted among the grown-ups this time.' At this point, Mrs Ellis's voice faded away. Felix let his eyelids fall comfortably over his eyes, but for curious moments he flickered into complete consciousness and caught phrases, '. . . a pathetic little thing,' and '. . . suddenly the ship lurched over;' '. . . a hellish row,' and 'the water icy cold.'

This was clearly a story about a shipwreck, but no effort could keep him awake to hear it. He must have fallen asleep, for, a long time after, he was startled by Mrs Ellis saying: 'Well, I helped with the canteens and the troops' entertainments; then I got a job at GHQ. I had quite a time. But I found I got worried at the cinema – the news films, you know. If I saw a ship on fire or sinking, I was liable to make a nuisance of myself.'

'Why?' asked Felix, awake now, suddenly cold, but full of curiosity.

The others took no notice of him. Nikky said:

'Then you got married.' He sighed. 'At least you have lived a little. For me – what? Waiting for the war to end. Then I return to my estate in Poland, then I am again a Count . . .'

At that moment the door fell open and hit the wall. Miss Bohun stood there staring first at Nikky then at Mrs Ellis with a look of incredulous anger. When she noticed Felix, her expression softened slowly into its old exasperation. She strode into the room and switched off the reading lamp: 'You must try to help me to save,' she said.

As the others watched her, startled and silenced by her intrusion, she said with a defensive irritation: 'I could see those two lights on as I crossed the wasteland. It really is too bad of you . . .' Then she swung round on Felix: 'What is the matter with Felix?' she said. 'Why, the boy is half asleep. It's long past his bedtime. I know I'm late, but really! I'm surprised at you, Mrs Ellis. *And* leaving the electric fire on downstairs. You ought to know better, Felix, if no one else does. And what are *you* doing up here Nikky? This doesn't seem to me at all the thing. Of course, I've no objection to your making friends with the servants, Mrs Ellis – it shows a very democratic spirit – but please don't carry these friendships beyond the sitting-room. Now, Felix – to bed! Nikky – downstairs! Good-night, Mrs Ellis.'

Ushering the two males before her, Miss Bohun shut the door behind her with a smart slam.

9

Next morning when Felix came down to breakfast he was surprised to find Mrs Ellis sitting alone at the table. She was drinking tea.

He said at once as he sat down: 'Wasn't Nikky funny?'

'Very funny,' Mrs Ellis agreed in an abstracted way. She looked pale and gloomy, but Felix sighed with satisfaction as he contemplated the great diversity of life that, as in a pantomime transformation scene, was raising gauze after gauze for him. He said:

'You know, I could never have guessed Nikky was so funny. It makes him much funnier somehow because I didn't know.' When Mrs Ellis said nothing he added: 'And wasn't Miss Bohun cross!'

'She was damned insolent.' Mrs Ellis's sudden violence took Felix's breath away. He was afraid she might be making up her mind to go.

When Miss Bohun came she shouted cheerfully from the bottom stair: 'Everyone here. How nice. A family party.' She looked at Mrs Ellis, who did not raise her head, then said: 'Oh, yes, *I* know,' and hurried out into the courtyard.

She came back with a little saucer on which sat a half-inch dice of butter. She placed this in front of Mrs Ellis impressively: 'I am giving you extra butter.'

Mrs Ellis, her elbows on the table, her cup held at her chin, stared at the butter and asked: 'Why?'

Miss Bohun kept her mouth tightly shut as she sat down. There was a short silence before she said: 'I would have spoken last night had you been alone. Actually, I was kept late talking to a nurse from the hospital – a very nice girl, one of our "Ever-Readies". She needed advice and during our conversation she told me something – in confidence, of course – that I must say I at first could not believe.'

'And what was that?' asked Mrs Ellis.

'That you are going to have a baby.'

Mrs Ellis, sipping her tea, made no reply.

'Well, I was amazed. I realized, of course, when I came to think about it, that it must be true – I had noticed you were – well, altering in appearance, shall we say? But, really, I was amazed. I said: "You must be misinformed, Miss Tarkatian: if anyone would be likely to know, I would. After all I'm Mrs Ellis's friend."'

'It is perfectly true,' said Mrs Ellis without expression.

'Well!' said Miss Bohun, 'I won't say that I'm not a little hurt, but I thought to myself: I respect her reticence – and if she *is* – well, I must give her something extra; she needs it and it is my duty. There's very little I can afford to give you, but I've decided to give you extra butter.'

Mrs Ellis, sipping her tea, murmured coldly: 'You are very kind.'

'I wish I could afford to give you a daily glass of milk, but, alas!' Miss Bohun sighed, leaving her sentence unfinished.

Mrs Ellis put down her cup: 'I was going to ask you – perhaps I could place an order for milk with your man?'

'Oh!' at first Miss Bohun seemed uncertain. 'That would mean his calling every day.' Then her tone changed: 'But why not? You see, I sometimes give him half a piastre for calling, but you wouldn't mind doing that, would you? I feel it pays to treat tradespeople well. The milk has to be boiled, of course, but the fire is alight anyway.' As she talked her enthusiasm grew, for now she brought her hands together and let her voice soar: 'Yes, what a good idea. I'll tell Maria to speak to the man and order it.' In her mounting enthusiasm she placed her hand on Mrs Ellis's arm and said warmly: 'And I want to tell you that I, for one, have no doubts at all – I'm *sure* it is your late husband's baby.'

For a few seconds Mrs Ellis sat as though she had not heard this remark; she had lifted her cup again, but without drinking suddenly put it down and turned on Miss Bohun, frowning. Miss Bohun smiled and tried to pat her arm, but Mrs Ellis stood up and away out of her reach. She said quietly, without anger but as though making an interesting revelation: 'I can only think, Miss Bohun, that you are mad.'

She went up the stairs. Miss Bohun flicked open her eyes to watch after her, then turned them, puzzled and pained, upon Felix. After a pause, she caught her breath and said: 'Of course, she thinks I should not have spoken in front of you, Felix. I wasn't thinking or I would have hesitated – but, dear me, what an exhibition! After all, you are quite a big boy – and it's as well you should know about Mrs Ellis's condition so you won't keep dragging her out at night to cinemas, or wherever it is you go.'

'Oh, I don't think she minds my knowing; she told me herself.'

'She told you?' Miss Bohun paused, then said: 'Heigh-ho! I seem to be the only person not in her confidence.'

Miss Bohun looked so upset that Felix attempted to mend the situation: 'I'm sure she must have thought you knew, Miss Bohun. After all, that's why she wants the whole house in the autumn.'

'Did she tell you she's taking the house in the autumn? Well, that's far from certain. I'd rather you didn't speak about it.'

'Oh, I thought it was all settled.'

'I don't want to discuss it, Felix, if you don't mind. I was quite ready to do Mrs Ellis a kindness if I could – but, dear me, it isn't everyone nowadays that's willing to have a baby in their house. I feel sorry for the poor thing – a widow and going to be a mother, it's very sad – but I have to consider myself, as well, and you, too, my dear boy. I offered you a home. I know young mothers think the world should revolve round themselves and their off-spring, but she can hardly expect to deprive you of your home.'

'She said I could live here with her,' said Felix eagerly.

'She did, did she?' Miss Bohun smiled a sour little smile. 'So it's all arranged! I'm afraid you don't know this town, my dear boy. You are under my protection and I certainly could not let you involve yourself in a situation that might lead to gossip.'

Felix was not clear what Miss Bohun meant by this remark so did not contest it, but out of his disappointment, he cried: 'But this isn't fair. You promised Mrs Ellis . . .'

'Don't be silly,' Miss Bohun interrupted irritably, 'the autumn is a long way off and many things may happen by then. Mrs Ellis and I will have to have a nice long chat about it all, but, meanwhile, Felix, I want you to promise not to discuss it, either with her or anyone else. If I find you discussing my affairs behind my back in this way, then I'll just have to ask Mrs Ellis to go.'

'All right,' Felix said ungraciously and left the table. As he went along the landing passage he heard Mrs Ellis sobbing inside her room. He tapped the door and whispered her name.

'What is it?' she asked from inside.

'What's the matter?'

'Nothing.'

After a pause he asked with deep interest: 'I say, do you really think Miss Bohun is mad?'

'Oh, go away,' said Mrs Ellis, and Felix had no choice but to go.

A bleak atmosphere, like that which preceded the going of Mr Jewel, haunted the meals, but now it was not Miss Bohun who controlled the discomfort. Mrs Ellis had shut herself off in a silence that seemed to put Miss Bohun completely at a loss. Once or twice, perhaps attempting to test the surface of this frost, Miss Bohun had repeated, tentatively and unconvincingly, remarks like: 'Well, here we are! Just a happy family!' or 'One day, Mrs Ellis, we really must have that cosy chat in my room,' but Mrs Ellis made no sign that she had heard. When she did not come in to meals, Miss Bohun would sometimes say to Felix, meaningfully:

'Mrs Ellis seems to be sulking about something. So childish of her. It spoils everything, we could be such a happy family.'

Felix tried to get Mrs Ellis to tell him why she had so suddenly retired into silence and anger, but she refused to discuss it. He did, however, hear from her the story of the half-litre of milk that Maria ordered for her and placed in a jug in her room. On the first day the jug contained three glasses of milk, on the second only two and a half, and after that never more than one and a half glasses or two. As the weather got warmer it was often sour. One day Mrs Ellis asked Maria why the quantity of the milk varied and why fresh milk so quickly became sour. Maria, who covered her lips with her fingers in her embarrassment, answered only the second half of her question.

'Ah, it is the man – so dirty; he will not wash his cans.'

'I see. And why is it that half a litre of milk one day makes three glasses and the next only two or even one and a half?'

Maria, after a long silence, shrugged her shoulders.

'I suppose there is a reason?'

Maria seemed to find the word she needed, for she said suddenly: 'I do not divide it.'

'Why divide it? Isn't mine bought separately?'

Maria shrugged her shoulders again, at a loss because questioned so sharply. She said, stammering a little: 'Miss Bohun said she get extra for the house. Now she gets every day and she divide it.'

'I see,' said Mrs Ellis. 'Then to-morrow tell the man I want no more. I cannot drink sour milk.'

At the table Mrs Ellis behaved as though she were alone. One day she picked up her fork, looked closely at it, then pulled the edge of the table-cloth between its prongs.

Miss Bohun tut-tutted and said apologetically: 'I suppose Maria's using a dirty dish-cloth again. I wish I had time to keep an eye on her, not that it would do much good. She's old and I think it's our duty to consider the old, don't you?'

Mrs Ellis stared before her, blankly unhearing.

Miss Bohun would often chatter on, ignoring this lack of response, but a sort of plaintive shrillness, that Felix found painful, would come into her tone. Although neither Miss Bohun nor Mrs Ellis considered his presence, he was probably the most discomforted person at the table. This caused him at times to break into the silence or into Miss Bohun's monologue with a remark not only irrelevant but irritating to Miss Bohun, as when he said suddenly: 'My mother had the softest skin in the world.'

She snapped back: 'How do you know?' and Felix, nonplussed, felt he had achieved nothing. But even if he had some success its eventual result would be unfortunate, as when Miss Bohun asked him:

'Well, Felix, what do you think of the sardines today?'

Felix, who had been wondering what he was eating, replied with dishonest enthusiasm: 'They're very good.'

At which Miss Bohun cried out in triumph: 'There, you see, you could not tell the difference. I forgot the sardines today so I got Maria to slice some aubergine, dip the slices in batter and fry

123

those instead. They *are* good, aren't they? And such an inexpensive substitute.'

After that they had fried aubergine until Felix was nauseated by the smell of it. Miss Bohun would say: 'Now, Felix, won't you have another one of these little fish-things?'

'No, thank you, Miss Bohun.'

'And you, Mrs Ellis?'

No reply from Mrs Ellis.

'Of course, they're not really fish, but I'm sure aubergine is just as good as fish. I believe firmly in vegetables. The best Indian sages eat nothing else. Don't you find they agree with you, Felix?

'Yes, Miss Bohun.'

'And you, Mrs Ellis?'

No reply from Mrs Ellis.

Miss Bohun's satisfaction at having discovered this fish substitute lessened a little the table's desolation, but in the end Felix cried out in spite of himself: 'Oh, Miss Bohun, aubergine again?'

'Why!' Miss Bohun opened her eyes with surprise, 'I thought you liked it.'

'But not for every meal.'

'If you knew the bother and expense of housekeeping these days, Felix, you would not be so finicky.' Miss Bohun sighed: 'Heigh-ho. I had hoped if there was another woman in the house we could take turns with the housekeeping, but . . .'

At this Mrs Ellis, surprisingly, spoke: 'I am quite willing to take my turn at housekeeping, Miss Bohun. After all, if we are, as you say, sharing expenses, you must have over £60 a month to run this house. I feel I could do something quite impressive on that.'

Miss Bohun gave her a startled look and for some moments seemed to be reflecting in a perplexed way on what Mrs Ellis had said. She did not mention the subject again, but Mrs Ellis mentioned it to Felix: 'Nikky says she runs that house on less than twenty pounds a month – so can you imagine she would let me do the housekeeping?'

She no longer spoke of Miss Bohun as a joke, but instead with a contemptuous anger that troubled Felix because it seemed to prove Mrs Ellis to be unreasonable and involved in pettiness. He supposed Mrs Ellis had been upset by Miss Bohun's remark about the baby belonging to her late husband, but he could not see the remark as being, after all, so very important. Miss Bohun was obviously trying to be kind and reassuring, but Mrs Ellis, for some reason, behaved as though she had received a deadly insult. One day he asked Mrs Ellis: 'Why are you so cross with Miss Bohun?'

She said: 'I'm not going to tell you.'

'Not ever?' asked Felix.

'No, not ever.'

Felix was sorry for Miss Bohun and touched by her show of indifference to rebuff, but his adherence now was to Mrs Ellis, and when, without any reference to Miss Bohun, she said across the supper table to Felix: 'Like to come out to-night?' his embarrassment was completely lost in his delight.

'The cinema again?' asked Miss Bohun with hurt casualness. 'I do hope, Felix, you'll not stay out too late,' but she received no reply beyond Felix's: 'No, Miss Bohun,' and then they were gone.

After that Miss Bohun's manner changed. She, too, retreated into grievance and long periods of silence would descend on the meal tables. When she spoke it was with sudden outbursts of aggressive cheerfulness: 'Well, I must be off to my "Ever-Readies". Dear me, how nice it is to have something to *do* . . . to feel that one is really of use in the world. And there are such splendid people at the "Ever-Readies" – such a jolly crowd. No sulking there.'

Felix felt these innuendos to be very unfair. He had no wish to sulk; his silence came from the feeling that now Miss Bohun had somehow got back into the right, not only Mrs Ellis but he himself was in the wrong. For some reason he felt guilty whenever he went out with Mrs Ellis, but this guilt was suddenly lifted when Miss Bohun one day announced in loud, decided tones: 'I'm sorry to have to tell you, but I am forced to put up the rent.'

Mrs Ellis's head gave a startled, upward jerk and she looked at Miss Bohun in spite of herself. Miss Bohun seemed satisfied with this result. Felix, waiting in some dismay to hear more, saw her lips set momentarily with placid composure, then she said quietly: 'I do not want to do this, of course, but milk has gone up

125

another piastre – the summer shortage, of course – and yesterday we had eggs. I want you to eat well, but everything has to be paid for. Now there's some talk of raising the price of fish. There seems no end to the increase in expenditure; so, I'm afraid I shall require five pounds extra from each of you this month.'

Felix looked at Mrs Ellis, but she did not speak. He wanted her to protest, but could think of nothing to say himself. For the rest of the meal, during which Miss Bohun kept humming to herself the tune of 'Jerusalem the Golden', he wondered miserably whether the Consul would be willing to pay this money.

Towards the end, when Miss Bohun was least expecting it, Mrs Ellis asked in a remote, cold voice: 'I believe there is a Government control on *pension* prices. The price of a single room with meals is controlled at twenty pounds a month.'

Miss Bohun replied: 'I'm afraid the people who fix those prices know nothing about the expense of running a home these days.'

'But most prices are controlled, and you never deal on the black market.'

Miss Bohun gave a slight click with her tongue and replied irritably: 'If you mean you cannot see your way clear to pay the extra five pounds, then I shall be forced to make further economies.'

'Heaven forbid,' said Mrs Ellis. She had finished her meal but she sat still for several minutes, then she said rapidly and not without effort: 'And are you putting up the rent of the front bedroom as well?'

Miss Bohun had been about to lift her fingers from her finger-bowl. Now, although she stared at them, she seemed to forget to move them. Suddenly she said accusingly: 'Who told you I receive rent for the front bedroom?'

Mrs Ellis smiled to herself and rose from the table. Before she could go Miss Bohun, remembering her fingers and lifting them out and drying them on her handkerchief, said with calm dignity: 'I am not a rich woman, Mrs Ellis. No doubt you are used to those fortunate people whose worldly wealth permits them to *give* their services to their faith. I wish I were one of them. I am not. My private money is very small – just two hundred pounds a year. . . .'

'Really,' interrupted Mrs Ellis, 'I wish I had a private income of two hundred pounds a year.'

'As I said, Mrs Ellis, I'm not a rich woman, neither am I a young one. My mother left me my little income and it's all I've ever had given me. I have never had a husband to keep me, or even to die and leave me a comfortable pension. No, I have had to rely on myself all along. I have had to build up for my own old age. Having no wish to be dependent on others, I must work while I can and work hard.'

She stood up, paused to glance at them in silence, then, turning slowly, went up the stairs. It must have seemed to her, as it did to the others, that she had administered an unanswerable rebuke. A few moments passed before Mrs Ellis roused herself and said: 'Well, I'm damned.'

Felix, recovering from Miss Bohun's censure only to remember its origins, said: 'How awful! Another five quid a month. I won't have any pocket money at all now.'

'Why should we pay it? Whatever she says, she can't justify charging twenty-five pounds. This wretched service, these workhouse meals – I shall send her a note and tell her that I'm not eating in any more. I'll pay only for the room.'

'But I can't do that. You see, she was kind and . . .'

'You'd better let your Baghdad friend deal with her.'

'Yes,' Felix agreed despondently, afraid the Consul would tell him to move to the YMCA. Now it was no longer a debt of gratitude, but the presence of Mrs Ellis that kept him in Miss Bohun's house; he worried for some time, expecting to be presented with the ultimatum that either he left or gave up his pocket money.

The Consul must have paid up without question, for Felix heard no more about it, but something else occurred that seemed to him worse. Mrs Ellis, without warning him, disappeared from the meal table. Miss Bohun made no comment and Felix, left alone to suffer her censure, had not the courage to ask about Mrs Ellis. Sometimes he heard Mrs Ellis leave her room but he did not run out to intercept her – he kept to his room if he knew she was in the house; he did not go into the garden if she were there. He was hurt and yet he felt cool and aloof from her, as though he had thrown off a burden. He decided he would not attempt to speak to her again. He cared for nobody – nobody and nothing in the world except Faro; he said to Faro again: 'I love you; I love you.' He knew he really did love Faro; he would often lift her in his arms to the level of his face and rub his smooth cheek against the very tender fur of her throat; then he would carry her round the room, she purring, her eyes, oblique to watch him, half-closed in ecstasy. Faro was natural and genuine and would never disillusion him or put him unfairly in the wrong.

After a week had passed, it seemed to him that his own aloofness from her. had somehow cancelled out Mrs Ellis's indifference; now he could see her again and start afresh without any danger to his pride. He knew suddenly, then, that he did want to see and speak to her again; and in an instant he was possessed with the idea and could not bear the thought of waiting until she returned. But he had no idea where to find her. During the afternoon he kept going to his window and watching for her; at last, about six o'clock, as the sun was dropping in the sky, he saw her coming over the wasteland. He went back to his desk and composed himself so that he could appear the more naturally out of his door as she came along the passage. At last, scarcely able to bear his own excitement, he burst out of the room and said, 'Hello' into her face.

She answered casually: 'Hello. Where have you been all this time?'

'Where have *you* been? You haven't had any meals here for ages.'

'Well,' she answered reasonably, 'I told you I was going to stop having meals in. I didn't see why I should pay so much for her beastly food. The trouble is she is making me pay sixteen pounds a month for the room alone – so it's damned expensive . . .'

'But how can she possibly charge sixteen pounds?' asked Felix, drawn at once into the entrancing game of discussing Miss Bohun. 'She told me the food cost most.'

'Well, she does charge sixteen pounds,' Mrs Ellis shrugged a little, seeming rather bored with the game at the moment. 'What did you do at Easter?'

He copied her slight shrug. Easter had come and gone since he last saw her. 'Nothing,' he said. 'Miss Bohun may be religious, but she doesn't seem to think much about those things. I mentioned it and she said: "What, Easter already! There's always something . . ."'

Felix's attempt to copy Miss Bohun's exasperated uninterest made Mrs Ellis burst out laughing: 'Come in,' she said as she opened her door.

Felix had not been in her room since the night Miss Bohun had burst in and ordered him and Nikky out. He entered happily, sniffing the scent in the air as though it were something on which he could get a tangible hold.

'Well,' said Mrs Ellis, 'if you'd been around I'd have taken you to see the Holy Fire.'

'What Holy Fire?'

'A ceremony in the Holy Sepulchre on Easter Saturday. The Greek patriarch produced fire from Heaven – I've never seen such a crowd. People went quite crazy; they almost set the church alight.'

'No! And you didn't take me?' His distress was so poignant he could scarcely keep it from his voice.

'Oh,' Mrs Ellis was remorseful now that she saw his suffering, 'I would have asked you if I could – but one of Nikky's friends at the café gave me the tickets so I had to ask Nikky to come.'

'But . . . but *couldn't* you have got another ticket?'

'No. They're very difficult to get. But don't look so miserable. I promise you if we're both here next Easter I'll take you.'

It was poor consolation. Felix sat on the edge of the bed trying to pull himself out of his hurt; it was like a bitterness of disappointment inside him although he had expected nothing. Somehow it was related to the past when the year had been so beautifully hung, like garlands, on the four secure props of Easter, his birthday in July, his mother's in September, and then Christmas. The sense of security had gone quickly enough when the Shiptons had forgotten all about him last Christmas. He had expected nothing this Easter – and yet here he was, wretched because there had, after all, been something, but not for him. He made an effort to say with interest, betraying nothing:

'What is this Holy Fire for?'

'I don't know. I think it's Pentecost.'

'What's Pentecost?'

'My dear boy, don't ask me. You are incredibly ignorant,

Felix. People ought to know more at your age than when they're grown up.'

His indignation at the unreasonableness of this statement raised him from his dejection and they argued happily enough for half an hour. When she told him to go because she wanted to change her dress, she said: 'Would you like to come to the café to-night?'

'Yes, of course.'

'Come along after dinner. I'll look out for you.'

When he arrived Mrs Ellis was sitting alone at a table where she had had dinner. She was smoking and drinking coffee.

'Hello,' she said. 'You are the first.'

'Are other people coming?'

'Nikky probably – and his friends. They usually drop in.'

Felix was glad to have Mrs Ellis to himself for a while. Almost at once he started to talk about his mother, feeling in some way that his devotion to Mrs Ellis left him in debt to his mother's memory. Mrs Ellis, her elbows on the table, her eyes narrowed against the smoke, watched him with a sleepy half-interest that he found exciting. He told her about his mother's lovely dresses and how she would sometimes ask him to choose one for her, but she never accepted his choice because he was not good at choosing; she would say: 'Yes, darling, that is a nice dress – but I think I had better wear the pink,' or 'the black'; how she was rather religious, but not a lot; she would read C. S. Lewis aloud to him, but would play bridge on Sunday afternoons with the Shiptons and Mr Turner-Tufley and say: 'I am sure God has no objection to our having a little fun'; how Mr Turner-Tufley was very nice and had a wife in England whom he had not seen for years; how Felix's mother would sometimes sigh when Mr Turner-Tufley went, and put her arms round Felix's neck and say: 'Anyway, I always have my little boy.' And she was terribly artistic and good at interior decoration and could paint table-mats and make lamp-shades . . .

'Did she make that frilly thing in your room?' asked Mrs Ellis.

'Yes, and she was terribly clever at buying things. She always bought the right things, and she didn't pay much, either. People were always saying: "How clever you are, Mrs Latimer", and she used to say to me, "You wait, Felix, with all these things, we'll have such a lovely home in England." She had *boxes* of things. I wanted to keep them but the Shiptons sold them; they said I'd need the money for my education.' After a pause, he asked her: 'Did you have a lovely home in Cairo?'

'Good Lord, no; we had no home at all. I had a job at GHQ and I lived in the Pyramids *pension*. The Americans bought up all the flats in Cairo. We couldn't compete. The best we ever had was a double bedroom at Shepheard's, but that was luxury.'

The words 'luxury' and 'Shepheard's' and 'double bedroom' filled Felix's imagination with visions of such splendour and passion that he breathed fervently: 'Oh, yes, like the films,' and Mrs Ellis burst out laughing.

When Nikky arrived he came at once to their table, and he and Mrs Ellis discussed some scholarship to England he seemed to hope to receive. Indeed, though he would, if persuaded, repeat his stories about the 'Ever-Readies', Felix later found he was never as funny again. Felix became rather bored with Nikky's scholarship and the question of where Nikky might or might not stay if he went to London. Felix did not know London. Places called Bloomsbury, Euston and Chelsea had no reality for him. He was not interested in them, because in England he would live in the country. They could not have had more for Nikky, but his interest in them seemed at times almost like a drunken excitement. He kept saying: 'One thing I must see, it is Piccadilly . . .' or 'the Strand,' or 'Fleet Street.'

Felix was glad when other people began to arrive and they talked of something else. By nine o'clock six or seven young men had arrived – Jews, Arabs and Poles – and a profound discussion followed about some people called . . . Felix got these names right because when he whispered to Mrs Ellis: 'Who are they talking about?' she broke up an empty cigarette carton and wrote on the inside: 'Kafka, Palinurus, Sartre'. 'But who *are* they?' Felix whispered, desperate to penetrate the mysteries of this rapid, excited talk; but Mrs Ellis, on the point of saying something to the table, shushed Felix aside and years were to pass before he discovered.

During the following weeks, when Felix went to the Innsbruck as often as he dared, he became used to the curious names that came and went in everyone's conversation, unquestioned as clichés and apparently pertinent to everyone except Felix. No one here –

Jews and Arabs though they were – ever spoke of Palestine's private war that was marking time now until the World War ended. Felix soon discovered that these young men were proud of the friendship that held them together and aloof from the political tension that kept Jews and Arabs apart. One or other of them would usually point out to Mrs Ellis during the evening: 'Madam, you see here a most unique. What are we! Myself, an Arab, my friend a Jew; and so the others, Jews and Arabs, mixing in intellectual amity. Were all to act in such a way, the problems of Palestine would be solved. My friend here, Mr Finkelstein, is an intellectual, and as such his sympathies are naturally with us Arabs. He does not much like other Jews. To him, they are narrow, stupid, full of religious prejudice. Myself, I see the shortcomings of the Arabs – how are they educated? To recite the Koran, no more. Such is not enough in a world of this size where there are paintings, so many literatures, the telephone, Professor Einstein, the radio, the films and Salvador Dali.'

Nikky, when he was away from them, would affect to find shortcomings in the intellectuality of this circle, but Felix was completely dazzled by it. He had never before known people whose conversation was devoted exclusively to sex and the arts. The young Moslem Arabs were fervent in the support of the freedom of all Moslem women (except perhaps their own close relatives), and the young Jews deplored as embarrassingly vulgar the licence of the settlements, whose women drove the repressed and ignorant Arabs wild by the swing of their breasts and buttocks and the briefness of their shorts.

Mrs Ellis, who seldom did more than help the conversation with an occasional question, was regarded as the group's chief ornament – a brilliant and beautiful woman; an Englishwoman who, unlike almost all other Englishwomen, was not stiff, narrow, proud, prudish and contemptuous of 'the natives'. When she assured them that the young women in England were more often like her than like the wives of Government officials, they laughed uproariously and said: 'You are making the propaganda, are you not?' and they were all more or less in love with her originality.

Felix, who lived in the same house as Mrs Ellis and had seen her first, felt he must be much more in love than anyone. Now he listened like a dog for her comings and goings and could scarcely bear to let her go out without him, yet beneath his adoration there remained like a bruise the fact she had gone to the Holy Fire, taking Nikky and not him. Something within him was shaken and ready to fall.

At the first opportunity he asked her to tell him the story she had told Nikky about the shipwreck. 'I couldn't hear it,' he said. 'I kept going to sleep.'

'Not now; you must never ask anyone to repeat cold a story he's told when warmed up.'

'But couldn't you get warmed up again?'

'Perhaps. But I'm not warmed up now.'

Several times later he tried to get the story from her, but she would not tell it. Whenever he thought of it he was jealous that she should tell it to Nikky and not to him. Sometimes he would hurry through his work in the afternoon so he would be free to go out with her on the following morning and walk in the sunlight, on the pavements crowded with shoppers.

Everything she said and did delighted him. Although she did not use much slang herself, she occasionally approved of something with the words 'smashing' and 'bang on', or disapproved by describing them as 'foul' or 'bloody'. These terms entranced Felix and soon displaced his own 'super' and 'beastly'.

It seemed to him that the smallest of incidents experienced in Mrs Ellis's company could help change his view of life. He had accepted without question his mother's philosophy, which described everyone as 'rather sweet' or 'fundamentally really rather nice'. If his mother came into contact with anger, rudeness or dishonesty, she somehow shook those things off with a little movement of the shoulders, a little lift of the head, that placed her above them. 'Poor darling,' she would say, 'no doubt something's worrying him (or her). Always remember, Felix darling, that everyone has his troubles.' This attitude carried her through life with the minimum of hurt and anxiety, but Felix felt that even if he could convey it to Mrs Ellis, it would not work with her. Life itself seemed to change within her aura. People in contact with her were not always at their best. He began to wonder if those 'rather sweet' and 'fundamentally nice' people who had peopled his mother's world had a real existence anywhere at all.

One morning, walking in the Jaffa Road, they were stopped by a little English couple – the wife plain and badly dressed; the husband a junior and never likely to be much more. As they spoke, their four eyes were fixed on Mrs Ellis as though they wanted to hypnotize her. They had a perambulator for sale and Miss Bohun had told them Mrs Ellis might be interested.

'Well, I might,' she agreed cautiously, 'how much do you want for it?'

'Twenty-five pounds,' said the husband promptly.

Mrs Ellis smiled without friendliness; 'I was thinking of buying a pram, not a small car.'

Their faces fell as they realized this was a refusal. Felix's mother would probably have said: 'Poor things, no doubt they need the money'; and now the wonderful chance of making money out of someone – not another official, just an outsider – had faded. The wife was explaining how her husband had improved the perambulator, perhaps it hadn't been worth much when they got it, but now –

'Oh, I only want an ordinary pram,' said Mrs Ellis and as they moved off she said without lowering her voice: 'Bloody little scroungers! You could see their eyes fairly popping with avarice!' and Felix thrilled, realizing that that indeed was the truer comment.

She said: 'Of course all the dumbest types end up in the Colonial Service – people without sparkle, poise, depth, intellect, or anything but that smug mediocrity that makes them think themselves the salt of the earth. God, no wonder the Arabs and Jews despise them. And the nearer the top you go, the more frightful they are. Take the Radletts . . .'

'The Radletts!' breathed Felix, awed that she criticized these important people.

'What a charming couple! They're notorious, of course – as mean as cat's meat. He's a sour little fellow who drinks whisky in front of his guests and only offers them beer. She's the quintessence of suburbia. She looks like a charwoman and has the manners of a butcher's wife to whom rationing has given the upper hand . . .'

Felix squawked with delight, elated by Mrs Ellis's candour. Miss Bohun had spoken of the Radletts with respect, telling Felix that the fact she was, once a year or so, invited to their house showed she ranked in their view with persons of senior grade. When Mrs Ellis spoke he suddenly, with the instinct of youth, of a creature with unblemished eyes, recognized truth, truth, truth, and he knew that truth was the thing he wanted.

Gazing at her, adoring her, he said: 'You're smashing. You're the most smashing person I know. I wish you'd marry me.'

She smiled as though he were joking.

'But,' he pursued her, 'you're only five or six years older than me. Lots of people marry people six years older . . .'

'Don't be silly,' she said vaguely, and no argument would persuade her to give the matter more consideration than that.

Now he suffered moments of desolation, thinking they would be sent home on separate ships, that when she was in London and he in Somerset they would almost never meet, perhaps *never* meet –. It was beyond thinking that a time could come when they would never meet again, but he had experienced her indifference. He knew she would make no effort to keep in touch with him. She would never stay anywhere for long. He felt the quality of her as something drifting, almost intangible so that he felt a need to keep close to her; when with her he would cling to her arm if she let him, but usually she shook him off. At times she showed her impatience with him or, half as a joke, half as a statement of fact, would describe him to the others as 'my shadow', or 'the limpet'. He would have painful clairvoyant moments in which he knew that to Mrs Ellis he was rather more a nuisance than not, and when they separated she might feel relief. But those were only moments, for she treated him with tolerance and good nature and perhaps felt for his youth a certain pity. Whenever she went to the hospital he would go with her and, while waiting for her, he would visit Mr Jewel. One afternoon as they left he remembered to tell her about Mr Jewel's paintings. 'Do you know,' he said, 'Mr Jewel is an artist, and he's terribly good!'

He was pleased to see he had surprised and interested her but she did not sound very convinced when she said: 'Really! What does he paint?'

'I'll show you when we get back. I know where Miss Bohun put his things.'

At the house Felix, making sure Maria was occupied in the

135

kitchen, slipped into the wood-shed and came out with Mr Jewel's pictures under his arm. Mrs Ellis was waiting under the mulberry tree. She looked at the paintings one by one, but said nothing.

'Don't you think they're wonderful?' Felix asked. 'Those are primroses. They grow in England.'

'Very nice,' said Mrs Ellis, handing the pictures back, but he knew from her tone that she did not think so.

'Don't you like them?' Felix felt deflated.

'I expect he enjoyed doing them,' said Mrs Ellis and would say no more, but as Felix looked at the paintings a light seemed to go out of them. He knew suddenly that she was right; they were not good, but he was sorry. He would have liked Mr Jewel to be a good artist. His mother would have liked it, too; she would have said: 'Oh, yes, darling, they are wonderful. To think of that poor old man making such wonderful pictures up in an attic, all by himself,' but the story, hanging in the air romantic and golden would not have been true. It would have belonged to the story-book world which his mother always somehow produced around her and which he knew he must leave now he was growing up. Venturing into reality, Mrs Ellis was the guide for him. Almost every time he was with her some incident widened his understanding of life, or of himself.

One morning, as they were out in Princess Mary Avenue among the shoppers, she took him into a shop to buy wool. She was unable to knit or sew herself, but she was employing Maria's daughter-in-law to make baby clothes for her.

She examined some skeins of dark wool – for there were no pale colours left in the shops – and said: 'But this is Botany wool. It washes badly. I must have real wool.'

The man behind the counter lifted the skeins close to his thick spectacles, and read the label in a German accent. ' "Botany",' he became scornful, 'that is the Mark. This is, of course, wool like all wool – "Botany" they call it as a – a – what is it?' He snapped his fingers irritably at his fat wife, who supplied the words he sought:

'It is the Trade Mark.'

'So,' he threw down the wool, 'the Trade Mark.'

'No,' said Mrs Ellis, 'you're wrong. "Botany" wool is not like sheep's wool. It is made from plant fibres.'

'Not so, not so,' declared the shopkeeper and all in a moment he seemed to leap in a hysterical rage, shouting at Mrs Ellis and Felix: 'Not so. Do you tell me that I do not know. I am selling wool since four years,' and breaking off now and then to give little laughs of pure rage; sometimes swinging round to his wife, who shrugged her shoulders in ridicule of a customer who would profess to teach them their business. The man put his thick, square finger-tips on the table: 'So – the *Mark*, you see . . . look for yourself . . .' He was now speaking slowly, with the infinite scorn and ridicule of an unbounding fury. 'Here,' he snatched another skein. 'Here a "Sea-shell", here a "Botany" – look for yourself!' He pushed the Botany skein under their noses.

'I recognize the "Sea-shell",' said Mrs Ellis coolly, 'but tell me – what is a "Botany"?' The man swung on his wife: 'What is a "Botany"?'

'It is a Trade Mark,' she repeated as before and from the loftiness of her self-control made the statement: 'All wool, madame, is from the sheep; where else is wool coming?' The man laughed unpleasantly. He and his wife fixed on Mrs Ellis stares of pitying contempt.

She said to Felix: 'Let's get out of here.'

In the street she seemed unaffected by the scene, but there was a slight colour in her cheeks.

'Why was he so cross?' asked Felix.

'Because he's crazy. Everyone's crazy here, perhaps because of living on top of a mountain. I don't know. Anyway it makes life very difficult.'

'Is that why you said Miss Bohun is mad?'

'Probably. Do stop asking silly questions. Sometimes you're a damned silly kid for your age. When are you going to grow up?'

Felix, startled and rather hurt by this, was also oddly awakened. He realized this naïveté did not go down with everyone. His mother had said: 'Oh, how I wish my little boy could remain a baby all his life,' or 'How I dread the day when my little boy loses his freshness and innocence.' His mother had been his world and he, out of touch with other boys, perhaps unconsciously to please her, had remained rather too 'fresh' and 'innocent'. Anyway, it didn't please everyone. He became conscious suddenly of his own developing attitude to life. Now he was alone in the world, it was just as well he couldn't remain a little boy all his life. The sooner he became as sensible as Mrs Ellis, the better for him.

The summer was coming. There was no more rain; the sun's heat grew, the spring flowers wilted, dried, turned to dust, and the fields grew bare. Now the beauty of the day came with the sunset and the sky turned from a pure, bright green to a peacock blue in which the stars shone each evening larger and more brilliant. The sunset translucence and colour lingered, perhaps until dawn. Felix was never up late enough to know; but the colour and the beauty of the sky filled him with excitement as though the iron rule of the night had been overcome. It was wonderful to go out with Mrs Ellis and to saunter beside her, with the red tip of her cigarette moving through the delicate air, and to see the crenellations of the old city wall cut romantically black against the brilliant sky.

If by chance at the Innsbruck Mrs Ellis and Felix (for Felix never let himself be separated from Mrs Ellis) were cornered by one of the Poles, the conversation would take a sombre and personal turn. There were two Poles, rather alike, with taut, yellowish skin strained over their skulls and pale eyes flatly set in their heads. They had got out of Poland into Russia and had recently, with several others, been sent to join the hundreds of Poles in Palestine. These two seemed always to be in the café; if none of Nikky's other friends had arrived, they would sit together silent, each having untouched before him a small *café turc*. One evening Mrs Ellis and Felix found themselves cut off from the main group by the Poles and the four of them sat for a long time without a word. Then the elder Pole murmured gloomily: 'Today I saw some blue flowers and they made me think of Poland.'

Mrs Ellis, who was beside him, made a sympathetic murmur and asked: 'Are there many blue flowers in Poland?'

'There are some,' he answered and added after a long pause, 'naturally.'

'I supposed there would be,' Mrs Ellis said.

At the other end of the long table, which comprised three small café tables pushed together, someone was being very funny. Felix, gazing across the two stiff emaciated bodies of the Poles, strained to hear what it was about, but he could only get a word here and there. At last Mrs Ellis asked: 'Did you have much difficulty in getting out of Poland?'

'No, I was near the Russian frontier – there were many of us in lorries and we drove across. But the Russians seized us. You would not believe it; they put us in a camp. "Where is my servant?" I asked. "Here, in our regime," said they, "you have no servant." "This," I shouted, "is an outrage. If you wish no servant, that is your own affair. I, I must have a servant. I am not of your regime. I demand a servant."' As he told the story, the Pole began to tremble; his lips shuddered with spasms of anger and he suddenly slapped the fragile table and upset the cognac to which someone had treated him. He made no comment on this, but sombrely watched the spilt cognac drip off the edge of the table. In a minute he whispered: 'They laughed at me. Yes, I have suffered.'

Here the other Pole joined in, although he had not appeared to be listening: 'I, too,' he said; 'in my camp we had to eat only potatoes! Frost-bitten potatoes. Day after day, potatoes. Believe me, my friends, that is to suffer.'

Mrs Ellis shook her head slowly in sympathy: 'And what did the Russians eat?' she asked.

'They also ate potatoes. There was a famine. But that was their affair. You cannot treat a Polish officer as if he were a Russian.'

'One is not used to such food,' said the other with a grimace of distaste, and after a long pause added suddenly as an afterthought, 'and every day they beat me.'

'Beat you? Why did they do that?'

He shrugged his shoulders: 'How should I know.'

Felix moved restlessly in his seat and looked at Mrs Ellis hoping she might catch his eye and agree to go. But she was sitting with hanging head as though there was over her, as over Felix, a deep depression. She said without looking up: 'Ah, well, the war will soon be over and then you can return to Poland.'

The nearer Pole shrugged his shoulders: 'To Poland! Such a thing is impossible. I have suffered too much, my health is not good. It is the chest, you know. The chest. I could not survive a northern winter.'

At that moment, on the order of one of the young Arabs or Jews, a waiter brought a brandy to replace the one that had been spilt. Without a glance to either side, the Pole picked it up and swallowed it, and Felix took the chance to whisper: 'Let us go.'

'All right,' Mrs Ellis agreed, 'we'll go to the King David.'

'Really!' Felix stumbled with excitement as he got to his feet, 'really the King David?'

'Why not?'

Nikky had not arrived. The others were so engrossed in an argument that they accepted Mrs Ellis's departure with no more than a few mild protests.

Out in the fresh spring air, she said: 'I'm getting bored with the Innsbruck.'

As they entered through the swing doors into the central hall of the hotel, Felix was almost as disappointed as he had been on first entering a café. There were a lot of people about – English officers, Levantines, even two Transjordan Arabs in full dress – but everyone was behaving with the utmost decorum. A breeze, too cool for comfort, came from the revolving fans. The light was not bright enough; the people sitting at the little tables seemed scattered and silent. It seemed to Felix that a slight chill hung over everything, and as he crossed the floor behind Mrs Ellis this impression was deepened as he noticed Frau Wagner sitting by herself, upright, a fixed artificial smile set upon her artificially-coloured face. A tiny liqueur glass stood on the table before her. In her eyes, as they drew near her, he saw for the first time in his life the ultimate despair of loneliness. He caught his breath, touched as though by death, and tried to hurry past unseen. But she recognized him. Hope came into her glance, appalling him. He smiled awkwardly and pushed Mrs Ellis slightly in his eager-ness to pass without being intercepted, but when he saw Frau Wagner look quickly away and lift her chin with a bright false stare of interest in something at the other end of the room, he felt ashamed of himself. He sat silent for a long time before he sud-denly said to Mrs Ellis: 'I know that lady over there.'

'Oh, which one?'

'The one with golden hair – rather – well, a bit old; with a purple silk dress.'

'How on earth do you come to know her?'

Felix told her the story of Mr Jewel and Frau Wagner and the unfortunate evening when Felix had failed to stay in the house as he had promised.

'She told you to stay in and play gooseberry. How disgusting!'

'Then you don't think Mr Jewel was wicked?'

'What do you mean by "wicked"? If you mean do I think he should be allowed to have a bit of slap and tickle with his old girl, I can only say it's not my business. And it's not your business either – or Miss Bohun's.'

Felix did not know what to say, and after a moment's pause Mrs Ellis burst out angrily: 'I suppose the poor old things were lonely. Miss Bohun wouldn't understand that – but everyone hasn't got a jack-in-the-box called "God" in their minds.'

Felix caught his breath, startled into admiration of Mrs Ellis's spirit, and yet worried by this irreverence about God.

'People, you know, can get unbalanced by loneliness,' said Mrs Ellis as she watched Frau Wagner. 'That woman'll go off her head one day.'

'Really?' Felix was deeply interested but felt more guilty than before. 'Do you think we ought to go over and speak to her?'

'Well...' Mrs Ellis gave Frau Wagner another glance, then said: 'We'll speak to her on the way out.'

Felix felt much relieved, but he kept glancing over at Frau Wagner, seeing her now and then put the small glass to her closed lips and return it undrunk to the table. Whenever he could see her eyes they seemed to have a mad, bright light, and Mrs Ellis's phrase 'unbalanced by loneliness' kept repeating itself in his head. He had a terrible urge to go over and say as they said at the Innsbruck: 'Drink that one up and have another on me,' but thank goodness, Mrs Ellis was with him and he could not leave her.

He said: 'Do you think she's mad because she's lonely?'

'I don't know.' Mrs Ellis had lost interest in the case, but in a moment she suggested: 'Perhaps she's lonely because she's mad.' After a pause she said as though she were quoting: 'The desolating loneliness of the mad.' She sighed and said: 'I suppose if we were really kind, we'd do something about her, but the boredom – I can't be bothered to be as kind as that. Besides, she wants a man.'

'Perhaps she wants Mr Jewel?' Felix suggested.

'I suppose he'd do as well as another,' Mrs Ellis agreed.

As she seemed so willing to talk, Felix took the opportunity to ask:

'Do you think Miss Bohun is wicked?'

'Don't use that silly word, Felix. Of course I don't. She's absurd and tactless and a busybody, probably no worse. She belongs to a generation that seems to combine thinking the worst of everybody with trying to do the best for them. I expect she's awfully innocent.'

'Yes,' agreed Felix, extremely flattered that he was by implication included among the less innocent. 'Still,' he added, 'she does do her hair like that.'

'In plaits round her head? What has that to do with it?'

'My mother said that women who do their hair like that want to seem more simple than they really are.'

Mrs Ellis gave a laugh: 'Did your mother say that? Perhaps she wasn't such a fool after all.'

Felix jerked up his head and looked at Mrs Ellis with such pain, she said quickly: 'I didn't mean "a fool", of course. How silly of me. I meant – what did I mean? "Unworldly" – yes, that's what I mean. My dear little Felix, don't look so upset.'

'It's all right,' said Felix. Despite the trembling of his hands and the tears in his eyes, he made an effort to drink the last of his lemonade.

'Have another lemonade?'

'No, thank you.'

'Then have a Peach Melba or an ice?'

Felix shook his head. He put down his glass and sat drooping, his hands clasped between his knees.

'Oh, come on!' Mrs Ellis rallied him. 'I hurt your feelings, I was silly – but worse things happen at sea. Much worse.'

'Yes,' he agreed politely.

'Shipwrecks, for instance.'

In spite of himself, he looked up: 'Will you tell me about it?'

'All right, if you'll be a sensible boy.'

142

He had to smile: 'Are you warmed up?'

'Not yet. If you don't mind waiting, I think I'll get a cognac first.'

As soon as the cognac came and she had drunk some of it, she said: 'This happened when they were sending the children home before El Alamein. I was about sixteen. We were all on a ship lying off Suez. We had to go round the Cape in those days.'

'Yes, I know.'

'Well, we older ones were put in charge of kids who hadn't got their mother with them. I was given a little girl of five or six. I wasn't too pleased – she was such a thin, pale, little creature – a bundle of nerves. I remember I was rather disgusted because her clothes weren't too clean. It wasn't her fault; she'd been neglected, but I thought then I'd never seen such a miserable-looking kid before. Her mother had gone off with a South African officer. Her father did not know what to do with her. He had got a divorce and wanted to marry again and the kid was only in the way. Then he had this heaven-sent chance of sending her home on this boat. She told me she was going to her grandmother. I had to be responsible for her in case there was any trouble. I was pretty fed up at first, especially as she seemed to take a fancy to me and wouldn't let go of me for a moment. I thought "I'm in for a journey, my goodness, three months of this . . ." But even though I didn't like her I felt sorry for her. You see, I knew what was wrong with her. No one had ever loved her. She just didn't know what life was all about. Anyway, we were lying off Port Said waiting for a convoy and I was taking this kid to her berth for the night and she was holding my hand – and we were struck. Suddenly the most hellish row and the boat plunging about and, d'you know, I wasn't afraid. I behaved in the most sensible way. I picked the kid up and said: "Nothing to be frightened of. We're near the shore." I remember saying those words: "We're near the shore." The kid just hung round my neck not yelling or anything. But the row that broke out! I've never seen such a pandemonium. In a minute there were kids everywhere, screaming and fighting, all terrified, and the grown-ups trying to get them up the stairs. I held on to my one and I got another one – a boy – by the hand, but he was lost in the crush somewhere. I turned to go back for him – but it was impossible; anyway, he'd disappeared. When we got on deck, we couldn't see anything, but we could feel the deck slipping sideways. We were going down so quickly, I knew there was no time even to get in a boat. People were throwing the kids up on top of one another like a lot of parcels. I heard afterwards some of the boats sank as soon as they reached the water. I knew I'd just have to jump in. I said to the kid: "Now hold on tight. I'm going to swim to the shore." The town was blacked out, but you could see a glimmer in the distance, two or three miles away. The water was black as hell. I jumped in, not even knowing how far I had to jump. It was icy. At first I thought I was the only person in the water and then, suddenly, there were hundreds of them all splashing about and shouting and not knowing what to do, and the poor brats . . . At one time I was swimming with half a dozen of them hanging on to me. I almost went under, but it was so cold, they couldn't hang on for long. They dropped off one by one, but my own kid hung on to my back without making a sound. I kept saying: "You all right?" She didn't answer – then she slipped off into the water. I caught her arm and said: "Move, move, try and swim," but I had to drag her along, then a searchlight went on. It lit up some boats that had come out to look for us and I made a bee-line for one of them and they hauled the kid and me on board and I took her on my knee. We went round for an hour or more taking people on board. It was strange. Although the sea had been crowded with people when I jumped in, we could scarcely fill the boat. We were still hunting for people when it began getting light and I realized the kid on my lap was dead. She looked like a wax doll. I remember one of her arms was stretched out stiff on my knee and her fingers were blue and they were curled up like this –' Mrs Ellis stretched out her hand and curled her fingers and sat for some moments looking reflectively at her own long, dark red nails; then she said: 'I went on holding her and all I could think of was that no one had loved her and now she was dead. Apart from thinking that, I felt quite indifferent really. I thought I was being pretty brave. It was only afterwards that I began to feel sorry about that kid just as though she'd been my sister or something, and also I began to be afraid. When they said I could go home on the next boat, I began to cry. They said: "You've been a very brave girl; you mustn't give in now. Come on, pull yourself together," but I couldn't. It was impossible. I said I couldn't go on a boat, again, and they had to let me stay. I got a room in a *pension* in Cairo and my father sent me an allowance. I lived just like a grown-up. After a while I began to enjoy it. And I got married.'

Felix sat and stared at her, his eyes fixed, still in his mind struggling in the black, night waters of the Gulf of Suez. After a few moments Mrs Ellis shook his arm:

'Come on now,' she said, 'we must go over and speak to your Frau Wagner.'

When they stopped at the table, Frau Wagner was pretending not to notice their approach. As Felix said: 'How do you do, Frau Wagner? May I introduce Mrs Ellis?' she jerked her head round on her crêpey neck that the sun had burnt to peony red, and her blue eyes bulged with pleasure:

'Please, please sit a moment. How nice it is. All evening I have been wishing a friend that I might discuss my fine new project.'

They sat on the edges of chairs, ready for a quick getaway.

'A new project!' said Mrs Ellis, 'how interesting.'

'Yes, to think – I have heard of a house to be let vacant. I shall hire it. Now I have learnt all, I shall start a *pension* and grow rich like Miss Bohun.'

'You are lucky! Where is the house?'

'Ah, that would be telling, would it not? But, can you believe me, I have already heard of a lodger.'

'Congratulations. But what about furniture?'

'I have my things lent at this moment to a friend in the censorship. And I have a packing-case with such fine linen, such glass and silver. They could not be found here. This lodger is a lady – I know, of course, today all are ladies – but this one, she is called Lady Evelina Lundy. It is a title, so I shall ask her to pay more, no?'

'Who told you about her?'

'My friend in the censorship.'

At this point Felix managed to get out the very grown-up remark he had had on the tip of his tongue: 'Drink that up, Frau Wagner, and have another on me?'

Coming in an unnatural voice, it now sounded a crude and silly remark, but Frau Wagner, her eyes bright, gave him an admiring, coquettish glance and said: 'Ah, a so polite young man, is not?' and drained the glass at a gulp.

Then they had an awkward few minutes while Felix tried to catch the eye of a waiter and give an order. Mrs Ellis was not helpful. Regarding himself as being under her orders, he had never thought to offer her a drink. Perhaps she was cross? – but surely she must realize this situation was different.

Frau Wagner, on the other hand, with one liqueur inside and another on the table, seemed to perk up and take it upon herself to do the entertaining just as when she had been alone with Mr Jewel and Felix at Miss Bohun's. She said: 'The house on which I keep my eye has many features but, alas, in the water-closet there is no water, and in the rooms only the jugs. So inconvenient to officers who have the lady friends. I shall tell them at once I can have here only those who make love without the h. and c.'

Felix, although he did not see the significance of this joke, thought it very funny. He laughed uproariously and Mrs Ellis, supposing he knew what he was laughing at, gave him a surprised look. Frau Wagner quickly put up a hand:

'Please, please – I am thinking to ask you. This packing-case of mine, full of such valuable things – I am concerned because they say there will be fighting here. You know, the Arabs and the Jews – so dangerous for everyone. The Arabs will steal all, I have heard it said. I was wondering . . . you English people will get safely away; you always get away – would you take for safety with you my packing-case with the silver, glass and linen?'

'Well!' Mrs Ellis looked doubtful, then asked: 'How big is it?'

'Oh, very big. So . . .' she stretched her arms to indicate the size of a cabin trunk, 'I have some good things, you know. In Vienna we were big people. If you take it, you must put it in the Bank of England. I will keep the key, of course.'

'Of course.' Mrs Ellis rose with a more decided movement, 'Now we really must go – or Miss Bohun will say I'm keeping Felix out of bed.'

Felix did not want to leave Frau Wagner so soon – now he had got over his first repulsion he realized again how entertaining she was – but Mrs Ellis seemed determined and he felt bound to move with her. As he went he waved to Frau Wagner and she waved back with a little fluttering movement of the fingers. In his annoyance at being forced to go, he began to feel again the guilt and wretchedness that had swept over him when Mrs Ellis called his mother a fool, but Mrs Ellis, as though relieved at having got away from Frau Wagner, was being very funny, describing how they would have to take it in turns to carry Frau Wagner's packing-case out of Palestine and guard it until they reached the Bank of England – but Felix could respond only with an effort and when they got back he was glad to shut himself in his room away from the sound of her voice. Some time during the night he awoke with the thought perhaps it was understandable that Mrs Ellis should think his mother was a fool. All she knew of his mother was what Felix had told her, and how inadequate that had been! Perhaps if he had tried to tell his mother about Mrs Ellis, his mother would have thought Mrs Ellis a fool. Although he could not quite convince himself of this last, he awoke next morning prepared to show Mrs Ellis that he no longer gave the matter a thought.

When he went downstairs to breakfast, Miss Bohun was brooding over a letter. The opened envelope with its Egyptian stamp lay on the table. She murmured to herself once or twice as she turned the pages over and re-read the beginning, then, putting them down, said: 'Here is a most charming person, a Lady Evelina Lundy with her little boy, looking for somewhere in Jerusalem so she can spend the summer here. She wants no grandeur – just a comfortable place at a reasonable figure. A gentleman she knows has written to me. He says he knew your father. How nice of him!'

Felix was aghast to realize that the information given Frau Wagner by her friend in the censorship must have come from Miss Bohun's letter.

He said: 'I saw Frau Wagner and she says she is going to rent a house and take in lodgers and . . .'

'Indeed!' Miss Bohun interrupted with a smile, 'no doubt she thinks she's going to get her employer's house. Frau Teitelbaum told me some time ago that they're going to Haifa – but Frau Wagner will be unlucky, I'm afraid. The Teitelbaums want key-money for that house, and, as a matter of fact, I've already put one of my "Ever-Readies" on to it.'

'Oh! And what will Frau Wagner do?'

'Get another job, that's if she doesn't want to go to Haifa with the Teitelbaums.' Miss Bohun's satisfied smile faded as she looked down again at her letter. She sighed: 'A charming person! And a dear little boy who would love the garden.' She reflected a moment before she said earnestly: 'I know, Felix, Mrs Ellis is a friend of yours! I like you to have a friend. I am glad you get on so well together, but – I dislike saying it – I'm afraid Mrs Ellis is treating me very unfairly. You have noticed no doubt that she doesn't come down for meals? Perhaps she hasn't told you that she doesn't pay for her meals now. She says her doctor – Dr Klaus, quite a good gynaecologist, I'm sure, even though he's not an Englishman – has told her she's suffering from malnutrition. She showed me a note about it. A lot of nonsense, I'm sure. Our meals may not be rich, but they're wholesome – and Mrs Ellis is certainly not too thin. But, there, she's made it an excuse to eat her meals elsewhere, and she just pays for her room. I don't want to put her out, in her condition, but it's very hard on me.'

Felix listened apprehensively but could think of nothing to say. Miss Bohun opened her writing desk and threw the letter in. The drawer was crammed full of papers and letters. When she returned to the table she brightened and asked in a lighter voice: 'I suppose Mrs Ellis does have some sort of breakfast somewhere, but I don't know where she gets it at the hour she rises.'

When Felix said nothing, Miss Bohun added in a pleasant, interested way: 'She doesn't drink intoxicants at night, does she?'

'Oh, no, she only drinks coffee.'

'Even coffee is not the right thing in her condition.' When Miss Bohun spoke again she lowered her voice: 'You know, Felix, I do not want to pry into your life; if you do not wish to confide in me, I would not seek to force a confidence, but I am your aunt, in a way, and I feel I *must* ask you – what do you and Mrs Ellis do in the evenings? You can't go to the cinema every night?'

'We go to the Innsbruck café.'

'The Innsbruck café! How strange to wish to spend the evenings in such a place! Does Nikky go there, too?'

'Sometimes. He has lots of friends there – Jews and Arabs and Poles, and they're very clever; they talk about art.'

Miss Bohun drew down her lips. At last she said with some

portentousness: 'I hope, Felix, when you are at this café you never do, say or think anything about which you would be ashamed to tell your mother.'

For some moments Felix contemplated this admonition with an easy conscience. The young Arabs and Jews were very frank about sex, but it was not a subject on which his mother had been secretive. The Freudian terms they used put the particulars of their talk beyond his understanding, but he had supposed they were saying very much what his mother has said when she talked to him from a religious viewpoint. Then he suddenly thought of something she often said: 'Sex, you know, Felix darling, is very beautiful; it is something to take very seriously indeed. I do hope my little boy will never grow up into the sort of person who listens to jokes about sex...' Remembering now the roars of laughter that often resulted from obscure remarks at the Innsbruck, Felix blushed. Unfortunately Miss Bohun chose that moment to raise her eyes and look at him. Seeing his dark and guilty cheeks, she looked down again. After a pause she spoke gravely: 'Felix, are you in the habit of going into Mrs Ellis's bedroom?'

'No.' He was surprised, as he had expected her to ask him something much more difficult to answer.

'You were in there the night I came home late.'

'I only went in then, and one other time. You see, that night we were talking and Nikky...'

Miss Bohun again interrupted. She spoke quietly and firmly: 'I must ask you another question. I want you to understand, Felix, that my position is a very difficult one. This is my house and my home. It is also *your* home: an important point to remember. I am responsible for its moral tone,' here she broke off to say in a rapid aside: 'And there I am stuck up in the attic. It is *so* inconvenient! What a pity I had that door put on. Anything could happen without my hearing,' then continued at once with measured solemnity, 'so, unwilling though I am, I feel bound, Felix, to ask you something. And I know you will tell me the truth.'

Felix, his hands clasped between his knees, leant with his chest against the table, his lips parted. The weighty nature of Miss Bohun's preamble filled him with fear. He had no idea what she was going to ask him to reveal, but again, when her question came, it seemed to have the simplicity of idiocy. She pronounced it carefully: 'Does Nikky go into Mrs Ellis's room at night?'

Felix frowned in his surprise: 'I don't think so. Why should he? He has a room of his own.'

'You all come home together, I suppose?'

'Yes, sometimes.'

'And Nikky parts from you in the courtyard?'

'Yes.'

'And you go straight to your own room?'

'Yes.'

Miss Bohun's interrogation of him reminded him of those witness-box scenes in films and he had to admire the sensible, straightforward way in which he played his part. His answers, however, did not seem to please Miss Bohun very much, and the cross-examination left him befogged as to its purpose.

'Now,' she said, as though she had been leading up to this point, 'I want you to think carefully for a moment, Felix...Do you ever hear anyone else coming up the stairs after you have gone to bed?'

Felix frowned more deeply and stared at his plate. He appeared to be thinking carefully as suggested, but indeed he was a complete blank except for a sense of the unpleasantness of this last question with its suggestion of the supernatural, the mysterious and, for some reason, the indecent. It came to him suddenly exactly what all these questions meant. He blushed with an acute sense of shame. Dropping his head he answered gruffly and angrily: 'No, never.'

Something in his changed attitude must have warned her, for, as she rose, she said quickly: 'Please don't mention anything I have said to Mrs Ellis. At a time like this it would be dangerous to upset her.'

When she went to the kitchen, he went out to the garden. It was the delicious time of the year before the sun became unbearable. The crinoline branches of the mulberry tree were now completely hidden in leaves. The seat beneath the tree was shut in as in a green tent. Instinctively Felix went to this seat as into hiding to reflect on Miss Bohun's questions. His face was still flushed; the shame he had felt was now curiously shot through with jealousy that Miss Bohun could imply, even imply, that Mrs Ellis could be so intimate with Nikky. He did not for a moment believe there was any basis for the implication, yet his jealousy made him feel sick. At the same time he felt for Miss Bohun a loathing that made the thought of her unbearable. If she had come near him then, he would have had to move away. As the thought of her passed through his mind, his face twitched with distaste as though he remembered with her an unpleasant odour. Curiously he felt something of the same distaste for Mrs Ellis. He did not want to see either of them for a long time, or Nikky either. He did not want to see any human beings at all. When he heard a movement in the tree and looked up, he called to Faro as though he were calling for her from the depths of his distress. She moved down slowly, her eyes upon him.

'Faro, Faro,' he whispered urgently, 'darling Faro...' She dropped easily and happily to the lowest fork of the tree and stood there purring. He lifted her into his arms and pressed his face into her fur. It seemed to him that since his mother's death, Faro alone had loved and needed him. The feel of her warm, living body beneath her fur comforted him and filled him with tenderness. He said: 'I love you better than anyone, Faro,' and after a few minutes he added: 'But I don't love anyone else, anyway.'

10

When he saw Mrs Ellis again, he believed he was quite indiffer-ent to her, but after he had been in her company a little while, the indifference was disturbed by the fact she was so clever and funny and so often said what, with a sense of baptism, he recog-nized to be the truth. He knew then that he was not indifferent to her at all; he liked her very much, but for all that the first excite-ment had gone.

When he looked at her now he realized she had lost completely her fragility, her paleness and her remote look. Her skin had turned golden in the sun and as her figure grew heavy, she began to look robust and more a part of the everyday world. She no longer when she sat, lounged as though too frail to hold herself upright, but she planted herself down, legs apart, with an un-gainly firmness. She was no longer very beautiful, but, strangely enough, he liked her better and felt more at ease in her company. She was a companion, a friend, someone he could trust, but the thought of the ultimate separation of their lives no longer filled him with despair. He would see her again somewhere sometime – why should he not?

Now that the afternoon sun fell so intensely into the back rooms of the house, he and Mrs Ellis took to sitting under the mulberry tree, she with a pad on which she wrote letters to friends in Cairo or reading a novel; he with his school work, which had become simpler for him as his brain adapted itself to the necessity for study. Mr Posthorn occasionally admitted now that Felix might scrape through the London Matriculation when he reached England.

One day in May, when the late spring had changed to the heat of summer and only the leaves on the trees and the protected garden flowers remained, the war in the West was declared to be at an end. No one seemed very happy about it. There was a bleak little procession with a band and speeches, and in the evening, after sunset, people trailed about the twilit streets. But there was no enthusiasm. Indeed, at the Innsbruck, there was apprehension, for many thought the really important war – the war for Palestine – would break out straight away. The young Arabs and Jews were more conscious than ever of the uniqueness of their friendship and some were indignant that they, of all people, might be dragged into the struggle in spite of themselves. The party was much disturbed by Nikky's describing how a couple of years before, when the Jewish authorities felt it politic for their men and women to join the Allies, tough members of a Jewish youth movement used to do the round of the cafés to 'persuade' young Jews to join up. They agreed if they stuck together, protecting one another, press gangs of that sort would hesitate to pick on them. But the days following the war's end were so like the days preceding it, people settled down again, forgetful that they were now supposed to be living in the midst of peace. The war, after all, was still going on in the Far East and this fact should give Palestine a respite.

Felix, however, was called to the Transport Office and told to see that his passport was in order. Hundreds of English people caught in the Middle East by war had now to be sent home. He said he was in no hurry, but the authorities seemed to think the sooner the civilians went the better.

Although he was disturbed and depressed at the thought of leaving Mrs Ellis, he was also a little excited and a little afraid. Pictures of England he had long forgotten began to come complete and brilliant into his mind.

He saw the crescent where he and his mother had had their flat in Bath. The houses had been massive and columned like classical buildings, but in his imagination they hung upon the grey English atmosphere like drawings on tissue paper. He had been a little boy then – seven or eight; he had had a bicycle. He saw clearly his own red knees as he sped round the crescent. There were football-boots tied on his handle-bars. When he rode out through the town he had always gazed up from among the streets to see the near hills with their smooth, misted vistas of greensward and the smoky tree shapes crowding round great columned house fronts. Suddenly, walking in the hot, sun-shrill Jerusalem streets, he smelt the English autumn. He came to a stop, feeling upon his hands the damp-cold and seeing the blue drift of wood smoke, the patch of squelching mud at the field-gate; the red of the boys' jerseys and the red berry clusters among the brown and yellow leaves. When he came to himself and realized how far away were these things, a nostalgia overwhelmed him. There had been Christmas. That came to him as something experienced indoors with the outside world green and wet. He saw logs on the fire, the glinting tree and, again, his mother. Without her, of course, Christmas would be another thing. At some time he must have seen snow, for the memory of the Jerusalem snow seemed to echo a memory of England. Then, realizing that one day Jerusalem would be only a memory, he felt regret for it . . . But this went when he saw – where had he seen it? – a flat field with a flat stream turning like a looking-glass snake between the pollarded willows. Although he was nervous of the distant country that had ceased to be familiar to him, he could remember how, neither privileged nor resented as he was here, he had once belonged there . . . But he had had his mother then; now, perhaps, it would be different. Perhaps he would take back with him a quality of strangeness; he might find he no longer belonged; he might be resented. He was touched by a nausea of apprehension and he wished he were not going alone. If only Mrs Ellis were going with him! Caught between desire to go and stay, nervous and alone, he made a desperate appeal to her:

'Do try and come on my boat. It'd be such fun.'

She shrugged vaguely and said: 'Oh, I don't want to go back so soon. I believe it's misery having a baby in England these days.'

Then, as time passed and no word came from the Transport Office, these thoughts and memories faded from his mind. But it was as though his life had been disturbed at the roots and would not settle into Palestine soil again. He did not find Mrs Ellis as satisfying a companion as he had done: her voice sometimes sounded harsh and unfriendly: her judgments hard. He knew now she was often bored with his company. Small, unimportant events could fill him with irritation so that he began to wonder, if, like the man in the wool shop, he was suffering from living on top of a mountain.

One day as he was working in his room, he heard an unusual rustle among the mulberry leaves below his window. Looking out, he saw that a Bedu woman and her brats were filling some large, flat baskets with mulberries. One boy, up in the tree, was dropping mulberries in handfuls to another. Three girls spaced round the tree were picking at a great rate, as though they meant to strip the branches. One small child was tearing off handfuls of the lower leaves and berries and scattering them about the ground. The baskets were nearly full.

Felix felt indignation swelling in his throat. As he leant from the window to shout he could scarcely get the words out: 'Yallah, yallah!' The woman gave him a casual glance, then they all picked the faster. Felix shouted again, and when they still ignored him, he ran from his room. Rage seemed to transport him in a flash into the garden. He expected the whole family to bolt at the sight of him, but the children took no notice at all. The mother, twisting her face in a second into a mask of whining misery, stuck out a thin, dirty arm with a jangle of silver bracelets and began to beg. The small child, copying the attitude of its mother, began to beg, too, but the other children snatched the last of the berries within their reach. The boy up the tree stuffed his last handful into his mouth. The tree looked torn and naked.

'Oh, yallah! Go on – yallah!' raged Felix and ran at the boy under the tree, who was about his own age. The boy darted off nimbly: his brother slid down and away. The woman and the girls, making no haste, propped the edges of their baskets on to their hips and adjusted their headcloths before trudging off leisurely to start selling the fruit in the main street.

Felix watched them helplessly. It was only when they had gone that he noticed Nikky lying full-length on the seat beneath the tree, open-eyed and gazing up through the pale, translucent leaves at the top. In his anger he forgot his usual deference towards Nikky and said:

'Didn't you see that crowd of Bedu stealing the mulberries?'

Nikky twitched his shoulders: 'Mulberries,' he yawned, 'a worthless fruit. Now, in Poland, we have raspberries...'

'I like mulberries,' Felix broke in and would not stay to hear about the Polish raspberries. When he returned to the sitting-room, he saw Miss Bohun coming downstairs and, sure of her approval, said: 'There was a crowd of Bedu stealing the mulberries. I drove them away.'

Miss Bohun clicked her tongue but she did not seem much concerned. 'It happens every year,' she said, 'you can do nothing with the Bedu. If you drive them off now they're back early in the morning before you're awake. But it's such a big tree. Thank goodness there's enough fruit for everyone. I often have to give it away; but I always feel that whatever I give comes back in some other way. If I let the Bedu take the mulberries, God will give me something much more useful in return.'

Felix, listening to this, on top of his indignation, felt at once irritated and in the wrong. He was relieved that Mrs Ellis, when she heard of the incident, was as indignant as he was. She said: 'Those disgusting Bedu. It's not only that they strip all the mulberries, but they tear the tree to pieces.'

They were both fond of the tree that, heavy in foliage now, was a refuge from the growing heat.

Sitting hidden beneath it, only a few yards from the open door of the house, they could overhear Miss Bohun giving a lesson or talking on the telephone. In this way they discovered she was organizing a new 'Ever-Ready' entertainment. Parts were being apportioned and pupils were required not only to buy tickets, but to sell them.

'Now I rely on you, Mr Liftshitz,' her voice came one afternoon through the door, 'to take four tickets for your family and I hope you will sell two more to your mother-in-law.'

'Ach, no,' breathed Mr Liftshitz nervously, 'I cannot my mother-in-law make buy any such things.'

'Nonsense, Mr Liftshitz. I'm sure you would succeed if you kept poking her.'

Mr Liftshitz, murmuring and sighing, was hustled from the room and went out of the garden gate with the tickets in his hand.

One pupil, a Greek, counter-attacked by asking Miss Bohun to help organize an entertainment that would bring in money for the Greek refugees encamped, she said, in misery down at Rafah. The appeal grew impassioned and was not brief. Miss Bohun apparently did not interrupt it, but when it was over she replied in coolly measured words: 'I would like to help you, Madame Babayannis, but I am forced to think of others. My time belongs to many things. First, of course, to the "Ever-Readies", then to my lodgers; fifteen hours a week of my time belongs to my pupils; it does not belong to me. And then I have this house – some of my time belongs to that. Besides, I know how much organization costs. I feel I owe it to myself never to take on that sort of thing without payment. It would not be fair to my other commitments.' There was a pause during which Madame Babayannis must have sorted out this reply, for her voice came in a sudden explosion: 'Ah, Miss Bohun, this is a new thing – the property of time.'

'I don't quite know what you mean by that curious phrase, Madame Babayannis. I have told you before that your English is good, but you tend to run before you can walk. Well, now – if time is a property, it is a valuable property, and we must not waste it like this.'

The Greek woman's voice cut in with the impatience of anger: 'That, Miss Bohun, is what you call in English, "the snub", is it not? But I am not accepting it. You live here – how? In an Eiffel Tower. You know nothing of the sufferings of my peoples . . .'

'I cannot discuss the sufferings of Greece today,' Miss Bohun interrupted with businesslike decision, 'I have no time to waste. If you do not wish to continue your lesson then I must . . .'

'Ah! You are well known, if I may say so.' Madame Babayannis in her turn interrupted with a cold intensity: 'Is there anyone who does not speak of you for this thing? For instance, do you know one Gradenwitz?'

'Gradenwitz! Never heard of him.'

'Did he prune trees for you? Yes or no?'

'Oh, that man! What has he got to do with the sufferings of Greece?'

'Nothing. He works for a Greek lady and thus I learned this Gradenwitz was shocked at the little you pay your Arab gardener.'

'Really, Madame Babayannis, *really!*' In her indignation Miss Bohun sounded out of breath: 'I refuse to be discussed in this way behind my back.'

'We are discussed without our permission, Miss Bohun. And I may say, the comment was made in company that so mean a pay goes ill with so much religiosity.'

Miss Bohun's voice and phrasing changed now as she felt herself at a loss: 'You don't know the facts. The gardener hardly does any work at all – really, I have to work almost as hard as he does keeping him at it. You don't know the trouble I have driving him all the time . . .'

'Then why do you keep him?' rapped Madame Babayannis remorselessly.

Miss Bohun regained herself as she answered this one: 'Because I have a theory one must support the aged. It is a duty. And now your hour is up, Madame; no doubt my next pupil is in the courtyard. So, good afternoon.'

While this conversation had gone on, its subject, the gardener, with fat, good-natured face sweat-slimy, was idly plucking off some withered leaves. When Madame Babayannis darted out from the door, he started to pick wildly, but seeing it was not Miss Bohun, he stopped and straightened himself with groans, and smiled, preparing to salute her. Her face looked dark and puckered. Mrs Ellis called to her. She swung round aggressively.

Mrs Ellis passed through the mulberry branches into her view and said: 'Would you let me help with your concert for the Greek refugees? When is the date?'

Madame Babayannis was too angry to give thanks, but she glanced at the tickets in her hands and said sharply: 'August 9th.'

'Isn't that the date of Miss Bohun's "Every-Ready" entertainment?'

Madame Babayannis was a small, thin woman, without charm. She replied: 'Yes – it is here on her tickets and now I fix mine for the same. If you can sell tickets for me, I will send them gladly.'

'I'll do my best.'

As Madame Babayannis stumped off out of the garden, Miss Bohun called on a high and pleasant note from the sitting-room door: 'Oh, Mrs Ellis, I wonder if you could spare a moment.'

Inside the room, Miss Bohun spoke quietly to Mrs Ellis, so Felix, straining his ears, could catch only the operative words, 'disloyalty', and 'Lady Evelina Lundy'. Mrs Ellis's reply, when it came, was in her normal voice:

'Oh no, Miss Bohun, I'm afraid I cannot move back to the King David. I can't afford it, but in any case I have no intention of moving from here or of giving up the chance of getting this house in the autumn. Also, I know Evelina Lundy. She's a thoroughly decent person. If she heard you'd turned me out to accommodate her, she would refuse to come here. You'd be left without anyone.'

Miss Bohun, replying, spoke now with less restraint: 'I am not turning you out for Lady Evelina Lundy, Mrs Ellis. There is no question of such a thing. I simply consider you an unsuitable tenant. When I took you in, you did not let me know you were going to have a baby. I have this young relative here – a boy, little more than a child. Really, you must see how unsuitable it is! And then, to add to it all, you take him off to . . . to low drinking dens where he listens to the most improper conversations. All this behind my back! I feel I'm deceived on all sides. I've always been a judge of people; I have an instinct about them – I am a genius in a rather unimportant and unobtrusive way; anyone who can handle people as I do, must be – but I would not have *dreamt* you could be capable of such depravity. The corruption of youth, Mrs Ellis, is a dreadful thing. Depravity is the only word I can find for it,' she paused in her growing excitement, then repeated: 'Depravity,' as though only a special emphasis could give it the meaning she had in mind.

'This is all nonsense . . .' Mrs Ellis was half-laughing, half out of patience, but Miss Bohun broke in, not listening:

'You'll *have* to find another lodging. I won't have this sort of thing going on under my roof.'

'What sort of thing?' demanded Mrs Ellis, but Miss Bohun in a mounting hysteria of annoyance still continued as though she heard nothing: 'Felix is only a boy. He's my dead foster-brother's child. It's my duty to protect him . . . I just won't have you here . . .' she broke off as she suddenly noticed Felix now standing in the doorway: 'Please go away, Felix,' she said irritably, 'this is a private conversation.'

But Felix was not to be dismissed. He was filled with an exalted sense of purpose that gave him rights in the grown-up world: he spoke with the dramatic force he had so often heard issue from the cinema screen: 'If Mrs Ellis goes, I go.'

159

Unfortunately, however, he got no more than a moment's attention, then Mrs Ellis gave his shoulder a push so that he stumbled back off the step on to the gravel: 'Don't be silly,' she said, 'I'm not going. If Miss Bohun wants another lodger, she can let the front room.'

'How dare you mention . . .' began Miss Bohun, but now it was her turn to be over-ridden. Mrs Ellis, continued, completely out of patience: 'All this nonsense about the Second Coming. True religion should give practical results. "I was naked and ye fed me; I was hungry and ye took me in." Here I am a widow. I'm pregnant, and I look it. If Miss Bohun turns me out, I shall jolly well see that the whole of Jerusalem . . .'

Mrs Ellis stopped as Miss Bohun's face began to work tragically before collapsing in tears: 'This is the return I get! I throw open my doors . . . I . . . I . . . And you, Felix. *You* of all people!' Unable to say more, she turned and felt her way towards the stairs. As she went she sobbed so loudly, the others knew that to speak themselves would be a waste of effort.

11

When Felix next set out to see Mr Jewel, his mind was full of the state of affairs at the house. They depressed him deeply and yet there was no one with whom he could discuss them. Mrs Ellis was so clearly avoiding him that he had not the courage to go to the Innsbruck. As for Miss Bohun, she behaved as though he did not exist. She took her meals in complete silence and when he discovered that anything he said was ignored, he sat bored and miserable, isolated in bleak consciousness that he had somehow got himself into the wrong with everyone. When he had announced: 'If Mrs Ellis goes, I go,' he thought he was being very impressive, but no one had been impressed, and he had done no good at all.

Now there was only Mr Jewel to whom he could talk. The sunshine and regular meals had so improved Mr Jewel that Felix felt he could now risk his discovery that the attic was no longer empty. Mr Jewel had put on some weight; he was sunburnt; he moved with briskness and decision, and he looked ten years younger than he had done in the summer. He enjoyed being looked after; he enjoyed the fuss the nurses made of him and he enjoyed having his leg pulled by the young policemen, but he had moments of gloom, knowing he could not stay there for ever. Sometimes he complained to Felix that a chap needed a roof of his own. He himself needed somewhere where he could do a bit of painting when he felt like it.

Felix had offered to bring his paint-pot, brushes and pieces of board to the hospital, but Mr Jewel said: No, he liked to feel they were there to go back to. It was as though he imagined they were keeping his place for him.

Felix wondered why Mr Jewel did not take the short walk down the hill to Herod's Gate and tackle Miss Bohun on the subject of his attic and his return. He did go out sometimes, to buy a paper or his weekly ounce of tobacco, and Felix had seen him once gazing into the window of a small shop that still had some artists' materials at scarcity prices, but it was as though an invisible barrier kept him from approaching the house. Once Felix had mentioned to Miss Bohun that he had seen Mr Jewel walking in the Jaffa Road and Miss Bohun had said with an air of self-congratulation: 'No one whom I befriend ever has cause for complaint. There's Mr Jewel living at the hospital as though it were an hotel, free to come and go, paying almost nothing, I'm told; and there's Frau Leszno in a splendid job. And neither of them ever comes near me to say "thank you".'

'Shall I ask Mr Jewel to come and see you?' Felix asked mischievously. Miss Bohun replied with composure: 'There's no need. He knows he will be very welcome any time he cares to drop in.'

Today Felix found Mr Jewel sitting out on a wooden seat in the paved, tree-planted square that was overlooked on three sides by hospital windows. The sun felt very strong here, but Mr Jewel, in an old shrunken tussore suit, sat blinking contentedly in the hottest corner of the yard. As soon as Felix arrived he started talking. Nowadays he was always full of the gossip of his companions in the ward, the young policemen, suffering from dysentery or bullet wounds, who came and went. This usually related to the growing tension in Palestine and the belief that one day soon there would be a special shot, a special bomb explosion – not the sort of thing that happened every day, but something significant – and, as Mr Jewel put it, 'all hell'ud be let loose'. He often swore he had heard shots at night out in the dark spaces of the Russian Compound. Last night in the silent sleeping hours there had suddenly been the ringing of a telephone and then footsteps hurrying along the stone corridors. Just when everyone was half asleep again, the ambulance had swung into the courtyard. 'What happened last night?' he had asked the nurses in the morning. They told him a Government official driving up late from Tel-Aviv had been caught in an ambush.

'Shot through the shoulder,' said Mr Jewel with sombre relish. 'If they get many more of 'em, they'll be turning me out. They'll want my bed; it stands to reason. Anyway I can't stay here for ever.'

'Where will you go?' Felix put a test question.

'Dunno,' said Mr Jewel and Felix was certain he knew he could not return to Miss Bohun's.

Felix said suddenly: 'There's another lady in the house now.'

'What!' said Mr Jewel loudly, 'not in my attic?'

It was as though the attic had become a joke they both understood, but Felix was glad to evade a reply that told him more than: 'Oh, no; she's not in the attic.'

Mr Jewel gave a shout of laughter: 'So she's let the front room, has she?'

Felix said: 'Well, Miss Bohun wants her to leave, and she says she won't.'

'She won't, eh? Good for her.' Mr Jewel seemed to think the matter a tremendous joke, but Felix remained serious.

'This lady's called Mrs Ellis and she's very nice. She's a widow. Her husband was a rear-gunner and he was killed and she's going to have a baby. Miss Bohun promised to let her have the whole house in the autumn. Now Miss Bohun wants her to go so she can get in another lady. But it's not funny, Mr Jewel, it's not fair. I said: "If Mrs Ellis goes, I go."'

'Did you!' Mr Jewel sobered at once, the first person to take this declaration as it was meant to be taken.

'Yes, but Mrs Ellis just pushed me out of the door and now Miss Bohun won't speak to me.'

'Don't let it worry you,' said Mr Jewel comfortingly.

'But why is she like this? Why is she so beastly to Mrs Ellis?'

Mr Jewel shook his head: 'Ah, she'll get over it.'

'She made Frau Leszno go and . . .' but Felix had to pause unable to make the further point that she had made Mr Jewel go, too.

'Well, Frau Leszno was a mean-spirited creature, I'd've got rid of her myself. But Miss Bohun – she's not a bad sort, you know. Not a bad sort.'

Felix remained silent. His feelings about Miss Bohun were changing – or, rather, not so much changing, he felt, as appearing out of a cloud of illusion. He could not agree that Miss Bohun was not a bad sort. He said:

'If it weren't silly to speak of people being wicked, I'd say she was wicked.'

'Ar, no,' Mr. Jewel shook his head again, 'to be wicked you've got to have wicked *intentions*. Now, can you say she's got wicked intentions? Can you?'

Felix did not reply. He felt no confidence in Miss Bohun's intentions. He wondered why Mr Jewel should comdemn Frau Leszno and yet stand up so stoutly for Miss Bohun. Somewhere in his mind he found himself suspecting the single-mindedness of Mr Jewel's loyalty. Miss Bohun had, after all, power to take him back or reject him. Felix put this suspicion aside almost at once, but he was left with the conviction that Mr Jewel was rather simple; perhaps he was simple because he was old. It seemed clear to Felix, from some of the things he had heard his mother and Mr Jewel say, that they had grown up in a simpler world; and, being simpler, a world in which hypocrisy had had things all its own way. But it didn't have things all its own way with Mrs Ellis and Felix. Oh no! They were young and knowing; they saw through Miss Bohun. This satisfactory conclusion, now reached, was jolted rather askew by Mr Jewel's next remark:

'The trouble with her,' he said, 'is that no one's ever loved her.'

'Oh,' said Felix; that was, of course, a new aspect of the case, but he could not consider it with much sympathy. 'Probably her own fault,' he said.

'I don't know. I don't know as love always goes to the most deserving.'

'Well, then, why hasn't anyone loved her?'

'I don't know. Do you love her?'

'No.'

'Why don't you?'

Felix opened his mouth to say: 'Because she doesn't love me,' but he thought that sounded childish: he wasn't a baby that had to be loved, so he said: 'She was kind to me; she gave me a home. Perhaps I would have – well, liked her, anyway – but I don't think she wanted me to. I'm not sure that's what she wants.'

'What else could she want?'

Felix did not know. On reflection he had to admit that Miss Bohun was beyond the range of his understanding. 'Perhaps she isn't a hypocrite,' he said. 'Or, perhaps . . .' and here he felt he was being really profound, 'perhaps she is and she doesn't know.'

164

Mr Jewel drew his eyebrows together and was about to make some comment when the luncheon bell rang and he got up hastily. 'Mustn't miss me grub,' he said.

As Mr Jewel went into the hospital, Mrs Ellis came out and was unable to pretend she did not see Felix at the door. She said: 'Hello,' without enthusiasm.

'Where are you going?' he asked.

'To get a meal somewhere.'

'Can I come with you?'

'I think you'd better not. Children nowadays seem to be so easily corrupted.'

'I didn't tell her anything . . .'

'I didn't know there was anything to tell.' Mrs Ellis turned and started walking to the gate, but she did not prevent Felix from following her.

'I didn't say there was anything to tell.' Felix was bewildered and wretched at this blame being put upon him. 'Do let me come with you!'

'Oh!' she made a small, petulant movement that suddenly made him see her not as the experienced grown-up he had always supposed her to be, but a girl; someone not much more grown-up than he was himself. He realized that, under her confident manner, life was probably as difficult for her as for him. He felt sorry for her. 'Please let me come,' he said.

She replied crossly: 'All right.' He did not know whether she was cross with him or merely wrapped up in herself and her pregnancy. She looked ill and tired. As they walked down through the crowded, hot main road her face grew damp and strained.

He said anxiously: 'You won't leave the house, will you?'

'I wouldn't please the old bitch.'

After that neither of them spoke until they reached the restaurant door, then she said: 'You can come in if you like.'

Another time Felix would have been delighted by this invitation, but now, feeling himself unwanted, he followed only because convinced that it was not his fault his friendship with Mrs Ellis had gone wrong: if he stayed with her long enough, the situation might be explained to her, he might justify himself, her anger might be dispelled and everything be as it had been before. But

Mrs Ellis showed no sign of doing the one thing that might start the process – directly accusing him. She looked at the menu blankly: there was only the controlled-price meal with very little choice: she ordered, not consulting Felix. When the waiter went off, Felix tried to start a discussion that should have interested them both: 'Mr Jewel says that no one loves Miss Bohun.'

'Are you expecting me to contradict that statement?'

'No, but I mean – he thinks that's what's wrong with her.'

Mrs Ellis gave an acid little laugh; she started fumbling in her bag for her cigarettes and matches, murmuring as she did so, not very distinctly:

> 'And we are put on earth a little space,
> That we may learn to bear the beams of love.'

Felix leant towards her and said: 'What did you say?'

She laughed again, more pleasantly: 'Don't you know that poem? I thought everyone learnt it at school,' and as she put her matches and her squashed packet of Camels on the table, she recited:

> 'Look on the rising sun – there God does live,
> And gives His light, and gives His heat away;
> And flowers and trees and beasts and men receive
> Comfort in morning, joy in the noonday.
> And we are put on earth a little space,
> That we may learn to bear the beams of love...'

Noticing his troubled, puzzled face, she broke off and said: 'Don't you know it?'

'No. Do go on. I don't know any poetry. My mother didn't like it much. She once said it was nonsense.'

'Oh!' her tone and expression implied she was not going to be drawn into any further criticism of his mother; she said in an offhand way: 'Well, that piece is something more than sense.'

'What does it mean?'

'I suppose it means that life is a sort of school for love.'

'But is it a ... what you said?' After a pause, he repeated self-consciously: 'A school for love?'

She shrugged her shoulders but would not speak. She swallowed in her throat: he thought her eyes were aswim but she shut them so quickly, he could not tell for sure. He felt completely mystified. He wondered if his experience could ever widen enough to bring within his understanding anyone who behaved and talked as Mrs Ellis did. One thing he did know, it would be useless to ask her for an explanation of herself.

At last he ventured to beg: 'Please recite it again,' but she shook her head and lit a cigarette. Knowing her obstinacy, he could only revert to Miss Bohun.

'Do you think that's what's wrong with her?'

'I don't know.' Mrs Ellis put out her match with irritable decision. 'If it is, she's past saving now. She's a frustrated, spiteful, power-mad old so-and-so. No amount of love could unpack that bundle of neuroses.'

Felix sighed unhappily. He felt Mrs Ellis's to be an extreme judgment: he was worried by her anger and the violence of emotion he felt beneath it. His mother had shown him nothing like this. In reaction he found himself about to repeat Mr Jewel's words: 'Miss Bohun's not a bad sort, really,' but he stopped himself, feeling that that was not true either.

After luncheon they went down to the bar below. The counter was shut: the small room was hot and stuffy and smelt of stale tobacco smoke, but it was somewhere to sit out of the afternoon heat. She said to Felix: 'What about your lessons?'

He said: 'I haven't anything much.'

'And what about Faro?'

'She'll be all right. Maria always feeds her.'

Mrs Ellis settled in a corner to read a book called *Put Out More Flags* and to smoke her way through her cigarettes. Felix read a shabby copy of the *Palestine Post* someone had left on the floor. He could not bring himself to leave Mrs Ellis, and when at last she decided it was tea-time he trailed after her to a tea-shop. After that they wandered slowly about the streets as the shops closed and the lights came on through the delicately coloured summer twilight. Now that the black-out was lifted, the streets were alive after dark and the café gardens were packed with people. Mrs Ellis took Felix to a large garden behind Zion Circus and bought wine for herself and lemonade for him.

'Aren't you going to the Innsbruck?'

'I don't know. I'm rather tired of it.'

167

Felix's heart leapt as though the fact that she was tired of the Innsbruck should reconcile her to him, but she showed no more interest in him and it was clear she was indifferent to his company. They were sitting near some coloured electric lights so she was able to read her book again; she seemed to find it funny, but when Felix urged her to tell him the jokes, she ignored him. At last she said: 'Shouldn't you go back to supper?'

He would not move. He said: 'I'm not really hungry.'

'Well,' she said with resignation, 'I suppose we can get something here.' She ordered an omelette for each of them.

Mrs Ellis finished her book and there was nothing to do, yet they sat around doing nothing until nearly eleven o'clock: then they walked home slowly. Felix, reflecting on the complete emptiness of the day that, despite her company, had stupefied him with boredom, supposed even that was better than not seeing her at all. When they got back to the house and she was about to enter her room, he tried to pin her down to another similar day.

He said: 'I say, what time are you going out to-morrow?'

'My dear boy, how on earth do I know?' She closed the door on him before he could speak again.

When he got into his own room he saw that Faro was not lying, as she always lay, on his bed. There was no dent on the counterpane and when he touched it, no warmth. He felt a sudden premonition of loss that was the more acute because of the frightening justice of its happening on this very day when he had left her so long alone. But perhaps she had merely grown tired of waiting for him. He had to find her. He could not sleep if he did not find her. He leant from the window calling her name. There was no rustle or movement in the garden below. He ran downstairs and looked for her in the room. She was not there. Then he went out in the pale starlight and found his way around the garden. He sensed the emptiness of her absence. He knew she was not there. He felt acute fear at the thought she might have run away, that she might have been stolen, that she might be dead. At last in despair he returned to his room and lay in bed, tensed and listening for any noise that might mean her return. At the back of his fear there was a desolation of guilt. He had been told that Siamese cats could not live without love – and since Mrs Ellis's arrival he had often forgotten Faro. He imagined her feeling deserted, suffering as he had suffered when his mother died. He was desolated in pity and self-accusation.

He slept at last, but woke early with the sense of some unbearable misery weighing upon him. As soon as Miss Bohun appeared at breakfast he said at once: 'I can't find Faro.'

She said: 'I must speak seriously to you, Felix. Yesterday you did not come in for lunch, tea or dinner. I was very . . .'

He interrupted her to ask: 'Where is Faro?'

'If you ask politely, I will be happy to reply.'

'Oh, Miss Bohun, *please*, where is Faro?'

'She has gone,' said Miss Bohun, brightly informative, taking her seat at the table.

'Gone? Where?'

'I have given her away.'

'But you can't,' Felix found it difficult to speak. He stammered painfully: 'You didn't say anything . . .'

'Did I have to say anything? You forget Faro is my cat.'

Felix, not knowing what to say, stood at the table, gazing at Miss Bohun with an expression of such dismay that an explanation seemed to be forced from her: 'She's gone to Madame Sarkis, who has a male Siamese. She'll come to no harm and one day perhaps, if you're a sensible boy, we'll have her back again.'

'Where does Madame Sarkis live?'

'Sit down, Felix,' there was an appeal in her voice to which he refused to listen. 'I'll take you to see her if . . .'

As Felix started over towards the door, Miss Bohun raised her voice: 'Sit down and have your breakfast.' He took no notice. 'Felix!' she suddenly paused him with a command and then changed her tone. 'Really, it is too bad. This is my house, but you'd think I was a nobody. Mrs Ellis refuses to leave when I ask her to go; you don't come in for your meals; you don't warn me – food is wasted. Now your breakfast – there's a fried egg, too. All the trouble of running this house and yet I'm treated like a mere – a mere housekeeper. Now, don't be a silly boy. You forget Faro is a cat, and a female. She's coming into season.'

Felix, paused by the table, turned on her a mystified face. He could feel no reassurance in her change of tone: he was fearful and filled with distrust. For a moment, seeing her sitting there calmly and running at will through the gamut of her tones of command, exasperation, self-pity and disapproval, he was suddenly certain of her falsity. His faith in her as a human being had gone and he could believe her to be capable of anything – perhaps even of cruelty to Faro or indifference were Faro suffering. He remembered suddenly the burning rats in the cage and an agony of apprehension seized him – but Miss Bohun, flicking up her eyelids in a momentary glance, saw only his bewilderment and she said with satisfaction:

'There! You see, you don't know what I mean by "coming into season". You think you're so clever, but really you're only an ignorant little boy. You don't know anything. Now have your breakfast.'

With a quick movement Felix got out of the room into the courtyard and closed the door after him. It had been in his mind to ask Nikky about Madame Sarkis, but he was afraid to stop so near the house for fear Miss Bohun caught him. He hurried out to the road and then made his way at a half-run to the Innsbruck, where he might get Madame Sarkis's address from one of Nikky's friends. There was no one there. He could, he supposed, ask Mr Posthorn at the Educational Offices, but he was due there for a lesson that morning so he could not risk being caught. He decided to try the General Post Office, where he stood in a queue for twenty minutes before he reached the counter.

'This is not an Enquiry Counter,' said the assistant, a young man with the hauteur that characterized junior members of the Administration.

But Felix, holding to his place and refusing to be pushed on by the person behind, said urgently: 'Haven't you a book or something you could look up? It's very important.'

Fortunately the young man was a Christian Arab so knew where each rich and important Christian Arab family was to be found. He jerked his head to his right and replied: 'She's in the Greek Colony. Ask down there.'

As Felix went, his relief and gratitude were so great he could scarcely control his tears. He hurried down through the olive groves to the German Colony. The day was already growing hot and a slight haze hung over the pink, stony hills with their patches of green-silver olives. In the main road of the German Colony he slackened his speed a little, to regain his breath. Here the houses, built by a German sect that like the 'Ever-Readies' had settled in Jerusalem to await the Second Coming, stood back behind trees. The road was heavily powdered with dust. Felix walked through the dust heaped at the verges silently as through sand. It rose in puffs over his shoes and coloured them fawn. The gardens were dry with summer but there was a delicate herbal fragrance in the air that came perhaps from the rosemary or the sticky, blue plumbago flowers that survived the early summer.

There was no one about. There was no noise except the hum of insects, monotonous as silence, and the thump, thump from the ice factory over by the railway line. The windows of the houses, half-hidden by trees, had the watchful look of windows behind which people are asleep. Felix started to hurry again, fearful because he could see no one from whom to enquire about Madame Sarkis. He could hear in the distance a thud of tennis balls, but the players were out of sight. He began to fear he might have passed the house. He was uncertain where the German Colony ended and the Greek Colony began. At last he came on a small café where two tables stood out on the pavement beneath red umbrellas. No one was sitting at the tables. A fat man leaning at the counter moved his face enquiringly when Felix entered, but when asked about Madame Sarkis, he shrugged his shoulders indifferently and looked the other way.

'What? What is it you are asking?' A young woman came from the inside room, 'Madame Sarkis? An Arab lady, no? Yes, you turn up the road there and on, on to the top.'

At last, at the top of the road, Felix wakened an Arab sleeping against a wall. The man opened one eye and waved vaguely at the garden within the wall.

'Aywah, Madame Sarkis, henna.'

As Felix went up the path between the rockeries and flower-beds, he repeated to himself: 'I love Faro; I love Faro; I love Faro better than anyone,' and that got him safely to the front door of the large, ugly house.

Felix knew and cared nothing about Madame Sarkis or her importance in the Arab social and political world. For him she was merely someone who had his Faro and, having her, might be induced to treat her well. He was let into the house by an Arab servant and left on a seat in the hall. The house was dark and very cool after the outer heat. Felix sat shivering slightly as he gazed up the mahogany staircase and at the panelled walls opposite him on which hung an enormous steel-engraving of a stag lifting its cry across a frozen waste. He felt concerned for Faro in this gloomy house. He stood up as Madame Sarkis, dressed in black and leaning on a silver-headed cane, came slowly down the stairs from the dark and cavernous heights. Without smiling, she came to a standstill opposite Felix and looked steadily at him, her head quivering all the time. She looked and spoke like an elderly English lady. Yes, she assured him, Faro was there. Would he like to see her?

In silence they moved at her pace across the black-and-white marble chequer-board of the hall into a mahogany dining-room full of massive furniture. How could Faro be happy here? But they went out through french windows into the garden at the back and Madame Sarkis lifted her stick and pointed to the glitter of a conservatory: 'I keep her in there,' she said. 'She likes the warmth and the plants.'

Felix let out his breath with relief at this understanding of Faro's tastes. When they reached the conservatory they could see the leaves of the plants pressing against the damp-pearled glass. Inside, the atmosphere, hot and steamy as a jungle, smelt of wet earth. Felix saw Faro at once. She was lying dozing along a bough shaded by ferns. Her fur, extremely soft and fitting like a loose glove, was pressed into folds along her legs and the line of her belly. Her summer coat had come in pale; there was a sheen over her whole body and a glisten of silver-white at her throat.

She was at her most beautiful, the languid leopard-curve of her body tapering off into the four seal-dark paws and seal-dark tail, and the delicate, small, dark mask. His heart leapt as he saw her there, safe after all his fears. Once, he thought, Mrs Ellis had had for him some of the beauty of Faro but now she had lost it. He did not believe any human being could be wholly as beautiful: he did not believe he could love anyone or anything as much. He called: 'Faro,' and she opened her eyes and gave a small, hoarse cry. She stretched her paws and then her whole body.

'Darling little Faro,' he said.

She jumped down to a shelf below and walked towards him, her purring thudding through the air. He lifted her in his arms and felt her fur hot with sunlight, but almost at once her body stiffened, and she broke away and gave a violent peacock squawk of a cry that repeated itself and died away like a bell note. He tried to lift her again but she struggled against him and broke away again. She went off round the conservatory giving sharp, piercing cries.

He looked with alarm at Madame Sarkis: 'What is the matter with her? She must be ill.'

A remote smile touched Madame Sarkis's grey and withered face: 'Oh, no, she is perfectly all right. It will only last a few days.'

'But what is the matter with her?'

'She wants to have some kittens.'

'Oh!' Felix had only the vaguest idea of what connection there was between Faro's wish and her curious behaviour, but he felt hurt and jealous that he had suffered this defection of both his female friends over a question of babies and kittens. He stared sombrely after Faro.

'Will she have some kittens?' he asked.

'Perhaps not the first time. Some day she will. Would you like to see my cat?'

Faro had wandered off, seeming indifferent to him, so they closed her in alone, and went to see the large stud cat with his dark coat and eyes of so deep a colour they were nearer purple than blue. He lay on the rim of a fountain watching the occasional red twitch of a fish's flank. He was not interested in Felix, who thought that compared with Faro, he was a heavy and dull creature.

Walking back to Herod's Gate, Felix began to feel a certain guilt towards Miss Bohun. Miss Bohun had, after all, been right about Faro. Perhaps he had misjudged her in other ways. He felt the more guilty because he himself had not treated Faro so well. No, he had neglected and forgotten her for Mrs Ellis's sake, but it was Faro who loved him. He knew that Mrs Ellis cared nothing for him at all: she would forget him as soon as he was gone. He did not blame her for that, but blamed himself that he had put her first. Perhaps she had not been completely right about Miss Bohun. But, despite his deepest reflection on this point, he could feel no trust in Miss Bohun.

When he got back to the house the luncheon was on the table. Miss Bohun was sitting there as though she had not moved from her seat since he walked out that morning. He was prepared for her anger, but instead she said in a friendly way:

'I suppose you've been to see Madame Sarkis?'

'Yes.'

'And did you see Faro?'

'Yes. Madame Sarkis says perhaps she'll have kittens.'

'Um!' Miss Bohun agreed amiably and added: 'If she does, they'll be quite valuable. I'm told the Peppers paid three pounds for Faro.'

After a long pause Felix asked: 'Would you sell Faro for three pounds?'

Miss Bohun looked less amiable: 'What a strange question!'

'But would you? Would you sell her to me?'

Miss Bohun frowned, and with the old note of exasperation back in her voice, said: 'I don't know. I can't possibly say. I should have to think about it.'

'Would you sell her for six pounds?'

'Really, my dear boy, what is the point of this vulgar bargaining? Faro is my cat, but I've never prevented you from having her in your room and treating her as a pet.'

'But she doesn't know she's your cat. She thinks she's my cat. How could I go and leave her?'

'You're being ridiculous, Felix. No one would think of taking a cat back to England, especially at this time. And as for asking me to sell her! What would people think?' As Felix opened his mouth to say something, she interrupted with decision: 'Faro is my cat. I have no intention of selling her, so please let the matter drop.'

Felix said nothing more then, but the matter remained fixed in his mind. It took on new urgency when, a few days later, he received a note from the Transport Office telling him to stand by for a passage to England. If someone gave up a passage during the next four weeks Felix would be next on the list. In the sudden jolt of seeing his return to England as a reality, he thought only of Faro. He scarcely considered Mrs Ellis now; what did she care for him? and, besides, she could look after herself. But Faro – even if he did not love her as he did – would have to be saved.

She was only a little cat. She could be sold to a stranger or starved or destroyed like the rats. Although he had no reason to suppose Miss Bohun would do those things – no reason except his distrust of her – Felix would take no risk. Anyway, his mind was made up. If Cook's said he could not take her, then he would smuggle her on board. If he were discovered with her and she put ashore, then he would return ashore himself. His determination had an almost mystical quality: he was so transported by it, he was convinced he could overcome any obstacle. But there were not many obstacles to overcome. The official at Cook's took his enquiries mildly. Some people were taking dogs back with them. They had to be quarantined in England. That cost money, of course, but if Felix was prepared to meet the expense and to be responsible for her, there seemed no reason why a cat should not go with him. The liners had been turned into troop transports and perhaps the pets' quarters had been dismantled – if so, there would be nowhere where he could shut her up at night. As a male civilian he would have no cabin. The army officers would have cabins to themselves on 'A' deck; the women and children would sleep about nine a cabin on 'B' deck; the civilian men, of whatever age and rank, would be allotted hammocks with the troops on the lower deck. Felix said that as Faro always slept in his arms, he thought she would be safe enough. And food for her? He was pretty sure he could scrounge something from the galley.

As he worked out his plans and at every step saw difficulties overcome, he began to be filled with a sense of achievement. He had no doubt that when the time came he'd get possession of Faro: he'd steal her if necessary.

As time passed, England became more real in his mind. Jerusalem paled to a shadow. His present was temporary, unimportant and powerless. Miss Bohun and even Mrs Ellis, once great figures blocking his whole horizon, were dwindled now almost out of sight.

He never gave them a thought, so he felt nothing when Miss Bohun broke into his reverie one evening at supper and mentioned a subject she seemed to think important to him:

'I suppose Mrs Ellis is all wrapped up in Madame Babayannis's concert.'

'I don't know.'

'She's quite deserted you, anyway.'

'Yes.'

There was a pause then Miss Bohun commented: 'An odd young woman! I hesitate to think what sort of mother she'll make. I don't know what's going to happen to her at all. She's so unstable, so, so . . . I don't know. She doesn't seem to have roots anywhere.'

'Hasn't she any relations in England?' asked Felix.

'I think not. Of course she's got a father somewhere, but from what I've heard of *him* . . .' Miss Bohun clicked her tongue. The conversation ceased, but, after a long silence, Felix suddenly said:

'I have my uncle in England.'

Miss Bohun, surprised, lifted her eyelashes an instant. 'Your mother's brother,' she said; 'are you attached to him?'

'I can't remember him very well, but he's a vet. He lives in Bath.'

'Are you looking forward to going back to England, Felix?'

'Yes, I am now.'

'Have you been happy here?'

'Oh, yes,' he said without expression, but, after a moment, added, 'thank you, Miss Bohun.'

Later, when he was looking through the cinema advertisements in the *Palestine Post*, Miss Bohun went up to her room and returned with an olive-wood camel, roughly carved, and put it on the table.

'There, that's a present for you.'

'For me?'

'Yes. I thought you might like to collect a few things like that to take home to England with you.'

'Thank you,' he was embarrassed and not pleased. He picked up the camel and looked at it from politeness – he had seen hundreds like it in the shop. His mother, he knew, had despised things like this. 'It's very nice,' he said, not wanting it, not wanting anything from her. Now he knew why Mrs Ellis would not take the gloves. Mrs Ellis had disliked Miss Bohun from the first. He looked up with the best smile he could and Miss Bohun, who had been watching him, looked away at once.

'I wonder,' she asked, 'have you ever thought you might like to stay out here?'

'No,' Felix replied without hesitation. 'Besides, Mr Jewel doesn't think anyone will be able to stay out here much longer. There'll be trouble.'

Her glance shot back at him and he realized how much he had alarmed her. 'But that won't affect us,' she said, 'I'm an Englishwoman. I'm not mixed up in these squabbles. I was here in 1939 when there was a lot of shooting and bombs going off, but we weren't perturbed. With the "Ever-Readies" it was a case of "business as usual".'

She gave a laugh at her own humour and Felix could see Miss Bohun, unlike Mr Jewel, had never given a thought to the problem of the future. He said, in case she should now start worrying: 'Mr Jewel thinks Cyprus a nice place. It's not far and it's warm and cheap. He thinks he'll go there.'

'Cyprus!' said Miss Bohun as though it were as remote as Bermuda, but after a long pause she added less disapprovingly: 'There is a branch of the "Ever-Readies" in Cyprus – in Kyrenia; a charming place I'm told, full of English gentlewomen. The Presiding Brother kept a room there for a while, just in case. There's never any knowing what's going to happen here in wartime. Armageddon, you know. I'm told they nearly had it last time. But I'm sure Mr Jewel is panicking unnecessarily, and, besides, I could never consider leaving my house. It's my *home*. One becomes very attached to a place that belongs to one.'

Felix thought of her promise to let Mrs Ellis rent the house in the autumn: as he wondered how he could remind Miss Bohun of it, his thought must have passed into her mind. She sighed, then clicked her tongue: '*And* there's Mrs Ellis. I really don't know what's to be done about that young woman. I feel a sense of responsibility, though dear knows why I should. And there's her baby! That's another thing. It will be arriving in two or three months. Just one worry after another.'

Felix went several times to see Faro. Madame Sarkis told him he need not ask for permission at the house, but he could walk round and enter the conservatory when he wished. The gardener, having seen him with Madame Sarkis, took no notice of him. Faro had suddenly lost interest in the idea of kittens and had not been mated after all. Felix was pleased about that. It seemed to him that circumstances were all on his side. He took so many trips to Madame Sarkis's house that for a week he forgot all about Mr Jewel. When he went to the hospital again, he saw Miss Bohun, her hands full of pamphlets, hurrying away from it.

As Felix reached the verandah where Mr Jewel sat when it was too hot to go into the garden, he heard the policemen laughing and one of them said with a strong Ulster accent: 'I don't mind an Arab with a gun, but I can't stand a woman with a tract.'

Mr Jewel's eyes were pink and wet with laughter. As soon as he saw Felix, he croaked out joyfully: 'She's been to see me.'

'Miss Bohun?' asked Felix in wonder. 'Really? To see you! Was she friendly?'

'Friendly?' broke in one of the policemen, 'why, I thought she must be his old woman.'

Mr Jewel joined in the laughter, but at the same time he was a little apart; there was a slight self-importance, a slight self-satisfaction in his manner. He pulled Felix towards him and said confidentially: 'She said: "Isn't it about time we saw you home again?" "What," I said, "have you kept my attic for me all this long time?" "Attic?" she said, "that's no place for old bones. I thought of putting you in *my* room."'

A tremendous roar of laughter followed this and Mr Jewel took out his handkerchief and wiped the gummy corners of his eyes.

'Did she really say that?' asked Felix, uncertain whether this was a joke or not.

'And he said,' broke in one of the policemen: '"Wot, in your room with you?"'

When the laughter died down again, Mr Jewel gasped and said: 'And she wasn't annoyed. Believe it or not, we had a bit of a laugh together, and then she said: "Seriously now, Mr Jewel, I'm thinking of letting you have my room and going up to the attic myself." Now, what do you think of that?'

What Felix thought was too complicated to be conveyed to Mr Jewel. From the depths of his mystification, he simply said: 'Did she know you were going to tell me this?'

Mr Jewel suddenly sobered and looked away with a worried movement: 'I forgot. She told me not to mention it. Now, young Felix, I look to you to keep it under your hat. You wouldn't spoil my chances, would you?'

'No,' Felix reassured him, but felt forced to say, 'as a matter of fact, she's been up in the attic herself for a long time. Mrs Ellis has her room.'

'That's right,' said Mr Jewel. 'She said something about having a young woman in the house. She said this young woman was going off to have a baby and she wouldn't be coming back, so the room would be free.'

'I see,' Felix said, and asked with a keen sense of his own practical coolness: 'And will she want you to pay?'

'That's just it.' Mr Jewel started to laugh again with a sort of sobbing excitement. 'She knows I can't pay for that room. She knows as well as I do. What's she up to, eh?'

That was something for which Felix had no answer, but he saw the mechanics of the plot easily enough. When Mrs Ellis went to the hospital to have her baby, Mr Jewel would be brought back to occupy her room. Felix could not see what Miss Bohun would gain by the change, but as he spent the evening wandering about the town, he was agitated by the equal claims to his support of Mr Jewel and Mrs Ellis. Mr Jewel had been an earlier lodger in the house: he was an old man, almost penniless, who, if he lost this opportunity to return, would stand little chance of finding another room. Mrs Ellis, on the other hand, would come out of the hospital with a baby and no home to which to take it. Her position would be bad enough, but, after all, she had some money to make things easier; Mr Jewel had none. But supposing Mr Jewel returned, how long after he had served his purpose would he be permitted to remain? Felix could only hope Miss Bohun would find it more difficult to turn the old man out a second time.

After he had walked for an hour or two he realized there was only one thing he could do. He could warn Mrs Ellis. Warned, she would have time to find a *pension* willing to accept her with her baby – not an easy thing! – or perhaps if she could afford to pay enough key-money she might even find another house. He went to the Innsbruck. She was not there. Nikky and his friends had not arrived. Felix wandered round again looking into shop-windows. There were the funny notices Mrs Ellis had pointed out to him: the trousers marked, 'Source of Trousers'; the notice of a sale in a back room 'Sale only backwards through the Court-yard', and the butcher who said 'I slaughter myself twice dai-ly', but none of those things seemed as funny as they did when she pointed them out.

Suddenly he had another idea and went off at a quick trot to the King David Hotel. He pushed in through the swing-door be-fore he had time to feel afraid. He appeared so sure of himself that no one took any notice of him. He found Mrs Ellis in the conservatory, sitting under the gloom cast by the long, oily green leaves of giant plants. It was getting dark inside, but out through the glass he could see the reflection of the sunset and the green glimmer of the garden.

Mrs Ellis was reading. She did not look up for some moments while he stood beside her: she was sprawling in one basket-chair, her feet on another. She had on high-heeled white shoes and a white linen coat that would not close round her now. Her white-ness flashed with a silken sheen through the half-light, but when she looked up and turned in her seat, she looked heavy and dull. She had stopped cutting her hair and, neither short nor long, it was lank and lifeless. All the dazzle had gone from her and Felix could feel for her only compassion.

She looked cross when she saw him and said: 'Well, what do you want?'

He said: 'I want to tell you something.'

She said nothing at all when he told her his news. He thought perhaps she was completely indifferent to it and after a pause said:

'But perhaps it won't be so difficult to find something. You have a lot of friends.'

She gave a slight, angry laugh and threw her book on to the table so that it slid across the glass to the other side. Felix thought how much she had changed. Her humour had gone: she seemed now to be shut away from him into a chilly irrita-tion.

'Friends!' she echoed and smiled acidly: 'what makes you

think they are friends? I came up with some introductions. Each person invited me to a party. I met the same people at each – then things came to a standstill. They all knew instinctively that I wasn't one of them. The Government people here are graded and each knows what he can and can't do inside his grade – or, rather, his wife does – and who he can invite to his home, and who's going to invite him. It makes things easy for them. You see, they're all people from a small world and things have to be made easy for them – so they can't afford to admit strangers, anyway not strangers who probably won't follow the rules. It complicates things too much.'

'Oh!' said Felix, interested and impressed by this summing up of a situation about which he knew nothing, 'do you mean they thought you wouldn't follow the rules?'

'They knew damned well I wouldn't, especially the women, and how right they were! I go to the Innsbruck, for instance, and no nice English lady would do that. But apart from all that, they didn't want to have me around.'

'But why?' Felix pursued. 'Didn't they like you? I don't understand.'

Mrs Ellis screwed up her mouth to one side, raised her eyebrows a little with one of her old comical movements: 'No. Perhaps because I'm different – and because circumstances have made me different. They've got homes – nice houses, low rents, ordered lives. Here they were, all nicely settled when the war started and here they'll stay till they're blasted out of it. Nothing has happened to them, except food's got a bit short and prices have gone up, but – and this is the funny thing – they seem annoyed about the things that have happened to other people. They seem jealous. One of them going home on leave said: "I wish I'd had a bit of excitement, too," and then offered to rent me her house for twenty-five quid a month. She pays five. One of the old boys, a nice old boy, said: "I don't know what's happened to people these days. Before the war no one would have dreamt of trying to get a profit like that from a friend," but that's the trouble, of course, I'm not a friend. I'm not fixed anywhere in the hierarchy. I'm fair game.'

'So it's no easier for you than for Mr Jewel?'

'Look,' said Mrs Ellis, lighting a cigarette and throwing the match over her shoulder, 'your Mr Jewel's nice and snug in the hospital. No one's going to throw him into the street. I'll soon have a child to worry about.'

'Well, perhaps if you tell Miss Bohun . . .'

Mrs Ellis grunted and then said suddenly: 'I'll walk back with you.' She got up with energy and decision. They walked together to Herod's Gate in the quickly disappearing twilight. The sky, in which the stars were appearing, was a pure green and from behind the great Damascus Gate came a bloom of light as the flares were lit in the market. Felix thought how exciting it used to seem going out with Mrs Ellis. Now, returning home with her, he felt slightly sick with apprehension of the scene that might occur when they arrived. Miss Bohun would blame him of course – not without justice – and she would blame poor old Mr Jewel. He could not imagine why Mrs Ellis need come back now to speak to Miss Bohun. There was no question of her leaving for some weeks . . . Then, from her silence, the nervous restlessness of her hands and the quick movements with which she was smoking her cigarette, he realized she was so possessed by anger that she had to attack something straight away, and she was going to attack the obvious person, Miss Bohun.

He said hopefully: 'She may not be there. She may be at the "Ever-Readies".'

Mrs Ellis took no notice of him. She was walking quickly and breathing heavily, her high heels clicking like tric-trac ivories on the tarmac. Nikky passed them with one of the Arab boys on his way to the Innsbruck. The Arab called gaily:

'Ah, Mrs Ellis, how you make haste!' but she seemed neither to see nor hear.

The light was on in the sitting-room: the table was set for supper. Miss Bohun was not yet down. Mrs Ellis gave the room a glance, swung round and went up the stairs without slackening her speed. Felix, helpless and miserable, followed her. As they ascended, Miss Bohun descended from her attic. They met on the landing.

Mrs Ellis, breathless, her voice having about it a sort of glow and confidence of fury, said: 'There you are, Miss Bohun! I hear you are plotting to let my room. I thought I'd let you know you are wasting your time. I have planned to have the baby here. Dr

Klaus is coming to the house and I'm having a nurse in. We are going to fix up a camp-bed and the nurse will stay with me for a few nights. Then she'll come in daily.'

Mrs Ellis had to pause for breath, and in that instant Miss Bohun raised her eyelids and looked at Felix. He looked away, expecting her to accuse him of making trouble, but instead she said mildly and pleasantly:

'Felix, go downstairs like a good boy and ring the bell for supper.'

As Felix went slowly down he could hear Mrs Ellis repeating, breathlessly and angrily, what she had said before.

'I thought I'd let you know you're not getting rid of me so easily.'

Felix lifted the bell, but held the clapper in his hand. He felt that to ring it would be an insult to Mrs Ellis, a sort of demonstration of fidelity to Miss Bohun.

Miss Bohun's voice was still mild, but her pleasantness had about it a quiet venom: 'I thought when I saw you there was something about you . . . something vulgar and immoral . . .'

Mrs Ellis broke in furiously: 'I wouldn't bring up morality or immorality, if I were you, Miss Bohun. What about you? A hypocrite, a liar, a cheat, a dirty-minded old maid . . .'

There was a sound of a slap, though who hit who Felix never discovered. He saw Mrs Ellis's heels slip off the edge of the stairs, then she tottered backwards into his view. She never actually fell, but somehow came from top to bottom of the stairs in a series of distorted movements, reeling from one side to the other, struggling to keep her balance, her face strained with astonishment. At the bottom she fell against the fumed oak dresser. Felix expected her at once to swing round in a rage, perhaps run upstairs again and accuse Miss Bohun of whatever had happened at the top. Instead she clung to the dresser, looking blind and completely defeated, then, slowly, she bent double and pressed her arm across her waist. She stared at Felix, tears in her eyes, opened her mouth as though to speak, but, instead, groaned and fell to the ground.

Miss Bohun came running down.

Felix, in horror and panic, shouted: 'You've killed her!' and he thrust furiously past Miss Bohun to kneel down beside Mrs Ellis.

Her face was pressed to the floor, turned sideways so he could see the greenish-white of her cheek; he could not move her. Tears ran down her face, but she did not make any noise. He held to her shoulder but could do nothing. She moved up one of her knees as though attempting to crawl somewhere. The red polish had come off one of her nails and lay like a complete finger-nail on the floor beside her hand. Felix picked it up as though that, anyway, were something he could do. He kept saying foolishly:

'Mrs Ellis, what's the matter? What can I do for you?'

'It's all right.' Miss Bohun crossed to her desk and lifted the telephone receiver. While she was dialling a number, she spoke calmly, but she looked pale: 'It's probably nothing serious. I expect her baby is coming – they often come early. Nothing to be afraid of. It's quite a *natural* process. I'll ring the hospital.'

Felix, looking at Mrs Ellis, could not believe there was nothing to be afraid of. Her very slow movements frightened him. She looked like an animal that had fallen from a height and, shattered and in agony, was writhing in spite of the pain it must cause itself.

'She's dying,' he said.

'Nonsense!' Miss Bohun, having dialled the number, began rattling the receiver in a nervous way. At last someone answered and she spoke, firmly and sensibly: 'This is Miss Bohun. I want you to send an ambulance for Mrs Ellis. There's been a *slight* accident. Yes, I'm afraid her baby is being born prematurely. You've got a bed ready? That's splendid.'

Mrs Ellis moved with a sudden spasm and caught at a rag rug which lay near her face. As she raised her knee again Felix noticed a trickle of blood running down the inside of her leg.

'She's bleeding,' he said.

Miss Bohun came over and looked at the blood as though she disapproved of it, but said nothing.

'Can't we lift her up between us?' said Felix wretchedly.

'No, no,' Mrs Ellis gasped, her voice very hoarse. 'Don't touch me.'

'Better leave her,' said Miss Bohun, in control of the situation. 'You can't do any good down there, Felix... You'd better... I know,' she suddenly sounded quite cheerful, 'you go and fetch Dr Klaus. He's Mrs Ellis's own doctor. I'm sure he'll want to know about this. Get a taxi and bring Dr Klaus straight back in it.'

'But where does he live?'

'Wait,' Miss Bohun ran rapidly through the K's in the telephone book: 'Dr Emil Klaus, 60 Queen Melisande Way... Here, I'll write it down.' She pulled open the writing-desk drawer and snatched up an envelope; it was a new one. 'Not a new one – an old one will do.' She put back the new envelope and took a used one from among the chaos of old letters. Felix watched her as he might watch these movements in a film. 'Here,' she scribbled on the back of the envelope and held it to him. He took it but did not move. As he stood stupidly, staring at Mrs Ellis, Miss Bohun crossed over and, putting an arm round his shoulder, pushed him to the door.

'Hurry,' she said, 'or the ambulance will be here before you get back. They said twenty minutes.'

Her voice, bright, confident, almost happy, went on repeating itself in his head as he stumbled into the courtyard and ran to Herod's Gate where the taxis stood. He held the envelope in his hand. When he found a taxi he read out the address loudly and clearly. The house was not far. A maid said Dr Klaus was at supper and she left Felix for a while in a small front room that was oppressively crowded with furniture. He sat staring at Dr Klaus's address on the back of the envelope and then, as time passed, he turned the envelope over and stared at the address on the front. He read:

To 'X',
   c/o Miss Bohun, Herod's Gate,
    Jerusalem, Palestine.

It was several minutes before he realized what he was reading... But he was the 'X' to whom the letter was addressed. He had a right to read it. He took it out and read:

Sir or Madam,

We were glad to receive your communication of February 9th which will, we hope, put us at last into touch with Mr Alfred Mordecai Jewel. His brother, Alderman Samson Jewel, died four years ago leaving the whole of his estate of some ten thousand pounds to his brother Alfred Mordecai. Many attempts have been made to trace Mr Jewel...

As Dr Klaus, putting his coat on, threw open the door and said: 'Come along now,' Felix thrust the letter back into its envelope.

In the car Dr Klaus said: 'What is this so unfortunate accident that has occurred?'

'Mrs Ellis fell down the stairs.'

'How did that happen?'

'I don't know. I think Miss Bohun hit her.'

'Did you see such a thing?'

'No, I was downstairs.'

'Ah, then it is as well to speak with caution.'

When they reached the house the ambulance was at the gate. The men were putting the stretcher inside. Mrs Ellis, wrapped in dark blankets, had her eyes closed. Miss Bohun, coming through the courtyard with a young nurse, was saying:

'. . . a slight argument about a trivial matter, but she was not herself. She got worked up and . . . well, I hardly like to tell you, but she made to strike out at me. We were at the top of the stairs and she stumbled backwards. I made an effort to catch her . . .'

'It's terrible,' said the nurse, a break in her voice. 'Mrs Ellis was always so nice.'

'I hope you'll save the child.'

The nurse gave her head a distracted shake. Dr Klaus called from the ambulance: 'Come; come at once,' and the nurse and the men jumped in, the doors were shut and the ambulance drove away.

'Come in, Felix,' said Miss Bohun cheerfully, touching his shoulder as he went in through the gate, 'we've done all we can; and I think we've earned our supper.'

Felix never saw Mrs Ellis again. The day after the accident he was called to the Transport Office. A passage had suddenly fallen vacant and he was given two days in which to pack and catch a boat at Port Said. The first thing he did was to buy from a shop in Princess Mary's Avenue a tin tray for sand, a cat basket, a lead and a small collar. These were, in Palestine at this time, articles of supreme luxury, and he had never spent so much money in his life before. Then he went to Madame Sarkis's house: Madame Sarkis was out. Felix left a note for her and returned to Herod's

Gate with Faro on his shoulder. He had behaved all the time with deliberation and complete confidence of success. It was as though he had suddenly grown in stature and strength. He knew no one could prevent his taking Faro with him when he went, but from politeness he decided to ask Miss Bohun's permission first.

She was talking on the telephone when he went into the room. She turned and made a slight movement with her brows as she noticed Faro on Felix's shoulder, but when she finished her conversation and put down the receiver, she spoke to Felix as though prepared to overlook the fact that her cat had been brought back without her permission.

'You'll be sorry to hear, I'm sure, that poor Mrs Ellis has lost her baby. Such a tragedy. She'll pull through, they think. She's young, after all. She's really rather lucky as I hear they're flying her back to England as soon as she's well enough. Only the most privileged people get air passages. Unfortunately you won't see her before you go. She can't be visited yet.' Miss Bohun moved to face Felix squarely and she gave him a serene smile. He did not return her smile. He said: 'Miss Bohun, I want to take Faro back to England with me.'

The smile dwindled on her face but she did not seem annoyed, merely sorry for him in his folly.

'My dear boy, that's impossible, you know. You can't take animals into England just like that. They have to be put in quarantine.'

'I know. I've been to Cook's about it. They say it costs about thirty pounds to quarantine a cat and I can pay that. And my uncle's a vet. They think she may be allowed to stay with him. It's all arranged. I only want your permission.'

Miss Bohun turned back to her desk and began fidgeting with some papers; after a moment she said fretfully: 'Really, I don't know. She's useful. She catches rats. She's only been away a fortnight and already Maria says she's heard rats in the kitchen.'

As she spoke Miss Bohun glanced round at Faro without affection or humour, but with a sort of cold reflection. It seemed to Felix he could see Miss Bohun's mind as clearly as the works of a skeleton clock. He could see her calculating Faro's usefulness and subtracting the cost of her keep; calculating Faro's value for breeding purposes and subtracting the loss of Felix's goodwill.

She repeated irritably: 'I don't know.'

Felix lifted Faro from his shoulder and held her in the hollow of his arm. Her coat, in the brilliant afternoon light, had the sheened silver and gold of grebe feathers. She was drowsy and kept her eyes shut. Gently, he gathered her front paws into his hand.

Miss Bohun, watching him, frowned slightly; her face gave an odd twitch, but Felix did not notice it.

'All right,' she said abruptly, and returned to her desk.

He said 'Thank you,' and as he moved away, she called after him: 'And don't forget, Faro is a valuable cat.'

'Let me pay for her,' he said.

'Oh, no, of course not.' Miss Bohun sounded very irritable. 'If you want the creature, have her.'

Felix knew he ought to show more gratitude, but he could feel only a chill, almost, indeed, a sort of rectitude because he had carried out the formality of receiving Miss Bohun's permission to take Faro away. No, he could show no ghost of gratitude; Miss Bohun had given him nothing. Faro, because he had always loved her, had always been his.

As he moved off, he put his hand in his pocket and found the letter to 'X'. He paused, wondering if he should return it; then she called him again. Turning, he saw she had taken from her desk a polished olive-wood box on which was stamped in Gothic script: 'A Present from Jerusalem'.

She said: 'I might as well give this to you now. I bought it for you as a parting gift.'

Felix looked at the box; he swallowed, and said miserably: 'I don't really want it.'

'But . . .' her surprise and hurt made it clear to him she had no suspicion of his feelings, 'you can't refuse a gift, a *farewell* gift. Perhaps you think it's too much after my giving you the camel, *and* Faro . . . Now, don't be silly. It's just a little reminder of the days when we were a happy family here together. Perhaps you don't realize it, but I feel quite sorry to see our little circle breaking up like this. Don't *you* feel sorry?'

After a pause, there seemed to be forced from him the reply she expected: 'Yes,' he said, but he could feel only that as Mrs Ellis would never return to the house, he was fortunate to be getting away from it. As for parting from Miss Bohun – it was as though he were parting from someone who had injured him. He felt numbed by a sense of injury, but what the injury was he did not really know.

As he put out his hand to take the box, he noticed he was holding the letter to 'X'. He said: 'Here is the envelope on which you wrote Dr Klaus's address.' She took it from him and threw it back into the drawer without a glance.

While Felix was packing the last of his possessions and closing his cases, he heard Miss Bohun and a pupil come out into the garden. He looked and saw she was with Mr Liftshitz. While he watched, she suddenly brought her hands together in a sharp little clap of excitement and her voice rang out gaily:

'I know what we'll do. We'll pick the mulberries. I'm afraid the Bedu have been at them again. Dear me, naughty people! Now, Mr Liftshitz, if you'll first get the ladder . . . It's over by the shed. The ladder . . . *ladder* – over there, over there – that's right . . .'

Felix watched Mr Liftshitz walking unsteadily under the ladder's weight. He was wearing a dark suit, too thick for summer, and his face shone with sweat. Miss Bohun directed him: 'Now, put it against the tree. The tree, the *tree* – the baum. Yes, that's right . . .' They passed out of sight beneath the wide leaves, but Miss Bohun's voice still encompassed the garden: 'We have lost a lot of mulberries this year; dear me, yes. But, there! God will no doubt repay. He always does, Mr Liftshitz. He always does!'

'Please?' asked Mr Liftshitz.

'Sometimes, you know, He works in the *most* mysterious way. Only recently I received a . . .' she broke off and her voice became peevish: 'What are you doing here, Nikky? Who's getting the tea today? It's *always* Maria. Do go in. Here I have a Jewish pupil, what will he think of you lying on the seat asleep, just like an Arab!'

Nikky appeared from under the tree, his hands in his pockets, and started to move away, then, suddenly, with a peculiar smile on his face, he said: 'Oh, by the way, I have had no occasion to tell you. I am going to London.'

There was no reply from under the tree, but in a moment Miss Bohun parted the branches, holding them like a curtain and stared at him with annoyance: 'Did you say you are going to London? What do you mean?'

'You are surprised? So? You think it is not possible. Well, I will tell you. I have been given a scholarship by the Cultural Mission and I leave next week.'

She caught her breath: 'This *is* a surprise,' she said. 'Of course I am very glad for your sake, very glad indeed. It is splendid – and you *want* to go?'

'But, of course.'

'Of course,' echoed Miss Bohun and her voice faltered, 'then you are all going – the last of the happy family. But,' her tone regained itself, 'Mr Jewel is coming back.'

'So?' Nikky turned on his heel and with a sudden hoot of laughter, he went off round the side of the house. Miss Bohun let the branches drop. At once her voice, clear and controlled, came from inside them:

'That's my houseboy. He tells me he has won a scholarship. Now, there's an example for you, Mr Liftshitz. Such a curious thing! One of my "Ever-Readies" tells me he's really a Count. I can't understand it. His father wasn't a Count. I meant to ask him about it.'

'Please?' asked Mr Liftshitz.

'Oh,' Miss Bohun now became impatient. 'Do get up the ladder, Mr Liftshitz, or your hour will be over and nothing done.'

When his last bag was closed, Felix made a last trip to the hospital to say good-bye to Mr Jewel. He took Faro on her lead with him: she rode on his shoulder. He was determined not to let her out of his sight until he had got her safely away.

Mr Jewel said 'Hello' to Felix and admired Faro's new red collar and lead, but his mind was clearly on something else. Suddenly he started to giggle and he caught Felix's wrist and shook it:

'You won't believe it,' he said, 'but she was in this morning, and what do you think she said? She said the room's all ready for me, and she said: "Well, Mr Jewel, two old people under one roof, both lonely, both single – well, well, well!" and she gave me such a look. I could see just what she'd got in mind.'

'What?' asked Felix, vague and not very interested.

'Can't you guess?' said Mr Jewel. Felix could not guess, so at last Mr Jewel was forced to say coyly: 'Marriage.'

Felix was aghast: 'But you couldn't marry Miss Bohun!'

'Why not? Marriage might be the making of her. She's still got a bit of life in her, y'know. See her nip up them stairs! You think she's odd, don't you? but all she wants is a bit of loving. She wants someone that belongs to her.'

Felix stared at him so blankly, Mr Jewel became disturbed and protested: 'She's not a bad sort. I've always told you that. After all, she gave you the cat.'

'Yes,' Felix agreed, 'it was very kind of her; and she gave me an olive-wood box and a camel.'

'There now!' said Mr Jewel happily.

Felix could not respond. He put Faro down on the ground and let her wander the length of her lead; he watched her intently as she sniffed the floor and chair legs. He did not know what to say and suddenly brought out:

'What about Frau Wagner?'

'Oh, her!' said Mr Jewel in a mildly hurt tone, 'haven't seen much of her since I came here. Miss Bohun says she's gallivanting no end. People have seen her at the King David – not that I've anything against a girl having a good time, mind you; but Frau Wagner, she needs a chap a bit younger; someone who can take her out and about. I don't blame her. The girl needed a bit of fun, a bit of company. The last thing I heard she's going to Tel Aviv with the Teitelbaums. Fine junketings down there.'

Felix, reflecting on Mr Jewel's faith in Miss Bohun, wondered if it could lead to any good. After all, Mr Jewel, if he did but know it, was a free man now: a man with money: one who could stay in expensive hotels if he liked. Suddenly Felix broke into Mr Jewel's talk, to say with discomforted sharpness:

'Did Miss Bohun tell you that your brother left you some money?'

He could scarcely bear to look at Mr Jewel, expecting him to be so astounded, to be so painfully struck by the motive behind Miss Bohun's advances – but Mr Jewel showed not even surprise. He shifted a little in his seat and turned his head to one side. After a pause, he cleared his throat once or twice and then said very casually:

191

'She did drop a hint like about some money coming my way. Quite a tidy sum, she said. Apparently she's been working on my behalf and somehow she got on to Samson's solicitor. She's a cute one, y'know, and no mistake. I could do worse for myself – a wife and a fortune, they go together.'

Felix opened his lips to tell Mr Jewel how his money had come to him, but before he spoke he realized that Mr Jewel was no more deceived than he was. Whatever the truth might be, Mr Jewel did not want to hear it. He was willing to be deceived.

Mr Jewel, glancing up uneasily, met the aware, critical stare of Felix's young eyes. He looked away at once and said with a sort of grumbling self-pity that hid nothing: 'I'm an old man, y'know, Felix. I might have a bit of cash now, but I've got no one of my own; no flesh and blood. That's what you want when you're old – flesh and blood. You don't understand. You're young. You're strong and independent. You've got all your life before you. You young ones are a bit hard on us old ones – you don't know what it's like to be old. I'm a lonely old man; she's a lonely old woman. All she's ever wanted is for life to give her something, just to show she's not out of it all, not neglected. We're all human; it's not for us to be too hard on one another. You'll find that out some day.'

Mr Jewel looked at Felix as though appealing for his support, but Felix would concede nothing. He lifted Faro on to his shoulder and stood up. Meeting Mr Jewel's bleary old eyes, he did his best to smile. As he shook hands and said good-bye, it seemed to him that Mr Jewel was little better than a child, while he, knowing all he knew, would never be a child again.

OTHER NEW YORK REVIEW BOOKS CLASSICS

For a complete list of titles, visit www.nyrb.com or write to:
Catalog Requests, NYRB, 435 Hudson Street, New York, NY 10014